The ALTAR *of* GOLD

by
LINDA BROTEN STRALEY

ENDICOTT
HUGH
BOOKS

The ALTAR of GOLD
Copyright © 2020 Hugh Straley for the Estate of Linda Broten Straley
Cover image: Pirate Ship © Digikhmer - Dreamstime.com
Panama map by Peter Straley

Proceeds from the sale of *The Altar of Gold* will be donated to Grandmothers Against Gun Violence.

Book design Masha Shubin

ISBN: 978-0-9993646-3-5 Trade paperback

Printed in the United States of America

2 3 4 5 6 7 8 9 10

The ALTAR *of* GOLD

To my grandchildren who will have many adventures,
Georgia, Oliver, Maggie, and Peter

Table of Contents

INTRODUCTION

In the seventeenth century, when English colonists in Massachusetts and Virginia were founding small towns and wilderness plantations, the Spanish colonies far to the south were already more than one hundred years old. Spain used the riches of the New World to pay for her wars against France and England. Twice a year, large, heavily guarded fleets of huge sailing ships known as galleons were filled with silver and gold from South America and sailed from Cuba for Spain. Those treasure ships were at the mercy of English, French, and Dutch buccaneers—pirates who stole from foreigners with the blessings of their own kings.

The buccaneers captured Spanish galleons and plundered them. But when there were no valuable ships to attack, they raided Spanish settlements around the Caribbean Sea. The colonists were threatened constantly by the presence of those lawless men.

This is the story of Edward, an English boy from the island of Jamaica, and Marta, a Spanish girl from Panama, who both lived during those dangerous times. Her letters and his journal entries tell us their stories.

Few people today bother writing such long, detailed

descriptions of day-to-day events. But in the seventeenth century, educated people often wrote about their lives. With no cameras, writing was the main way to record what you had seen. With no telephones or internet and slow, slow travel by land or sea, writing was the main way to communicate with relatives or friends. For Edward and Marta, writing was also a link between the world they considered real and the unreal world in which they were forced to live.

Edward's Journal

LATE SEPTEMBER 1670, LEACH PLANTATION, JAMAICA

Today I begin this journal. Today I begin a lot of things. My leather satchel is all packed. I'll write something short here at home before I leave.

Mother sits silent in the next room, but I know she is crying. Father waits for me at the stable. I wonder what he is thinking. Because of him, I must go to serve as cabin boy for Captain Henry Morgan.

Mother is angry with Father. Last night, she called him weak and worthless. She said that it should be him going away, not me. I don't know. Father likes to drink and he likes to gamble. He used to win sometimes. But lately he has lost.

The other night in Kingston, he lost everything. He lost the plantation, houses, and slaves to Captain Morgan.

The Captain agreed to take me as his servant on his next voyage in payment for half of the debt. He has given Father until I get back to come up with the rest of the money.

I wish Mother wouldn't cry. I'm not afraid anymore.

She acts as if I were leaving forever. But how long can it be before I am home again?

—Edward

Edward's Journal

LATER THAT DAY, SEPTEMBER 1670, PORT ROYAL, JAMAICA

Early this morning Father and I started by horse on the ten-league journey from the plantation to Port Royal where Captain Morgan's ship is anchored. The day was hot as usual, and I soon felt drops of sweat rolling down my back under my shirt, but heavy clouds kept the sun off us so we didn't have to stop and rest in the shade. Even so, the horses' hooves kept a cloud of dust around us. While I wasn't in a hurry to get there, it seemed a long, long way down that dusty road with nothing but cane fields and brush to look at. Father hardly spoke a sentence to me and he kept pulling a jug from his saddlebag and taking a drink.

I got tired of watching him, so to get his mind off the jug, I asked him what a cabin boy's job was. I'd been wondering what a cabin boy is expected to do ever since the night before when he told me that would be my new job.

My question caught him in the act of reaching for his drink, but he stopped, looked at me, and paused to think. Finally he said, "Why, he's the Captain's helper ... yes, his helper."

"Helper? What kind of helper?"

"Oh, he brings the Captain his dinner things; like that."

Then he put his hand in the saddlebag for his jug. I knew he didn't want to tell me any more.

I suspected he didn't know much more. Finding the jug empty, he corked it and put it back, carefully closing the flap. I was glad the rum was gone.

"Where'll I be going with Henry Morgan?" I asked. I thought he might be more willing to talk now.

He shook his head and said, "I don't know, son. Maybe Santa Marta, maybe Cartagena, maybe Panama. He's commissioned by Governor Modyford to hit the Spanish anywhere he can." Father started to reach for his jug, but remembered it was empty and stopped.

He thought a while. "You know, Ed," he said, "those Spanish devils have got to be taught they don't own the Caribbean."

"Am I going to fight Spaniards?" I asked. A funny feeling shot through me.

Father turned his eyes away. "I don't know, son," he replied. Then, as if he had just thought of it, he said, "The Spanish are cowards. They run away or surrender if anybody stands up to them. And believe me, if half of what they say is true, Morgan is the man to stand up to them. I can't say that I like him much, seeing as how he allowed me to sell my own son to him, but as a fighter, I guess there ain't none better. In fact I've heard the Spanish are so afraid of him that just the mention of his name turns their hair white."

Father shifted his weight in the saddle and he rode on, quiet as before. We must have gone a league or so before he spoke again. When he did, I guess I shouldn't say this, but he sounded like a man trying to sell a lame horse.

"Son, I want you to know that I wouldn't be sending you off this way if I thought it would do you harm. Morgan is a good one for you to learn soldiering from. That's really why I'm letting you go. You'll learn something about sailing and soldiering, and, God willing, you might come back rich."

"Rich? How?" I thought the rum had gone to his head.

"You never heard of 'No purchase, no pay'?" I shook my head.

"That means the King won't pay you to fight for him, but whatever you can take from the enemy is yours. Morgan made himself wealthy under that plan. A poor man he was when he came here a few years back. Now he owns land on the island and ships in the harbor...and if we ain't careful, he'll own you and me." He took a handkerchief from his pocket, pushed his hat to the back of his head, and wiped his forehead. Then he said, "You serve him well, son, and you'll get a share in what you capture."

It sounded like thievery to me, but I didn't say so. I didn't want to sound ignorant, and I guess if you're at war it's all right to steal.

About an hour later we rode into Port Royal. Father had told me that it wasn't a place where decent folks wanted to spend much time and it looked like he was right. The town was all wine shops and stores selling ship supplies. Fancy ladies leaned out of upstairs windows calling to fellows in the streets below. Dogs so skinny you could count their ribs wandered the street looking for scraps. Most everybody I saw was drunk. Tough-looking men wove their way up and down the street from one wine shop to the next.

Father stopped in front of a place called The Tortuga that had a big wooden turtle hanging over the door.

"Wait here, Ed," he said getting down from his horse.

"You stay and watch the horses so they don't get stolen. I'll be back in a minute."

My heart sank. I knew "minutes" could last until the sun crossed a good part of the sky. And just like I thought it was a while before he came out of The Tortuga grinning, looking relaxed, and weaving some when he walked.

"Here, Ed," he said, handing me a mug of ale. "Here's something for your thirst." While he mounted his horse he said, "I set up a game for tonight. My senses tell me I'm going to be lucky, Ed." I didn't answer him. I felt embarrassed. I was glad I wouldn't be around to see the fight he and Mother would have when he got home.

The docks lay at the foot of the main street. There must have been twenty ships tied up there. From a distance, the masts looked like a forest growing right out of the water. Even from where we stood, it was easy to spot Captain Morgan's ship. It was the biggest one, and its name, *Satisfaction*, was written on the bow in big yellow letters. Two rows of square, shuttered windows for cannon ran from the bow to the stern. The *Satisfaction* had three tall masts each with a small platform that looked like a basket way up at the top. The masts were held up by rope webbing that ran from the baskets and fanned out to each side of the ship where they were fastened with more rope to huge iron rings. It crossed my mind that climbing up that webbing to the baskets at the top wouldn't be any harder than picking coconuts. In truth, it would be easier since the ropes would give you foot and handholds more sure than the trunk of the coconut palm.

Once Father and I went aboard the *Satisfaction*, we almost tripped over a baldheaded fellow lying on the planks, his head pillowed in his arms, sleeping like a dog in the shade. He snored so loud it was a wonder we hadn't heard him from the dock. We looked up and down the deck for somebody to talk to but we were alone with the sleeper.

"You don't suppose this chap is on watch, do you?" Father said, looking down at him. Then he shouted, "Say, fellow, is the captain on board?" The snoring man didn't move. Father shouted again, "We're looking for the captain!" The fellow's snoring sputtered to a stop, but he slept on. We both watched for a minute, and then Father kicked him with the toe of his boot. I half expected the man to leap up with a drawn knife, but he didn't. He just raised his head a little and tried to focus his eyes. "Huh?" he said in a thick voice.

"Is Captain Morgan here?" shouted Father bending down close to the man so their noses almost touched.

"Damned if I know," muttered the fellow before he hiccoughed, sunk back onto the deck, laid his head on his arms, and closed his eyes.

Father muttered something about "drunkards," which made me feel embarrassed again. Then he chuckled and said, "Come, Edward, let's look around for ourselves."

A voice called from behind us, "Who's there?" I jumped and turned around. A man stepped out of the cabin at the front of the ship and moved toward us with a curious look on his face.

"Hello, I am Clarence Leach," said Father very formally, holding out his hand to the man. "This is my son, Edward. He's come to be your cabin boy."

"Glad to meet ye," said the man taking Father's hand. "Thomas Potts is the name. I'm mate on this ship."

He was about the same size as my father, medium, I guess you would say, but he looked harder. He wore a pair of brown pants and a white shirt with a green sash tied around his waist. What I noticed most about him was the gold earring in his ear. It was a big one, and it glistened in the sun.

"I see ye made the acquaintance of Moon, here," he said, nodding toward the man lying on the deck at our feet. "When he don't let the drink get to him, he's as good a hand as there is. He's been around, he has."

We looked down at the man who was snoring again louder than a pig in a barnyard. I couldn't picture him as a good hand, whatever that was. "Hoy! And can he put up a racket with that snoring! The mates who know him put themselves through any kind of contortions so's they don't have to sleep with him." Mr. Potts shook his head and grinned. "The boy's lucky he'll be sleeping off by himself." Then he looked at Father and said, "The Captain ain't here. I don't expect he'll be back 'til tomorrow. You just leave Edward, that is his name, ain't it?" My father nodded yes. "You just leave the boy here with me. I'll show him where to sleep and where to stow his gear if he's got any."

"That's good of you, Mr. Potts," said Father handing me my satchel. "Now you be good son, and mind you, don't cause any trouble for Mr. Potts here and the Captain." His voice sounded very formal, but I could see his eyes watered.

"Yes, sir," I answered. I suddenly felt afraid. I was afraid of whatever was coming, and I was afraid my father would start to cry right there in front of Mr. Potts.

He didn't. He looked away, gave me a solid pat on the back, then turned and left the ship faster than you could say goodbye.

"This is yer first time goin' to sea, ain't it?" said Mr. Potts, looking at me for the first time.

"Yes, sir," I answered.

"Well then, ye've got some learnin' to do." He started

down the deck towards the back of the ship and I followed along. "First, I'll show ye where ye'll be sleepin'."

We climbed down a ladder through a hole in the deck and walked toward the back of the ship. It was hot and dark, and there didn't seem to be much air for breathing, like the time back home that Father shut me up in the smokehouse for emptying his rum down the privy. Mr. Potts led me past coiled ropes and chains in piles and in the dim light I saw a row of black cannons sitting by the shuttered windows with a crate full of iron balls beside each one. When we reached the back of the ship, Mr. Potts stopped and pointed at a clear space on the deck just big enough for me to lie down.

"This is where ye'll sleep, Edward. If the bare planks are too hard for ye, grab a bundle of that sailcloth over there and put it down for a mattress." He pointed at a pile of white canvas stacked against the wall.

Mr. Potts grabbed a bell the size of a cowbell that hung from the ceiling by a rope. "This here's the way the Captain can call ye if he needs ye in the middle of the night." He rang the bell. "The other end of this rope is in his cabin. All he has to do is pull it and ye hear it down here. And let me warn ye, boy. When ye hear that thing ring, ye better turn to quick. Quick!" He yanked the cord again ringing the bell so loud it hurt. I knew I'd never miss the Captain's call for lack of hearing it.

Mr. Potts led me back on deck and showed me around. The sun had set by the time he took me to the galley and told me that since the cook wasn't on board, it was up to me to fix my supper. He left me there to do for myself without telling me where to look or what to eat.

The barrels, boxes, and cupboards were locked tight. I had to look hard until I found a few biscuits, some tea, and dried turtle meat in a greasy wooden box stuck under the stove. I felt like I should ask somebody if I could eat that food, but there wasn't a soul around so I helped myself, fearing that any minute someone would bust in and ask me what I was doing there. But there was never a soul and never a sound. It was like I was the only body alive on the ship.

After I ate, I went below to the dark, lonely spot by the bell. The hot, heavy air smelled like tar and wet clothes. I was glad I remembered to put a candle and flints in my pack. With the light from the candle I could see to make a bed for myself. After that was done, I sat down in the stillness and wrote in this diary. Now, to sleep.

—Edward

Edward's Journal

TWO DAYS LATER, SEPTEMBER 1670, PORT ROYAL, JAMAICA

Today about midday I was wiping kettles for the cook when Mr. Potts called into the galley, "The Captain wants to see you, Edward. Look alive and get yer arse down to his cabin quick."

He swatted me on the seat of the pants and I started off. My heart beat so hard in my chest, it felt like it was trying to bust out. Quick as some tea, and I could, I climbed the ladder to the deck and ran to the rear of the ship where Captain Morgan had his cabin. Out of breath, I hesitated in front of the door. "He's nobody to fool with," Potts had told me. "Sometimes he likes to joke around and be treated like me or you, but other times he acts like some kind of prince. I've seen him laugh and joke with a man in the morning and run a sword through that same fellow in the afternoon for showing disrespect. It's best to learn to read his moods." I took a deep breath and knocked.

"Come in," said a deep voice.

When I opened the door I was struck by how fancy the cabin was. In the center of the room stood a big wooden table painted bright, shiny gold. The legs were carved from top to bottom, and there was a matching gold chair whose seat and back were covered in red velvet. The bed to one side was gold like the table. From all I saw, it looked to me like the Captain was richer and lived fancier than Governor Modyford. I wondered if all this was the "purchase for his pay" Father had told me about.

Captain Morgan stood beside his golden table. On his feet he wore the finest pair of shoes I ever saw. They were black, shiny as a looking glass with bright gold buckles. He had white silk stockings, pantaloons, and on top of these, a bright red coat only half made. It was missing the sleeves. A man, his tailor, was busy taking a stitch here and there, pulling the material tight in one place and loosening it in others. The Captain's black wavy hair fell to his shoulders and it curled all around his face. I saw a moustache oiled and trained reaching out to each cheek like horns. There was a beard shaped like a V on his chin, and over one of his eyes he pasted a little black spot made out of cloth. His face was puffy and he looked tired, but I could feel his blue eyes inspect every inch of me.

"So you are Leach's son," he said. He didn't talk like the rest of the sailors on the ship who cursed and spoke what Father calls gutter talk. Captain Morgan spoke like a gentleman. "You don't look as big as I expected from your father's description. What's your name?"

"Edward, sir."

"And how old are you?"

"Fourteen, sir."

"Well, Edward, I assume your father told you about being a cabin boy." He held out his arms while the tailor smoothed the cloth at his waist. "While we are in port, I want you to run errands and be handy." He raised an arm so the tailor could put some pins in the side of his coat while he admired himself in the gold-framed looking glass next to the bed. A little smile came to his lips. "Tomorrow we sail." He still looked in the glass. "Once we are at sea, you will serve my food, keep my cabin clean, take care of my clothes, and do any other jobs I have for you. When we meet the enemy, you will stay by my side and follow orders."

He lowered his arm and stared right at me, "I expect you to be fearless. There's no room for cowards."

"Yes, sir."

"If you do your job well, you will be rewarded. If you fail me, you won't live to see your mother again. I am a hard master and I expect to be obeyed. Cabin boys are easy to replace. Remember that, Edward. Now be off until I send for you. Make yourself useful around the galley."

He turned away from me and started to talk about the fit of his coat with the tailor who was kneeling beside him doing something to the hem. I left the cabin as quietly as I could. My legs shook and my stomach was upset. I knew I'd better try my hardest to please him.

—Edward

MID-NOVEMBER 1670, SOUTH
SIDE OF TORTUGA ISLAND

This journal hasn't felt my pen tickling its pages for a good while. What with working sunup to sundown and losing the book in the folds of my mattress, I haven't had much chance to write. But I'll make up for it. At least I'll try. It isn't so good writing down here where it's close and you can feel the ship rocking and swaying; the smells, the temperature, and the motion make me sick. I'd go topside and write, but I don't want them to make sport of me.

We sailed out of Port Royal the day after I met Captain Morgan, and we came here to Tortuga. There must be twenty ships with us. Most of them are full of fellows who have sailed with the Captain before. The men are muttering that they want to stop all this fussing and waiting and get started. But the Captain won't hear it. He says he won't be ready 'til every ship is painted, tarred, and packed to the gunwales with food. He told Mr. Potts that no ship of his would fall into enemy hands because of a torn sail or a leaky bottom. So I am painting and tarring and sewing sails. I've been to the top of the mizzenmast, and I stood in the basket. It's called the crow's nest, and crow I was, perched a long way up there looking down on the deck beneath me. The fellow, Moon, worked on the rigging just below, and I was sore tempted to aim a spit ball at the top of his shiny head. But I didn't for fear he had no play in him.

Except for Tortuga Island with its coconut palms and sandy beach, there's nothing but water as far as you can see. On this side of the island, a reef offshore makes a kind of harbor for the ships. Inside the reef the water ripples gentle like blue frosting on a cake; but the other side of the reef is home to the wind and waves, and the water crashes against the reef sending white froth into the sky. The water out there, a dark unfriendly blue, is deep and mysterious. I'm glad for a good solid ship under me.

Sometimes I feel like the only slave on a farm with a passel of masters. There are days when every breathing soul on the ship has something for me to do. Like yesterday: I had just finished straightening up the Captain's cabin and was thinking about breakfast when Mr. Potts stopped me on my way to the galley.

"Edward, fetch the tar pot on the larboard side and run it up to the chaps on the foremast."

"Yes, sir," I hoped Cook wouldn't lock up the food before I finished the chore. I delivered the pot and just as I was climbing back down onto the deck worrying how there would be nothing but cold biscuits left for me, Moon came over, all red in the face and sweating, his bald head covered with a dirty white bandana.

"Ed, the scuttlebutt is near empty. How's a thirsty fellow to get a drink of water?" He pointed at the water barrel, "Be a good lad and fill it up real speedy so poor old Moon can wet his throat." He grinned at me showing a lead tooth.

I went below, fetched the fresh water, and was climbing out with the bucket in my hand when they called me to scrape tar off the deck. I never did get my breakfast.

But it's not all work. The men wouldn't stand for it. I get the feeling none of them likes to work too hard and the Captain knows just how hard to push them; then he stops. Like this afternoon, when some ships sailed up with provisions they stole from the mainland, the Captain called for a celebration and ordered rum all around.

It was near sundown. The afternoon breeze had quit and the sea inside the reef was flat and shiny as a china plate. Fellows brought out cards and dice and settled down in groups for gaming. I lowered myself into the middle of a rope coil next to where Moon sat on the deck in a circle with two other fellows. He leaned against the mizzenmast and boomed in his big voice, "I hear we sail for Tiburón at dawn," so loud that I felt the deck shake.

"I'll be believing it when we raise sail and no sooner," answered an older man named Higgins who had patches of white in his hair. The skin on his face was baggy and his cheeks sagged pulling down the corners of his mouth making him look mournful like a man who saw the sorry side of everything.

"Well I can't think there's much more to do here," put in a short nimble fellow everybody called Monkey because of the way he climbed up and down the rigging faster than anybody else and so easy you'd think he belonged there. "Everything on the blasted boat is so clean and neat the anchor chain's even been scraped free o' rust. It makes me uncomfortable, it does." Shaking his head, he said, "Reminds me of the woman I lived with in St. Kitts. She was always after me to leave my boots outside and she got riled when I spit on the floor, but what finished it off was Sundays when she wanted me to wear a clean suit o' clothes. I couldn't take that. A little dirt puts a man at ease. So I up and left her. That was five years ago." He put his hand on top of his head, fished around with his fingers, and pulled out a mite. "Ain't been back to St. Kitts since...these blasted lice itch though, don't they?"

He held the bug to his face and squinted at it in the fading sunlight, rolling it back and forth between his fingers. Finally, he squashed it with his thumb and flicked it toward the railing.

Right then Mr. Potts came up and sat on the barrel next to Higgins. He carried a pitcher of rum and handed it around to the men in the circle. The last rays of the sun bounced off his earring.

"Well, Potts, is it to Tiburón we're goin' tomorrow?" asked Moon as he took the pitcher from Higgins.

"Aye, to meet up with the rest of the fleet."

"And then where to, Potts?" asked Monkey leaning toward him.

"I'll be damned if I know. I hear talk of Cuba or Cartagena or even Panama."

"Panama?" All three answered at once. "Morgan ain't turned crazy is he?" Moon's voice was quiet for a change. "There ain't no man's ever tried to go to Panama and come back alive."

Mr. Potts shrugged. "Let me say this," he leaned in toward the circle and pointed his fingers at Moon. "I was with Mansvelt in his prime before they hanged him and I even sailed once with L'Olonnais before the Caribs ate him and I can tell you here and now that there ain't never been a man smarter or better at this kind of fightin' than Henry Morgan. If there's a man on earth who can take Panama, he's the one."

"Well, maybe," Higgins looked sad at Mr. Potts. "But if you ask me, there ain't a man on earth who can do it.

Not even the great Henry Morgan." There in the dusk
with the shadows falling on his baggy eyes and his sagging cheeks he looked like a hound dog. "I hear stories
about the city being surrounded with walls so thick that
nothin' could break through 'em. And that ain't all. They
say there's a ditch half a mile wide around that wall filled
with sharks just waiting to taste English blood." He shook
his head and his jowls jiggled like a beached jellyfish when
you poke it with a stick.

"Morgan's been in places tight as that," Mr. Potts said
to Higgins. "I was with him in Maracaibo," he chuckled,
sat up straight, and slapped his knee. "Now *that* was a
time! There was more than once on that expedition that
I thought we were goners, but I'll be damned if that sly
old Morgan didn't get most of us out o' there without so
much as a hair on our heads bothered," Mr. Potts smiled
and shook his head. "And he done it by pure brain power.
I swear that man's got more sense than the Almighty."

"So tell us what happened. I ain't heard this one,"
Monkey stretched out on the deck and put his head on
the rope next to me. The sun was gone, so Moon lit a lan-
tern and set it in the center of the circle.

Mr. Potts began his tale. "Well, I guess you might say
we was 'patrollin' off the coast when Morgan decides to
pay the Spaniards a visit in Maracaibo. He was there with
Mansvelt and he said we might make ourselves rich, the
town havin' been built up again and the citizens restocked
with plate. We knew it would be dangerous since Maracaibo sits on a big salt water lake and you have to pass
through a narrow strait not more than a mile wide to get
inside. That strait is guarded by a castle with big cannons
pointed out over the water ready to sink any vessel trying
to enter the lake uninvited." He pulled on his earring and
paused like he was trying to remember what happened

next. Then he said, "Well, we all had a meeting and decided the pelf waiting for us was worth the risk, so we sailed into the strait expecting to be shot at. But fortune was with us; the castle being under-manned, the few soldiers who were there fled fearing for their lives."

Mr. Potts motioned at Moon to pass him the jug. He took a big gulp and wiped his mouth on his sleeve. "We couldn't believe how easy it was for us to land in Maracaibo without havin' to fight. When we got to the town, everybody had run off with most of their possessions. It took us some days but we finally found most of the citizens and held them 'til they came up with jewels and plate and money." Mr. Potts chuckled and took another noisy gulp of rum. "Then it came time for us to get out of there and that's when the fun started. Morgan sent one of the boats on ahead to check the castle to make sure it was still deserted, but our luck turned. They sent out three big men o' war from Cartagena with forty or so cannons on each one and they sat in the channel blocking our passage out of the lake. Most of us on hearing the news was sure that our time was up, but not Morgan. He thought to make a fireship, *brûlot*, the French calls them."

He took another drink and passed the jug to Higgins. "Well, we all turned to and fetched some big logs that we found on the shore. Some of them we stuck out of the portholes of one of the ships and we fixed them up to look like cannons. Then we pitched and tarred that ship and set piles of brimstone and powder here and there. Last, we stood some of them logs up on the deck and put hats on them and muskets by them to make it look like the deck was full of sailors. Then we just sat and waited for the light of day when we could start down the channel toward the Spanish ships sitting there in a row like pheasants on a log. The fire ship was in the lead. At just the right moment, the men aboard her set the fuses and abandoned her. We watched her sail straight for the largest of the men o' war. When she hit, there was the prettiest explosion you ever saw. That Spanish ship went to the bottom faster than a stone in a well. One of the other ships lit out for the safety of the fort, but we managed to capture the third. Morgan boarded her and led the way back to Maracaibo where he fixed her up to be his flagship, which just so happens to be the *Satisfaction* here." Mr. Potts patted the barrel he sat on. Then he continued his story.

"Well, we were feeling real jolly at besting the popish Spaniards like that, but we were still in a pretty tight fix since we were still caught inside the lake and had to pass that castle with all its guns guarding the entrance. But Morgan had another plan for gettin' away. Next morning in broad daylight, the sun was shinin' down on us and it was even hotter than usual. We sailed up to where the Spaniards at the castle could just see us. Then we anchored and sent the small boats ashore loaded with men. Once they reached the shore and they were out of sight of the Spanish, all the men in the boats, save one or two, laid down in the bottom and the supposed empty boats were rowed back to the ships making it look from the fort like we landed most of our men on the beach. The Spanish, from seeing that maneuver, expected that we were going to attack them by land that night, so they moved most of their big cannons and defenses away from the water side of the fort and directed it all out to the land side."

Mr. Potts slapped his knees and chuckled. "Now here's the best part. As soon as darkness fell, we let the ebb tide carry us out that channel smooth and quiet. Not one of us made a noise. We was nigh past the fort when somebody spotted us and sounded the alarm. So we quick raised sail and got out of their reach before they could rearrange their guns to fire a single shot at us." He slapped his knee again. "And if that wasn't enough insult for them papists, Morgan stopped the fleet just out of range of their guns and fired a sort of salute at 'em, seventy shots it was. They didn't even bother to answer us." Mr. Potts sat up shaking his head and laughing.

"You're right, Potts," said Monkey. "Morgan has wit. If he says he's going to Panama, I'll wager he does it and returns to tell the story. They said Portobelo was impossible, but Morgan proved them wrong there."

"He sure did," said Higgins.

"Gave those papists a little surprise," said Moon.

Monkey sat up and crossed his legs, "If he goes to Panama, I for one go with him."

Moon nodded his head, "Me too."

"Well, I guess I'll be going too," Higgins added. "But I'm near fifty now. I'm getting too old for this life. This'll be my last trip, and I won't throw my share away this time on drink and wenches." He shook his head making his cheeks shake. "No, by God, this time I'm going to buy me a piece of land and settle down."

"Ho, ho!" bellowed Moon, "That's what you said last trip."

"Well, Higgins," said Mr. Potts, "if this is to be your last raid, you've picked a good one. I hear they've got warehouses of two and three floors there in Panama." In the air he drew the outline of a big building. "Bigger than any on this side. And they're full to the ceilings with gold and silver."

"Clear to the roofs?" asked Moon, sitting up and staring at Mr. Potts.

"And that ain't all," said Mr. Potts shaking his head. "Word is they've got an altar there in one of them papist churches that goes across the front and clear up to the ceiling and it's made of solid gold."

"Wouldn't I like a piece of that to bring back?" boomed Moon. "That'd bring a pretty price in Port Royal, wouldn't it?"

Everybody got silent then, each man thinking about what he was going to do with all that gold. I pictured myself in a suit of clothes like Captain Morgan's, riding on a fine chestnut horse. A girl my age, in a fine silk gown, was watching me pass.

—Edward

Marta's Letter to Rosa

FEBRUARY 1672, PANAMA

Dear Cousin Rosa,

You write from Seville asking me to tell you about myself and my family here in Panama. How I wish I could tell you in person. I long to see Spain, the great stone cities, the cathedrals, the hillsides planted in vines. Here, we have our cathedral with its Altar of Gold and our Governor's Palace, but beyond that it is mostly wooden houses and muddy streets and everywhere the jungle. The birds and flowers are very beautiful, but my dreams of Spain are beautiful, too, in a different way. The journey to Spain is long and dangerous, though, so for now, our letters alone must bring us closer.

Even for letters, the journey is long and dangerous. I write this not certain you will ever read it. When the letter leaves me, it must travel across the jungle-covered isthmus to Portobelo, where it must wait for the departure of a fleet. Sometimes, letters—and people—wait for weeks or even a month before the ships sail. Then at the very least, my letter—our letter —will stop several days in Cartagena and a week or two in Havana before it begins the long ocean crossing. If fortune smiles, the fleet will come safely through great storms and foreign pirates, and you will read my letter in Seville. If the fleet is unlucky, as many are, this letter will tell my story to the fish at the bottom of the sea. I write for you, my friend, not the fish. I hope that the fleet is a lucky one.

Rosa, you have written that my life here in the New World sounds exotic and exciting. I am going to tell you what happened to me and my family just a year ago and after you have finished reading my story, you will be thankful that you live in safety in a Spanish city where you have large armies and plenty of weapons to protect you. Here in the colonies we are at the mercy of ruthless foreigners who take no shame at murder and plunder. Our small number of soldiers proves no match for those heathens who do any unspeakable act for a handful of gold or silver. The most despicable villain of them all, English, French, or Hollander is Henry Morgan.

I first heard of Henry Morgan five years ago, when I was eleven. It was the dry season. The breeze from the sea gently blew across us as we sat at the table eating the afternoon meal. The entire family was there, my brothers, Roberto and Jaime, Grandma, Mama, Papa, as well as our tutor, Señor Ortega. Eulalia, the Indian girl, kept our plates and cups full. It is remarkable that I can still remember what we had to eat that day. There were fried platanos, arroz con pollo, mangos, and papaya. It was so hot that I ate the juicy mangos and very little else.

The dining room in our house, a favorite place of mine, was always one of the coolest spots because the breeze blew directly through the windows, which looked out on the bay. On another side of the room, heavy mahogany doors carved with wonderful floral designs opened onto the courtyard. As I sat at the table, I could see the fountain in the center of the courtyard, its water bubbling softly from the top and flowing down into the basin below, making a lovely cool sound. Our two parrots, Juan and Chichi, sat on a perch in one corner while purple and red flowering vines made a background for them. On the walls of the dining room hung large paintings of holy scenes, which Mama and Papa brought from Spain. I especially liked the painting of the Virgin ascending to heaven. She stood like a queen on a fluffy cloud held up by a number of fat little cherubs. I stared for hours at her beautiful pale face and the graceful folds of her blue robe. I always wished I could look like her.

I remember that Papa was upset that afternoon. At first he did not eat at all. He sat staring at a spot on the wall directly behind Grandma and he twisted the end of his moustache with one hand as he drummed his fingers on the table making a nervous, impatient tapping sound. Grandma narrowed her eyes and asked him what he was looking at so intently, but he did not answer her. Instead, he looked down and took a bit of platano, chewed the soft, white fruit once or twice, and spit it on his plate. I was shocked.

"Eulalia!" he snapped at the maid. "Tell Luz to come here!"

Eulalia, frightened at his unusual outburst, quickly ran for the kitchen to find Luz, the cook. Her bare feet made no sound as she crossed the tile floor and ran out of the dining room to the cook house, which was a separate building a few yards away. Soon the two Indian girls hurried into the dining room, Luz leading as Eulalia hung back not wanting to catch Papa's wrath. Luz moved silently toward the table, her single braid swaying from side to side across her back.

"You called for me, Señor?" Her voice quivered and there was fear in her dark eyes.

"Luz, the food is terrible! It's so dry I can't swallow it." Papa's eyes flashed. He pushed his plate away toward the middle of the table. "I won't put up with this any longer. You are dismissed." Then he looked at my mother and said, "Find us a new cook."

Luz, looking hurt and confused, bowed her head and left the room. I wondered at Papa's behavior. He usually never talked with the servants except to say good morning or good evening. If he was pleased or displeased with something they had done, he told Mama and she took care of it. It was also strange that Papa who is a just man should treat Luz so unfairly, dismissing her like that over such a trifle. Besides, the food was the same as always.

I watched him as he sat leaning with his elbows on the table holding his wine goblet in his fingers. He frowned and slowly turned the silver cup around and around. Then suddenly he stood up and without saying a word stormed out of the room. Mama went after him while the rest of us sat there looking at one another. When we left the table, I followed Roberto out into the courtyard.

"Roberto, what's wrong with Papa?" I asked. "What happened at the docks this morning?"

"Oh, it's nothing for a girl to know."

He grinned at me knowing talk like that would make me angry. He was only a year older than I. We look very much alike and we had always done things together until a year earlier when Papa had begun to treat us differently. Roberto went to the fair in Portobelo with Papa, and he was allowed to go out into the city alone. I was expected to stay home and sew or read or play on the harpsichord Papa ordered from your city, Seville. I liked doing those things, but I also liked getting out, going down to the docks with Papa, riding with him to the yard where his ships were built. He still took me riding, but I was not allowed to go to the docks anymore, and it seemed like the only time I went out in the city was to mass or to visit friends with Mama and Grandma.

I glared at Roberto. Then I gave him a good kick on the leg.

"Ouch!" He grabbed his shin just as I raised my skirt to kick him again.

"Tell me, or I'll do it again!"

"I'll tell," he laughed, backing away from me. We moved to the edge of the fountain and sat in the sunlight. Roberto told me news came that morning that an English pirate, Henry Morgan, had captured Portobelo. I had never been to Portobelo, but Papa went there at least once a year when the galleons came in with merchandise for him from Cadiz or Cartagena. He always came back with stories about how unhealthy the climate is there: it rains constantly, there are too many insects, and many people die from the fever of the plague. Often the warehouses in Portobelo are filled with gold and silver waiting for His Majesty's ships. It was this treasure that Morgan was after.

Roberto said that the docks that morning hummed with talk about the raid on Portobelo. His account of what happened to the unfortunate souls who were living there made me forget that we were sitting in the hot sun in the middle of the day.

Morgan attacked at night. The town, totally unprepared, was caught by surprise. The people awakened, terrified by screaming cutthroats running up and down swinging cutlasses and firing pistols at everything that moved. The pirates forced Don Geraldo Avila, the governor, his soldiers, and many of the townspeople into the main fortress which lies at the mouth of the harbor. There, the governor and his men fought heroically from daybreak until noon, preventing the pirates from capturing the fort. In fact, it looked like our men would triumph. They bombarded the attackers with hot oil and pots full of explosive powder which blew up upon hitting the ground. Then Morgan thought of a plan that was so cruel and evil that it sickens me to tell you.

He gathered all the priests and nuns of Portobelo, there were thirty or forty, and he made them build ladders and drag them in front of his men as they stormed the fort. The religious people were supposed to get the ladders to the wall and stand them there for the pirates to scale. Morgan was certain that Governor Avila and his soldiers would not fire on the holy ones. With the ladders against the walls, the pirates could climb up and gain entrance to the stronghold.

Poor Don Geraldo! How it must have broken his heart to have to make such a decision. But at last he knew that the only hope of saving the town was to keep the pirates from the fortress, so he ordered his men to fire on them. Naturally, many of the priests and nuns who were at the front were killed, but Morgan kept on with the attack. Eventually some made it to the walls with the ladders. In no time, the pirates were inside the fort fighting hand to hand with our soldiers. After a ferocious struggle our men were beaten and Morgan asked Don Geraldo to surrender. When the Governor told him that he would never surrender to an English devil, Morgan shot Don Geraldo right there in front of his wife and daughter who had begged him to surrender to save his life. The women were then taken prisoner and held for ransom along with the other people in the town.

Messengers had come to Papa that morning asking

him to give money to ransom the townspeople of Portobelo. Morgan had them all gathered together in the
cathedral. He was torturing one or two of them each day
in front of everybody, vowing that he would spare nobody
if he did not get his ransom.

Just as Roberto finished his account, Mama called
from the shaded area of the patio. "Marta, come in out of
the sun. You know it's not good for your skin."

"Yes, Mama," I stood up and walked toward her, suddenly realizing that I was awfully hot.

"Marta, Marita, what am I to do with you if you
insist on going out in the sun without a hat? Here you
are growing into a young lady and you must start acting
like one. Your skin is your best feature. If you let it brown,
what will people think? Do you want them to say you look
like an Indian or a slave?"

Mama always worried about my skin. I suppose she
was right about it being my best feature. According to her,
the whiter it was, the prettier I was. She was not alone in
that belief, and she was not as foolish as some of the other
Creole women around here like Señora Ines de Zavaleta
and Señora Ana de Borallo whose stupidity nearly killed
them the year before when they ate pieces of earthen pots
which they thought would turn their skin even paler.

Everyone said that Mama was the most beautiful
woman in Panama, and she was. People also said, when
they thought I couldn't hear them, that it was unfortunate that I looked more like my father. It was true that
my hands and feet were big like his and I had his square
jaw and his long pointed nose. I was a plain girl, and when
I stood side by side with my beautiful mother, I looked
even plainer. Mama wanted me to be pretty like her, but
God has made me otherwise.

"I am sorry, Mama," I said, "next time I'll wear my hat."

"But dear, please stay out of the sun altogether unless there is absolutely no way to avoid it. You know, Marta, soon young men will be courting you. You must always strive to look your best." She had started saying things like that a lot. She made me feel embarrassed, and I wished she would stop. She tucked a curl of hair behind my ear, "Now both of you, get away to your rooms. It is siesta time." She pushed me along in front of her.

Usually during siesta time the house is as still as the middle of the night. But while I lay on my bed that afternoon thinking about Henry Morgan, I heard three men enter the house and go into Papa's room. I recognized the voices of two of them who were fellow merchants with Papa. The third man, I learned later, was Don Fernando Piñula y Fuentes, the Governor of Panama. I could hear quiet voices coming from Papa's room for an hour or so before the men left. When the door closed behind them, I arose and went to Papa.

"Come in, Marita," he called when he saw me standing at the doorway. He was sitting at his writing table with one of his account books open in front of him. He held out his hand and motioned for me to come to him.

"Were those men here for the ransom?" I asked as I crossed the room toward him.

"Oh, so you know, princess?" He always called me princess. "I gave them the ten thousand ducats I was saving to build the new house in the country. It looks like we will have to do with the old one for a while longer. Your mother will be disappointed." He leaned on the table and put his face between his hands.

"Papa, are we in danger?"

He sat up, reached out, and pulled me to his side. His arms were strong and steady and I felt safe. "Of course not, princess," he said, "What makes you ask that?"

I looked up at him and said, "How can we be sure that Henry Morgan won't come to Panama?"

At first, he said nothing. Then, he said, "Roberto must have told you about that vicious man. I am sorry he did. You worry needlessly. Morgan will never get to Panama. He would be a fool to try. There are thirty leagues of jungle between us and the North Sea where he is, and the road between here and Portobello is so well protected that it would be suicide for him to bring his band of infidels along that route. Suicide. And if he tried to hack his way through the jungle, the Indians would kill him, or the bugs and the fever would." He hugged me. "No, Marta, Henry Morgan may be a beast, but he is not foolish enough to try to invade Panama. Do not worry. We are as safe here as if we were sitting in King Felipe's court." He kissed me on the cheek. "Now go play me a melody on the harpsichord. It makes me happy to hear you play so well."

I felt much better when I left him. That was five years ago. Perhaps I remember that day so clearly because even though we didn't know it at the time, it was a sign of what would come. Rosa, I must end this letter and go to mass with Grandma. You will hear more from me tomorrow. My love to you.

Your cousin,
Marta

Edward's Journal

LATE NOVEMBER 1670, CAPE TIBURÓN

I guess I should mention my parrot, Gus. I bought him while I was ashore. A lad wandered down the beach and sold him to me for a red bandana and a handful of pennies. He said he captured him in the jungle. Gus is real pretty with his green body and his blue head, and I think he's taking a liking to me. He's smart. Already he can say my name.

Usually, I like that. Today, I didn't.

Since we anchored two nights ago, more ships have come from Port Royal. I counted thirty, and I heard the Captain tell Mr. Potts that there are over 2,000 men. Today, the Captain called a meeting of all the leaders. They came over to our ship in the late afternoon when it was cooling off some. I watched them as they came up over the side, two or three from every ship. I've been on board for a long time now, and I'm used to some rough looking chaps, but the group this afternoon was rougher looking than I'd ever seen. One day on our way to the horse market, Father and I walked past the prison in Kingston and I looked through the gate at the inmates. Father told me that the men in there were murderers and rogues; they would just as soon run a knife through you as pass you on the street. Some of the chaps who came aboard today could have been twins with those criminals.

But with all those evil looking fellows, there was one that stood out from the rest. He was big, so tall he'd have to stoop to go through a doorway. He didn't wear a shirt, and his arms and chest were nothing but muscle. In his belt he had stuck a curved dagger, the kind you use to rip open flesh. His hands were so big, I'm sure they could kill somebody with a swipe. But his face was the meanest part of him. There was a purplish red scar that started at the corner of his mouth and ran straight across his cheek to where his ear used to be. His long brown hair was tied back with a piece of hide. It covered most of the side of his head, but I could see that he had no ear on his left. It was ugly to look at, but that wasn't all that was wrong with his face. His left eye was missing too, and he wore a patch to cover the hole. When I first saw this man, I felt sick like I was seeing a monster out of the stories my mother used to tell. I tried not to stare, but I couldn't help it.

"Don't let that fellow catch you lookin' at him like that or he'll put yer lights out fer good," Mr. Potts whispered in my ear.

"You know him, Mr. Potts?"

"Aye, that's Blackwort. Behind his back he's known as the Executioner. He sailed with Morgan when they took Portobelo and Maracaibo. They say he killed more of them Spanish dogs single-handed than the rest of the crew all together. He was Morgan's right-hand man for gettin' the prisoners to cough up the ransom and tell where the treasure was. I never seed it, but I hear that he has ways of torturing a man that would make Christ himself talk. He's a mean un, Edward. Stay clear of him."

"What happened to his face?"

"A few years back, he got into a fight over a woman in Port Royal. He was caught from behind by surprise, and before he could put a stop to it, the other party carved up his face real good."

"What happened to the other fellow, Mr. Potts?"

"He met his maker quicker than you can spit." He spat on the deck. "That fellow didn't have a chance, he didn't."

By this time, everybody was on board. When the meeting started, I stuck around leaning against the fo'castle. I figured I should be close in case the Captain called for me. Gus, my parrot, sat on my shoulder where he is most of the time now.

The Captain was getting down to business, speaking to his visitors about the battles ahead, when that stupid bird started to talk. And he didn't talk quiet, he screeched.

"EDWARD! EDWARD! EDWARD!"

I told him to shut up, but he kept on going like a lunatic. I remember thinking that everybody was grinning at me until I saw the Captain. He stood there scowling and growled, "Make that blasted bird shut up, or I'll keel-haul you."

I felt my face turning the color of that red bandana I paid for Gus with, and I was wishing I had the bandana back instead of the loud-mouthed bird. All the time Gus went on screeching. I grabbed him from my shoulder, and he bit me hard on the thumb. It hurt so bad that I almost dropped him. But I held on and finally after what seemed like an unhealthy long time I shoved him into his cage and threw a piece of sail over it. With that cloth blocking the light, I guess Gus thought it was night, because he finally shut up. I suppose he went to sleep. I didn't care what he did as long as he quit that racket. Feeling relieved, but still hot in the face, I stood up and looked around me praying not to be the center of attention anymore.

My prayers were answered: the men were all looking back at the Captain and the Captain was talking about the battles to come. So I guessed he wasn't going to keel-haul me after all. Then I saw one person still looking at me with a big grin on his face. He was a lad, maybe a couple of years older than me. At first I felt kind of mad that he should laugh at me, but though his smile was mocking, there was something friendly about it and I found myself grinning back at him.

Meanwhile, the Captain was organizing the leaders of the other ships. Since there were so many men, he divided them up into two squadrons. They elected Captain Morgan admiral of the whole fleet and the head of one of the squadrons. He passed out to each captain letters which he said were from His Majesty, King Charles II. The letters gave the King's permission for us to carry out any manner of hostilities against the Spanish nation.

Captain Morgan and Blackwort stood facing the rest of the men. Blackwort was so big next to everybody else, he stood out like a horse in a herd of goats. But the Captain began to talk, and as he spoke you knew that he might not be the tallest, but he was really the biggest man around. You knew he meant business and he expected to be agreed with. Everybody in that unholy looking bunch listened to him with interest.

"I have here the Articles for each of us to sign. I think you will find them agreeable." He smiled at the group and then he read, "I, being the organizer and leader of this expedition, will take the share of fourteen men." He looked around to see if anyone would dare to disagree. "Each captain of a ship will get nine shares." The visitors smiled. "The surgeon, besides his ordinary pay will receive 200 pieces of eight for the use of his medicines, and the ship's carpenter will get one hundred pieces of eight besides his regular pay. For each man on the expedition, one fair share of the take. Now here are the special bonuses: if a man loses both hands he can collect 1800 pieces of eight or eighteen slaves, whichever he chooses, and depending on whether or not we take slaves this trip. Any soul unfortunate enough to lose both legs will get 1500 pieces of eight or six slaves. There will be fifty pieces for any man who is the first into battle, or for the first to take down the Spanish flag and fly our colors." He stopped reading and looked over the group gathered before him. "Is there any man here who doesn't think these Articles are fair?" There was silence. "Then I pass them to you to fix your marks."

He handed the paper first to Blackwort who made his special mark—one box on top of another looking a little like a square letter B—with a slow, jerky motion.

The Captain called me, "Edward, fetch brandy for everybody. We'll seal the agreement with a drink."

When I heard the part about the losing of limbs and eyes, I got a little nervous. I hadn't really thought much about getting hurt. There was a man in our crew who has a hook where his left hand was. I wondered how it happened. I tried to imagine what it would be like to have only one hand.

I went below, fetched the brandy, and had just finished filling the last cup when somebody spoke from behind, "I'll give you ten shillings for that bird."

I turned around to see the same lad who had been grinning at me earlier. "He's not for sale yet, I'm going to give him one more chance."

"Well if you ever want to get rid of him, remember my offer. My name is Ned Green. I'm sailing on the *Fair Maid*."

"I know your name, Edward," he said as we shook hands.

"How can you know it?" I asked, surprised. "I don't think we've ever met."

"Every man here knows your name," Ned said pointing at Gus' cloth covered cage. We laughed.

Ned was a couple of inches taller than me. I liked the way he looked, especially his freckled face and his bushy eyebrows. "How'd you get connected with this crew?" He waved his arm at the men who were sitting around drinking and talking.

"I'm paying off my father's gambling debt. What about you?"

We sat on some barrels of dried beef.

"Well," Ned said, "I was hanging around the Silver Flagon in Port Royal one night about a month ago, when I heard these two chaps talking about Morgan's new expedition. It sounded appealing to me so I asked them how I could get signed on. They told me, and here I am." He shrugged and spread both arms out wide, palms up.

"The Silver Flagon," I said, surprised. That tavern had a name as the location of murders and stabbings when the ships were in. Father told me to stay away from there. I didn't doubt that was the place where Blackwort had been cut up. "What were you doing in there?" I asked.

"I've been in worse places than that," he said, and a far off look came into his eyes. He spoke fine in tones like a gentleman.

"Judging from the way you talk, I bet you just came from England," I said, hoping he would tell me his story.

"Two years ago." He took the brandy jug they were passing around and drank. I don't know how he could stand the taste of the stuff. When he offered me the jug, I shook my head. I must have had a funny look on my face because he said, "Take some. It won't hurt you."

"No thanks."

"What's wrong? You afraid?"

"No," I said, but I really was, knowing what drink did to my father. "Just not thirsty."

"Oh." He put on a mocking look, and for a minute I wondered if I like him. He talked good English, but there was something rough about him.

"Did your family come with you two years ago?" I asked.

A forlorn look came over him and he said, "They did. But my parents are dead now, and my sister might as well be. We were on our way to Kingston to see my uncle when our ship was hijacked by the Spanish." His eyes got watery. "They took my sister and me prisoner and sunk the ship with my parents on it." He looked like he was struggling hard with his feelings.

"I don't know why I'm telling you all this," he said turning his face away.

I felt sorry for him. "Do you want to talk about something else?"

"No. I want to tell you." He looked at me with dry eyes and smiled. "It just got to me for a minute."

"The Spanish captured you. Then what?" My curiosity was taking hold.

He sighed and said, "I was sold as a bondsman to a plantation owner in Cuba for work in the cane fields. After a year of that they brought me into the house to wait on the owner. What a pig he was. He called me Miguel. 'Miguel, fix my pipe. Miguel, bring me my shirt. Miguel, help me make water.' He couldn't do anything for himself. He'd drop his hat and call me to pick it up for him and put it back on his head." All signs of sorrow were gone from Ned's face. He looked disgusted now. "He beat his slaves and the ones who were too worn out to work anymore, he refused to feed. They starved to death."

A fiddler struck up a tune and some of the men, feeling their brandy, started to dance a jig on the deck in front of us. I didn't much notice though.

"How'd you get away from there?" I asked.

"I made friends with a man they hired to add a wing to the house. He had a small boat and one night after everybody was asleep I sneaked down to the water where he was waiting. He sailed me to Port Royal. Then I walked on to Kingston, but my uncle wasn't there anymore." He slid off the barrel. The men from the *Fair Maid* were getting ready to leave.

"What about your sister?" I asked.

I guess he wasn't listening because he said, "Who?"

"Your sister. Do you know what happened to her?"

Then he said a funny thing. He gave me that mocking look again and said, like he didn't give a whit, "Oh, I don't know."

I didn't know what to think when he shook hands and he said good-by. If I had a sister, I know I'd care something for her.

—Edward

DECEMBER 1670, ISLE OF ST. CATHERINE

Since my last writing we sailed to the Island of St. Catherine, Providence Island, some call it. With a fair wind, it's a day's sail from here to the River Chagres where they say we start the march to Panama. The Spanish use this island as a kind of prison for criminals from Panama and other places. We came here to get some prisoners who would be willing to lead us to Panama.

Two days ago we sailed up to St. Catherine at night and anchored a mile or so offshore with plans to attack the island in the morning. About sunrise I went on deck. My head had just come through the hatch when Potts spied me and put me to work loading bags of shot and powder into the four boats they were readying to lower into the water.

It promised to be a hot sunny day without any wind. The blue-green sea was smooth as a fingernail. I counted twenty ships anchored on all sides of us and on every one, men rushed fore and aft readying more skiffs. Some of the small boats already floated in the water loaded with men who shouted and joked at the fellows still on the ships.

The island we were going to attack, St. Catherine, was bigger than most of those we passed on the way. It looked to be about six leagues long and it was flat. From the ship I could see no sign of humans. They told me there would be fortresses and guns, but I saw nothing save the white beach bordered with coconut palms. About two hours past daybreak our boats were finally stocked with guns and ammunition and swords. They ordered me to get into one of the boats and seeing Higgins in the stern of one, I climbed in and sat down next to him and held on tight as a leech because I didn't exactly like what was to come.

The ropes creaked through the pulleys as they lowered us toward the water and the front and back ropes didn't work together like they should, so one end of the boat would go lower than the other; someone would yell; we would jerk to a stop; get the boat level; start going down again only to have the other end drop. We stopped and started like that, and I was sure I was going to be thrown into the sea until finally I heard the splash of the bow hitting the water. A trice later the skiff was afloat, nice and level and safe, but I still held on tight because the last thing I wanted was to be thrown out of the boat. I don't like being close to deep water. I'd sooner be amid a herd of wild pigs. When I was aboard the *Satisfaction*, I didn't mind because she rides high above the water. She's big and you feel safe aboard, but in those little skiffs, it's no good.

There were ten of us in the boat and at first by all the joking going on you would have thought we were headed for a party. But when we got closer to the island, the atmosphere changed. The men quieted down and sat with their eyes on the white beach and the hedge of palm trees. The only sounds were the dipping and splashing of the oars. Those who had muskets held them in their laps ready to use.

On all sides there were other boats loaded with men. I looked for Ned Green, but didn't see him.

Once a bird flew up from the top of a palm and a dozen muskets fired at it.

"Easy men," someone shouted. "Don't go mistaking no bird for them devils. We can't go wasting shot."

It was midmorning by the time I felt the boat scrape against the sand on the shore. We saw no sign of the enemy, but I was edgy when I climbed from the skiff.

It felt peculiar being on land again. There was no give to the ground and I had to tighten up my legs when I walked. They were loose from going with the rise and fall of the ship. It smelled real good on shore, sort of damp and fruity like things growing. The sun blazed down and I licked the sweat away from my upper lip. The salt tasted good and I licked again.

By this time the beach was getting crowded. I looked for Ned, but had no luck. I spied the giant, Blackwort, climbing out of a boat nearby and I moved away. When I saw Higgins joining a line of fellows that was moving through the soft sand away from the beach and up into the coconut palms, I ran after him.

"Higgins, where are we going?" I asked, coming alongside him. He was barefoot and shirtless and he carried a sword in his hand.

"We'll be marching clear to the other end o' this island, Ed." His jowls shook as he walked along. "Them papists are hidin' out down there in their forts."

"How far is it? Five or six leagues?" I asked.

"Aye, about that."

"Do you think we'll be meeting up with any of them before we get to the other end of the island, Higgins?" I asked looking from side to side trying to catch sight of anything that might be hiding behind the round grayish trunks of the palm trees that grew everywhere. We had left the beach and now walked under the tall trees. It was easy going because there was no underbrush. There was nothing worse than dry grass and sand and dirt under our feet.

"I'm hopin' not, Ed. You know, I figure we've got more men than them three times over again. They ain't fools enough to fight us out in the open away from the protection o' their stone walls."

After awhile we broke from the trees into a clearing about twenty yards square where we came upon a group of thatched huts. I found some calabash gourds that someone used for cups and bowls, but the only real sign that anybody had been around lately was the smell of smoke from their cooking fires that still smoldered. I hadn't had anything to eat since before sunup and the thick smoky smell made me think of roast meat and yarns.

The clearing was fast filling with men who had stopped moving forward. Some milled around and others looked for food remains.

Mr. Potts yelled in a gruff voice, "Keep on movin' ye lazy hogs! We got to see the other end o' this island before nightfall. Captain's already gone ahead. Follow him!"

I was somewhere in the middle of the crowd as we filed out of the clearing along a path cut through thick brush and vines. The palms were behind us and I felt closed in by the greenery growing on both sides and overhead. It smelled swampy and not so healthy. I didn't like it much and I felt better when I saw a spot of bright sunlight up ahead. But it wasn't long before we passed through that clearing and ended up back in the jungle. It took us most of the day to march four leagues through woods and clearings until finally we came out of the darkest, longest stretch of jungle into a grassy field which must have been half a league wide and just as long.

It felt real good to have the sun on my back again and to lose that hemmed in feeling. We kept on marching across that field. The front of the line had already gone into the bushes at the other end and I was more than halfway there when in the distance, over the trees and bushes, I saw puffs of black smoke and flashes of fire. Then I heard muskets cracking and cannons booming like thunder.

A short fellow wearing nothing but a pair of trousers came running out of the thicket. As he ran, he waved his arms, crisscrossing them in front of his face. "Stop! Stop!" he yelled. He came as far as me, and seeing that the army was slowing down and looking his way he came to a standstill panting and trying to catch his breath.

"The Captain says wait here. Now that we've found the devils, he wants to save the attack until morning." The fellow threw himself down on the grass and sat there breathing hard.

"What did ye see up there, Will?" Mr. Potts ran up from behind and lowered himself to his knees on the ground next to the man.

"Well now, I seen plenty to worry me." The fellow named Will sat up straight and pointed down the way he had come. "Ye see where all that smoke and noise is coming from?"

By now he was circled by men who gathered round to hear him better. They gazed down where he pointed and nodded their heads.

"Well right there happens to be where the bridge lies that connects this here island to the smaller one. And right there happens to be a fort big as most I've seen in these parts and it's loaded with them Spaniards."

"What about the guns? How many? How big?" Mr. Potts asked leaning toward Will.

Will's eyes opened wide, "Aye, there's cannon big as most I've seen in these parts. They're sticking out of all the portals and they're pointing every which way. It don't look to me like there's a spot o' ground or air that them papists don't have covered."

"They'll put up a fight, then?"

"Most sure as I'm sitting here on this grass," he patted the ground. "And I would say it'll be a fight big as any I've been in yet."

The men, talking in an uneasy way, broke up into groups and sprawled out over the grassy field. I was thinking about making a serious search for Ned when Captain Morgan called me and told me to get the squadron leaders together. It took some running all over that field before I could locate everybody. The field was bigger than the market square in Kingston and there must have been more than a thousand men spread all over it, resting, talking, cleaning muskets, or searching for food. I looked for Ned, but I couldn't see him anywhere.

I finally passed word to the squadron leaders who came over to the edge of the field where the Captain waited. All sat down in front of him except for Blackwort who stood at the back, legs apart, fingering the handle of his dagger. Before I knew what was happening he turned his head my way and caught me staring at him. Then he yanked the dagger from its leather scabbard and I jumped as I heard it whiz past my ear so close my hair blew in the wind it made. I turned around to see the knife stuck in the grass a yard behind me. Blackwort motioned to me to pick it up. I pulled it from the ground and walked back to him, my legs soft as pudding. I felt the blade slice across my hand as he yanked the dagger from me, saying not a word, but glaring at me through his one eye.

I backed away from him quick, remembering Mr. Potts' warning that he didn't like to be stared at. When I was a safe distance, I turned and ran, checking the palm of my hand. There was a thin red scratch running across it from thumb to little finger. The bleeding wasn't bad and it didn't sting too much.

I felt hungry and I wondered when we were going to eat, but I didn't see anybody preparing food anywhere. There wasn't any fire smoke or pots and pans rattling or anything that hinted of supper. I thought maybe there was a rule about not eating before a battle, but there wasn't anybody around I felt I could ask. It was getting dark so I searched for the fellows from the *Satisfaction*. When I found some of them over to one side in a corner of the field, I threw myself down on the grass a little way from Monkey and Moon who were fast asleep. It was almost comfortable lying there in the grass with my shirt for a pillow after having slept so many nights in that close, stinking hole on the ship. I looked up at the stars that were just starting to come out and I felt real lonesome.

"Don't be a baby," I said to myself when I felt a lump growing in my throat. And I closed my eyes to fight off the tears that came anyway. I was glad for the darkness so nobody could see me. By and by I opened my eyes and stared at the night sky. What would happen in the morning? With the guns from the fort pointing right at us, I couldn't figure out how anybody could get across that bridge to the other island where the Spanish were holed up. Then I worried about what I would do if we did get across that bridge and had to fight the enemy man to man. Could I shoot somebody? Would I be able to get them before they got me? What was I doing there anyway? Why wasn't I home in my own bed with a belly full of cornbread and meat? Could I run away and hide? No, on this small island I couldn't hide for very long. And anyway, if I did that, Captain Morgan would see to it I didn't get off the island alive. He'd probably tell Blackwort to stick that dagger in my gut. I felt the scratch across my hand and shivered.

The next morning I felt a pain in my side and woke to see Monkey standing over me. His foot was drawn back behind him ready to kick me again. "Get up ye lazy cockroach. Captain wants to see ye."

As I sat up, the Captain came toward me. He looked fresh and groomed like he was going to call on a lady of quality.

"Edward, you sleeping scum!" he snapped as I got to my feet fast as my stiff body would let me, "Get over here!"

Under a heavy cloudy sky, I followed him across the field until he stopped and pointed at two firelock muskets and two pistols side by side on the ground. Next to them sat a big leather bag divided into two sections.

"Carry the guns for me." He motioned to the grass where they lay. "The bag's got powder and shot. Carry that too. Now here's what I want you to do: After I fire, I'll give you the gun to reload while you hand me a loaded one. Understand?"

"Yes, sir." I was glad Father taught me how to load and clean the flintlock he used for hunting.

"And you'd better keep up with me." He looked me up and down like he wondered if I could do it.

"I won't fail you sir," I said.

"You do and I'll rip the liver out of you. Now grab those weapons and the bag and follow me." He picked up one of the pistols and strode quick toward the far end of the field.

I hung the leather bag over my shoulder. Then I grabbed the two muskets and the pistol and started out after him. The guns were heavy. I could have managed if I had to carry only them, but the bag was heavy and it threw me off balance. I tried carrying both muskets under an arm to balance the powder bag hanging at my other side, but one of the muskets would always slip out from under my arm and fall to the ground. Then I put the pistol in my belt and balanced a gun on each shoulder, and that was better though it was still hard for me to go very fast.

Loaded up like that, I hurried after the Captain as quick as I could. I was not alone, for there were men moving along all around me heading for the edge of the field where the Captain waited.

The weather was dark and cloudy and the heavy air made any sound quieter and duller than usual. It hung so heavy it was hard to move fast, it was like a weight all over my body.

When I caught up to him, Captain Morgan snatched one of the muskets from me and held it in both hands above his head.

"Men," he shouted, "the scumbag papists are outnumbered and they know they're doomed. A purse of gold to the first man over their walls!"

"We'll roast a Spaniard for supper!" someone yelled.

The Captain took off at the front of the army, running toward the stand of palms which made a kind of fence between us and the beach. I stumbled along behind him trying to keep up, not thinking of anything but staying close to him.

We passed under the palms and there in front of me, just beyond firing distance was a stone fortress. It sat on the other side of a channel which was crossed by a narrow stone bridge. A big cannon stuck out every portal of that fort. Quiet came from there, and it was real unfriendly quiet.

The men with muskets and stonebows lined up on the

sand in ranks twenty across with the Captain in front row center and me by his side. Those who had only swords took up the rear, ready to scale the walls and fight close inside the fort. Arranged like that, we marched toward the fort. Still the fort was quiet. Where are they? I wondered. I knew they must be watching us from somewhere behind those thick walls. Why didn't they give a sign? I expected any minute to be blown off the beach by a cannonball. But still nothing happened. It took what seemed a year for us to cross the sand to the bridge. I kept trying to catch my breath, not from the marching, but from the fear I felt. What are they waiting for? I asked myself.

Then the answer came. The instant the first man's foot hit the bridge, that fort came alive. At the top of the wall, soldiers bobbed up, shoulder to shoulder and fired down on us in volleys of shot and stones. My line shot and then dropped to its knees to reload, except for the Captain who grabbed a loaded gun from me and fired again with the second line. I cursed my shaking hands as I reloaded the Captain's gun and handed it to him so he could fire with the third line.

Just about then, the cannons started to go off, shooting those iron balls like rocks out of a volcano. The explosions deafened me, but not long enough to cover the screams of the men who were hit and lay squirming on the sand.

"Keep it up men. We're gaining ground," yelled the Captain, but hardly anybody heard him above the noise.

The firing from the fort didn't cease, and they were hitting our men right and left, but we were hurting them too. We were hitting the heads above that wall like targets on a fence, and three men had made it onto the bridge. Then a second later all three lay dead on the ground.

I heard shot whizzing past my head and a cannonball

the size of a coconut landed behind me with a thud sending the sand spraying all over.

The air was full of the smell of burning gunpowder. Then as if the thunder of the cannons opened up the clouds, the rain started. At first it only sprinkled but then it got harder and harder until it seemed like a passel of washerwomen in the sky emptied their barrels right over us. The rain fell so hard we couldn't see more than three of four yards in front. Through the water the fort was nothing but a grey shadow, but the Captain kept on yelling for us to attack and capture the bridge. He ran forward, raising his gun to his shoulder, searching for something to aim at. He must have seen something through the sheet of water because he stopped, took aim, and pulled the trigger. Nothing happened. He pulled the trigger again. Still nothing. Just then, I heard a piece of shot whoosh between us, not more than an inch away from the Captain's head. He hurled his gun to the ground.

"Give it to me!" he snarled, yanking the other gun out of my hand. The Captain took aim once again and pulled the trigger. This time something happened, but it didn't have anything to do with the Captain's gun. I heard a scream and saw a fellow just in front of me put his hands to his face and crumple to the ground. He lay there with his eyes open while the blood flowed out of a bean-sized hole in his forehead. The rain washed the blood from his face down into the sand. I wondered at him lying there so still, when only a trice before he had been running and yelling like the rest.

The Captain shouted, "This is no good! Bloody rain! Retreat! Retreat!"

The rain put a stop to the fighting on both sides and the roars and booms of the guns gave way to splashing rain mixed with the sounds of voices yelling, "Retreat!"

The next I knew, I was turning around and trudging back toward the same field where I had spent the night.

I spotted Moon and ran over to him. We walked along together; the water made beads on Moon's bald head before it ran off onto his soaking shirt and pants. He held a pistol at his side.

"What happened, Moon, why are we going back?"

"Blasted powder's wet. Guns won't fire."

"What do we do now?"

"I, fer one, vote for turning back. We can get us a little town somewhere on the mainland, pick up enough swag to get us by fer awhile. This kind of fightin' don't appeal to me. It's too easy for a fellow to get killed if he don't starve to death first." He was quiet for awhile, but then he said, "No, I ain't goin' to turn back. I figure to get me some o' that pelf in Panama, maybe a piece of that altar they say is pure gold."

"Do you think there really is such a thing, Moon?" I asked.

"That's what they say, though I ain't never talked to anyone that's seen it."

The rain finally stopped; soon the clouds broke and the sun came out bright and warm. Men took their guns apart and spread powder on the ground to dry. I watched them and did the same with the Captain's guns. While they worked, the fellows grumbled about how hungry they were and how bad the fight was going for us. More and more men began to talk of heading back to the ships and chasing after easier prize.

Captain Morgan figured he had better do something fast to stop the talk about quitting. Frowning, he stared straight at a yellow-haired chap who spoke loud about going back to the ships. The chap got quiet in a hurry,

and decided he had business somewhere else. Then, the
Captain turned toward me.

"Edward, find that lad, Ned, who sails on the *Fair
Maid*. They tell me he speaks Spanish."

"Is he ashore, sir?"

"Aye, he's here. Try the squadrons to the back of the
field. Dutch John, his captain, brought up the rear. Find
him and get him over here fast if you know what's good
for you." He gave me a shove.

I ran toward the far end of the field. There were a lot
of men at this end. Most had no shirts, and it was hard for
me to tell one from the other in such a crowd. I worked
my way through them as they sat and lay on the ground
fiddling with their weapons and grumbling about their
empty stomachs. Finally I saw Ned sitting cross-legged on
the ground in a circle of men. Since he was the only one
in the group wearing a shirt and boots, he was easy to
spot. He had such a clean, respectable look about him, it
was hard to think he belonged there.

We traded greetings and then I said, "Ned, the Captain wants to see you. I hope you speak Spanish."

"That I do."

"Follow me."

We found the Captain down on the beach around a
point from the bridge. He was ordering Monkey to attach
two dirty white cloths to the top of a pole which stuck up
head high in the middle of a three-man dugout. When he
saw us, he waved us over to him with a jerk of his head.
Then he looked hard at Ned taking in everything from his
curly brown hair to the brown leather boots which came
up to his knees.

"Dutch John tells me you speak Spanish." He pointed
up the beach in the direction of the smaller island and
the fort.

"Yes, sir, I do." Ned stood up straight as a post but he answered the Captain in an easy tone like he was talking to me or any of the other fellows around. I had to admire him. I tried to talk to the Captain as little as possible, but every time I had to speak to him, I felt nervous and my words never came out like I wanted them to. Ned sure didn't have that problem.

"And under pressure, can you make yourself understood?"

"I guess so. For two years I spoke nothing else."

The Captain raised his eyebrows. "Then I want you to deliver a message to the fort."

When I heard him say that, my chest tightened up and I could feel my heart beating. How could Ned stand there so calm getting ordered to face the enemy on their territory with nothing but a white truce flag to stop them from killing him?

"Green," said the Captain, "I want you to tell the bastard over there in that fort that if he doesn't deliver himself and his men to me, I'll put them all to the sword, and grant quarter to none. Let him know if he surrenders he may live to see his old age, but if he resists, they're all done for." Then he smiled and said, "Mention that some of us are real inventive when it comes to torture. We learned it from the Caribs." He pointed toward the dugout. "Go now, and say exactly what I told you. Make sure they know the only way for them is to surrender."

"I will do it, sir." Ned started for the dugout.

"Green," the Captain called after him. Ned stopped and turned toward him. "Let me hear how all that sounds in Spanish."

Ned looked surprised, but he rattled off some peculiar sounds and the Captain looked satisfied that Ned really could speak Spanish. He nodded his head and said, "Fine. I think they'll get the message."

A grinding noise came from the boat as I helped push it across the sand in to the water. Ned stepped into the center of the canoe while a man holding an oar got in at each end. I watched the canoe glide out from the shore and head for the narrow channel between the two islands.

The canoe out there alone on the water made me think about my target sticks in the pond at home. I used to toss one into the water and when it bobbed to the surface, I would bombard it with stones pretending I was the English navy sinking Spanish and French ships. Was Ned going to be a target for the Spaniards like that stick was for me?

I stayed on the beach watching for Ned to come back while some of the men collected the dead and saw to their burial. Finally in the late afternoon I spied not one, but three dugouts traveling toward me close to the shore. Ned sat in the lead canoe followed by the other two boats both flying white flags of truce.

I ran to call the Captain who, when he heard Ned brought some Spanish fellows with him, said to have them wait on the beach and that he would be down to see them when he was ready. I went back to the beach, and we waited a long time; not because the Captain was busy at anything very important, but because he wanted to make the Spaniards wait.

Three Spaniards came from the fort with Ned. They wore faded brown doublets and they looked shabby. Their boots were old and the leather was cracked. One of the men's toes stuck out where the leather had come away from the sole. And one of them, a man shorter than me, cleared his throat every few seconds as if he had something stuck there and couldn't get it out.

We waited and waited on that beach. The three Spaniards got restless and they said things to each other that I couldn't understand, but by their tone I could tell they didn't think much of Ned and me. At first, Ned ignored them, so I did too. But they kept up their jeering and I could tell Ned was getting pretty hot. We were close to coming to blows with them when the Captain finally showed up with Blackwort.

As soon as the Spanish fellows saw those two, they sobered up real quick.

"Well?" The Captain looked them over. "They're as good as ours," said Ned in a disgusted tone.

"They surrendered to you?" The Captain arched his eyebrows,

"No, but they will to you."

"How?"

"The Governor says that he doesn't have the forces to defend the island against you. He's willing to surrender, but he wants to make it look like you took the island by force and like he and his men fought to the end. When word gets out that you captured the island he wants the world to think that he and everybody on his side fought like heroes to defend it."

"So!" The captain raised his dark eyebrows and pressed his lips together as if he was trying not to smile. "The pigs want me to help them hide their cowardice, do they?" He thrust out his arm and poked his finger in the ribs of the chap whose toes stuck out of his boots. The fellow jumped backwards looking pale like he might faint and bumped into Blackwort who shoved him onto the sand. The Captain turned to the next fellow, the one who was making those peculiar sounds in his throat. He smiled kind of mean, pointed his finger so it was no more than half an inch away from the man's chest and said, "I never run into such cowards, and crooked ones yet, as the pigs that are holed up on that island."

Captain Morgan faced the third Spaniard. This man stared at the Captain without any sign of fear. He was the one who led the jeering against Ned and me. The Captain dropped his hands to his sides and frowned at the man.

"Killing cowards isn't amusing. It is too easy. The challenge comes when they fight," the Captain said as he stared at the fellow. Then he turned to Ned and asked, "What does the brave little Governor want us to do?"

"He has a plan where you would bring your troops by night to the bridge that joins the two islands. You would then attack the fort of San Geronimo which is the one that guards the bridge. At the same time all the ships of your fleet should draw near the castle of Santa Teresa which lies at the other end of the island, and attack it by sea. While those two attacks are going on, you should land some troops near the battery called San Mateo. These newly landed men can intercept the Governor who will be on his way between San Mateo and San Geronimo. They can take the Governor prisoner and act as if they forced him to surrender. He urged that through all of the battle there should be continuous firing at one another, but without shot or at least into the air, so nobody would be hurt. He says that if you are agreeable to this plan, you may send your reply by these messengers."

"The man may be a coward, but he's no fool." The Captain looked pleased. "Ned, tell these curs that I'll carry out my part of the plan this evening after dark. I'll order my men not to fire directly on any of them. But if one of my men is harmed at the hands of any of them, I'll order the bloodiest massacre they've ever seen." He spat at the feet of the messengers. Then he turned to me. "Edward, call the squadron leaders together."

I followed him into the grassy field beyond the beach, wondering at how easy this pirating business was.

—Edward

Marta's Letter to Rosa

15 JANUARY 1672, FINCA LAS BRISAS

Dear Rosa,

I am writing you from our sugar plantation, which lies a few leagues from Panama toward Veragua on the South Sea. It was here that Grandma, Mama, Jaime, and I came in December last year with the intention of remaining until Papa and Roberto returned from Lima, where they had gone to arrange a shipment of silver and emeralds.

Ordinarily, nothing remarkable happens when we are in the country. I pass the days reading and sewing on the patio overlooking the ocean. Often in the early morning I ride with Roberto and Jaime through the cane and rice fields down to the beach. When it begins to cool off in the afternoons we play cards. Occasionally a neighbor comes to visit, or we call on someone, and once in a very long while, there will be a fiesta.

Last year I expected life at Las Brisas to be the same as always, but fortune decided otherwise. Several extraordinary events occurred during our brief time here, the first being that our neighbor, Don Gaspar de Ureña, came to court me.

Don Gaspar, a son of the noble Ureña family of Barcelona, was a widower nearly forty years old. People thought him a pleasant sort, always cheerful and courteous. Had he not been courting me, I might have thought so too; as it was, I could only find fault with him. He was a clumsy plain-looking man. His clothes were constructed of fine cloth, but they must have been in style when he was a boy. Instead of wearing the modern full pantaloons, he still dressed in short pantaloons which came scarcely below his doublet. With these he wore silk hose covered by heavy netherstocks which reached from his shoe to some ten inches above the knee. Don Gaspar was the only man I knew who still wore netherstocks. His favorite pair was brown leather with a series of bone buttons running up each side. The doublet in which he often dressed was a horrible shade of yellowish green like the color of water left too long in a cistern. The green of his doublet reflected onto his face giving him an unhealthy pallor somewhat like a corpse.

Rosa, have I given you an idea of how unappealing he was? If you are not convinced, let me tell you this. It was Don Gaspar's habit to blink his eyes incessantly. Mama said the poor man was nervous. Grandma thought he was in need of a pair of spectacles. Whatever influenced him to blink so, it surely was disconcerting. Each time he blinked, the flesh around his eyes wrinkled into tiny rays like rivulets running off from a pond. Watching him blink, I always forgot what we were talking about. When I caught myself blinking right along with him, it was difficult not to laugh. Often when Don Gaspar visited, Jaime liked to catch my eye and to imitate the poor man by carrying on a series of exaggerated blinks behind his back. There were times when I had to pretend a fit of coughing to hide my giggles.

One afternoon when we had been at Las Brisas for nearly a week, Grandma, Mama, and I sat on the patio around a circular wooden frame which held a piece of white linen we were embroidering for a coverlet.

I was knotting a strand of green silk to begin the stem of a hibiscus when Eulalia entered the patio. Quietly she approached us, bowed, and said, "Doñas, Don Gaspar de Ureña is at the door."

"Oh how nice!" exclaimed Mama as she rose to greet him. "Show him in Eulalia." She followed the maid to the door.

"What a calamity!" I thought. "Another afternoon spoiled." In one week he had already called on us three times.

Grandma and I pushed the embroidery frame back against a wall and were closing the thread box when Don Gaspar appeared with Mama. He was wearing his awful green doublet, and his eyelids worked furiously.

"Marta, Doña Ana, isn't it delightful that Don Gaspar has honored us with another visit?" Mama said as he bowed stiffly first to Grandma, then to me.

"Indeed it is," smiled Grandma curtsying. I curtsied and said nothing, forcing myself to smile through pursed lips.

Mama directed us to sit and Don Gaspar sat down too, gracelessly making his chair scrape loudly on the floor as it slid backwards. He stood up and pulled the chair back into its original position. Then he sat down once more, turned to his left and leered at me.

"Marta, you look lovely this afternoon. I can see country life agrees with you."

"Yes," I answered looking away from him. I knew I didn't look lovely. People said I looked healthy or pleasant, but never lovely. They saved that word for Mama.

"Marta adores the country," Mama said quickly. "She thrives here by the sea where she can ride and walk about freely."

Don Gaspar nodded and blinked. "It is a rare young woman now days who seeks pleasure in the rural life. So many I know prefer the city where they squander their time at the dressmaker and at parties and things."

"Oh, but I like parties too," I said, "and new dresses."

"Yes, dear, of course. Every young girl does," Mama answered hastily. "But at heart you are truly a country girl." Then she turned and smiled at Don Gaspar. I was beginning to feel betrayed.

"Don Gaspar is there any news from Panama?" asked Grandma.

"Nothing of import, Doña Ana." He crossed his legs and leaned back in his chair. "But I must travel there tomorrow for a few days. I will come to you with all the news when I return."

"What takes you there?" Grandma asked.

"A fellow in Lima is purchasing some of my bulls and I must arrange for their transportation." He took a glass of tamarind refresca which Eulalia offered him. "I should have made the trip a fortnight ago, but the rains left the road impassable." He sipped the drink, then held it in his lap. Beads of the rust brown liquid hung on the ends of his moustache.

"Is there any favor I can do you while I am in Panama?" he asked.

"Why yes," said Grandma, "how kind of you to offer. I'm awaiting some new books from Cadiz. Don Gaspar, would you be so kind as to see if they have arrived?"

He smiled thinly and shook his head. "Doña Ana, never have I known a woman as interested in books as you. I would think you have enough to do with your sewing and your work at the hospital without bothering about words on paper." He looked at Mama. "With all respect to Doña Ana, I have never seen the value in a woman being very involved in the written word." His eyes blinked with the regularity of a music master's tapping.

Mama opened her mouth to speak, but I interrupted. "I think books are wonderful. I enjoy reading too."

Mama gave me a look signaling me to be quiet. Don Gaspar turned toward me, smiled and said, "Oh, but you are young and idle now. Wait until you marry and are the mistress of a household. Then you will have no time for books."

He looked at me tenderly and I felt my face burn as I grew angry at his presumption.

"You are wrong there, Don Gaspar," Grandma said. "Marta is like me. She will always have time for books." I could see the color in her face rising also. "And you do women a disservice when you suggest that literature should not concern them. You are disdainful of the female who thinks only of fashions and parties and yet you would deny that woman any other occupation for her mind."

Don Gaspar threw up his hands and laughed. His right hand held the glass which was still half full. The juice sloshed back and forth violently and some spilled onto the floor, forming a small puddle. He didn't notice. Mama called the maid to come wipe it up.

"Forgive me Doña Ana," he implored as he blinked even more rapidly than was his custom. "I did not mean that *some* ladies should not read. I only meant that there is no need for *most* ladies to concern themselves with such activities."

Mama frowned at Grandma. Grandma said nothing more about women and books, and the discussion ended. Don Gaspar stayed on and on, talking of farming and the bulls he raised. I watched my hands, the stones of the patio, the shadows of the leaves. Finally he rose to leave, announcing that he would not visit for a few days because of his trip to Panama. When he left, Grandma pulled the frame with the coverlet back near us and we began to work on it once again. By his frequent visits, I was beginning to fear that Don Gaspar was interested in me. Mama had never said anything to me about it, but I decided it was time to ask her.

"Mama, I think Don Gaspar is courting me. Is it true?"

She put a final stitch in the petal of a yellow orchid and smiled as she looked over at me. There was excitement in her blue eyes.

"Yes, dear, I believe he is, although he hasn't mentioned it to me."

"But Mama, I don't like him!" I cried.

"Now Marita, don't be so hasty in your judgment." She poked her needle into the base of another flower and drew the thread through with her slender white fingers. "He is a good man from one of the best families of Spain. You could do much worse than to marry an Ureña." She took another stitch. "I have heard your father say that Don Gaspar's brother is one of the King's closest advisers. You should thank the Holy One that a man from such a background is interested in you." Mama looked at me with the same persuasive expression that she wore when she was trying to convince me I would be comfortable bound into the lead breastplate and corset which I had to wear under my best gowns.

"But Mama, I cannot abide his blinking all the time. And he is dull, always talking of nothing but bulls he breeds."

"Shame, child! How unkind you are! The poor man is nervous. Help him relax and you will find him charming."

We stitched in silence. The afternoon breeze rustled through the broad shiny leaves of the vines which grew across the ceiling over our heads. Our needles pierced the linen with tapping sounds, Grandma's was as swift as mine was slow.

"He is old," I muttered in a voice almost too low to hear.

Grandma stopped sewing and looked at me. Her lips parted slightly, but she said nothing.

Then Mama said, "Why Marta, older men are wonderful husbands. Your grandfather was Don Gaspar's age, perhaps older when Grandma married him." She turned to Grandma. "Doña Ana, tell her, do you think Don Gaspar is too old for her?"

Grandma, still holding her needle, put her hand in her lap and leaned back in her chair. "That is for Marta to decide." She reached over and patted my hand. "Your grandfather was a kind and considerate man and our years together were the happiest I have ever known. May his soul rest in peace." She crossed herself. "He was a wise man and he taught me many things." She smiled but a distant expression came to her face as she said, "Oh I wish you could have heard some of the discussions we had late in the evenings about music and poetry." She lowered her voice and looked at Mama and me. "And the Inquisition."

Mama asked, "And Doña Ana, you never felt that Don Roberto was too old for you, did you?"

"Oh my, no. But I often think that our time together was too brief."

Mama looked at me as if what Grandma had said settled it. I should not object to Don Gaspar's age. However Grandma was not finished.

"But you see, Carmen, Don Roberto was an educated man, an interesting man. I don't remember that we ever talked of breeding bulls." She paused, and then added softly, "and his eyelids did not flutter like the wings of a hummingbird."

I rose, put my arms around her and kissed her on the cheek. Mama began to sew again. Then she looked at me and said in a low voice, "Remember, Marta, that you are a plain girl."

I dropped my eyes and felt my face grow hot.

"Now Carmen," Grandma interrupted.

"Well, she is," retorted Mama, "and she has to realize that this may be the best offer she has. You know, there aren't very many men in Panama that can offer a wife what Don Gaspar can offer with his wealth and rank."

"But he's ugly and ignorant!" I shouted feeling the tears filling my eyes. "I hate him!"

"Do you want to be a spinster all your life?" Mama was shouting too. "Do you want to grow old caring for your brothers' children instead of your own?"

"Mama, you don't understand!"

"I understand that you are fifteen years old, and I understand that you haven't been overwhelmed by suitors. Marta, believe me, if you let this chance pass you by, you will regret it."

By this time the tears were running down my cheeks and falling onto my breast. Grandma took my hand and squeezed it.

"Oh child," said Mama coming to me and embracing me. "I didn't mean to make you cry. It's just that when I was your age, I was married and about to be a mother. I only want you to be happy." She handed me a handkerchief. "Now dry those tears."

"Mama?"

"Yes?"

"Would you and Papa force me to marry him?"

"Marta, dear, we want the best for you. Marrying Don Gaspar would make you the mistress of a large household and a member of one of Castile's best families. That is not an opportunity to turn away from lightly. Just imagine yourself as Marta Maldonado y Contrera de Ureña. What respect such a name would have. Your position in society would be unquestionable."

Because I was born here in New Spain, I am a Creole. Many of the Spanish here consider Creoles less well born than themselves. If I were to marry Don Gaspar, I would no longer be considered a Creole.

"Marta, at least give the man your consideration."

"Yes, Mama," I answered. But in my heart I knew that I would never like him.

We did not see Don Gaspar for a week, but after that, nearly every day in the late afternoon he rode the two miles from Las Cocas, his finca, to call on us. On the first visit he brought Grandma her books with more comments on his part about what a waste reading was for a woman. Each time he came to the door, I felt a tightening in my chest and a desire to take ill, hide in the chapel, or disappear in the cane fields. I would have done anything to escape sitting on the patio with him blinking furiously and telling over and over again about the qualities of his prize bull, Conquistador. I was secretly furious with Mama who did everything she could to encourage his visits. She listened, fascinated, to every dull word, and she laughed at his ridiculous jokes. And what was worse, every time he came she invited him to stay for dinner. It nearly brought me to tears when he accepted. Of course, he was included in our Christmas celebrations.

Finally, one afternoon as he was leaving, Don Gaspar announced that he would not be able to visit us for the next few days because he had to travel to Panama again. I tried not to show my joy as I bid him farewell.

The next day was particularly hot. There was not the usual breeze from the sea, and the air hung heavy and still, making me feel sluggish and tired. I lay on my bed trying to take a siesta and thinking about how angry I was at Mama. I had hardly spoken to her for two days. Then I heard a tapping sound at my door and someone whispered, "Marta."

It was Jaime.

"Marta, are you awake?"

"Yes, Jaime. Come in."

I sat up on the edge of the bed and put my feet on the floor as he entered the room. Jaime closed the door quietly behind him and his bare feet made no sound as he crossed the tile floor toward me. He was dressed in a white shirt, white trousers and he carried his shoes in his hand. "Jaime, why are you walking around barefoot like that?" I asked.

He held his index finger up to his lips motioning me to be quiet. Then he whispered, "Marta, it's so hot and dull here this afternoon, let's walk down by the shore while everybody is asleep."

His idea was tempting. I thought of how upset Mama would be if she discovered that I was out in the sun letting my skin brown.

"Well, maybe."

"Maybe? You mean you'd rather lie there dreaming about your lover!" Jaime taunted.

I threw my pillow at him, but he bobbed to one side and it missed him and hit the wall.

"Will you go?"

"Yes." I stood up and took a pair of soft cloth shoes from my wardrobe and we both tiptoed barefoot out of my room. We crossed the patio and crept through the gate to the garden. Bending down among the manioc bushes and batata vines, we quickly slipped on our shoes. Then we ran past the stable where we could hear the soft buzzing of flies as they swarmed around the stalls. Giggling, we raced past the sugar mill toward the cane fields, where we could hide among the tall green stalks. Once we reached the safety of the sugar cane, we stopped to catch our breath.

"Oh, Jaime," I gasped between breaths and giggles. "Mama is going to be so angry when she finds out."

"I know just what she'll say," laughed Jaime. "Marta, Marita, what am I to do with you? You conduct yourself more like a mischievous boy than a young lady."

"The fault is Jaime's, Mama. I'll reply. He's a bad child and he made me do it against my will."

"I don't think she'll believe you, Marta. You have never done anything against your will."

The ripening cane smelled sweet and fragrant. I broke off a long piece and divided it between the two of us. We walked slowly between the rows as we sucked the juicy nectar. I kept my eyes on the ground, fearing snakes might be lurking there, but Jaime didn't worry about such things. At the end of the cane field we had to pass along a path through a thick growth of bushes and trees before we arrived at the beach. It was dark and cool there because the broad green leaves of the trees and tall bushes shaded the intense rays of the sun. We ambled along enjoying the coolness and the humming of the bees which flew among the flowering plants. Approaching the beach, we could hear the constant rumble of the waves as they fell upon the shore. We climbed down a steep bank and stepped onto the gray sand.

As we left the shade and stepped out into the fiery sunlight I was nearly blinded by the flare from the water. I stood squinting trying to accustom myself to the blazing light. Jaime slipped off his shoes, left them where they lay, and ran along the beach toward an enormous boulder which formed a wall between the part of the beach where we were and a little cove which was our favorite place. I, too, discarded my shoes, then gathered my skirts and ran after him. When Jaime reached the boulder, he stopped abruptly, paused as though he were looking at something on the other side, then turned around and ran to me.

"Follow me and be quiet," he said.

We walked along the edge of the beach until we reached the boulder. Then we climbed up into the bushes and made our way around to the other side of the rock. Some of the plants were spiny, and they scratched my arms and legs as we progressed. I walked gingerly, not wanting to injure my bare feet. Once we were past the rock, Jaime grabbed my arm and pointed down onto the sand where not more than ten yards in front of us a man we knew as Pedro Garabito was shoveling sand into a hole. He was intent on his work and took no heed of us concealed in the bushes. It was clear that he had been hard at work for some time because his face dripped with perspiration. The blue cloth of his ragged shirt had dark wet circles on the back and under the arms.

Pedro was a dirty, sullen ladino who lived in a hut on the other side of Papa's rice fields. He worked for Papa once in awhile when he was in need of food or drink. Our overseer had warned Papa not to trust Pedro or even to leave him alone around the house or out buildings because he had no conscience about stealing and he was rumored to have killed someone once.

Pedro's clothes were in dreadful condition. His filthy bluish shirt hung on him in tatters and his trousers were in such shreds that when he stood with his legs together it looked like he was wearing a narrow skirt with fringe at the hem. He half smiled as he finished filling the hole. The he stood up, smoothed the top of the hole, lifted the shovel onto his shoulder, and turned toward us. We froze there crouched behind the bushes as he seemed to look directly at us. But it was plain from the grimace on his unshaven face that he did not know we were there. I held my breath and nearly died from fear when he climbed up the short bank into the bushes not more than six feet away. He walked a few yards in back of us, hid the shovel under a dense clump of bushes, then turned and climbed back down onto the beach. He paused briefly beside the place where he had dug, brushed his sandaled foot over it gently, smiled, and turned away. He walked toward the water, around the boulder, and back down the beach in the direction from which we had come.

We sneaked through the bushes to where we could watch Pedro retreating into the distance. When we were satisfied that he was truly gone, we stood up.

"What do you suppose he has buried there?" I asked, brushing leaves and twigs from the sleeves and bodice of my dress.

"I don't know," Jaime said, making his way down onto the beach. "Shall we have a look?"

"Are you certain he is gone?" I asked, glancing down the beach.

"No, I think he'll be back here any minute to hack us to pieces with his machete."

"Jaime, you're not amusing. But I'll get the shovel." I turned and made my way through the brush to where Pedro had hidden it. When I carried it back to Jaime, he was already on his hands and knees scooping up the sand. He stood up, grabbed the shovel from me and began to dig furiously. After a few minutes, when the hole was three feet deep or so, I heard the dull sound of the shovel hitting something solid. Jaime and I dropped to our knees and looked into the hole. Then we reached with our hands and cleared the gray sand away from the top of a large wooden chest which was fastened with a leather strap. We quickly cleared the sand from the top and down the sides far enough so we could unbuckle the strap and open the chest. This took some doing. The hole was so deep that we had to strain to reach the chest. Frustrated, I finally climbed into the hole and crouched on top of the chest so I could dig around the sides with my hands. The wet sand chaffed my fingers and the digging became painful, but finally we cleared enough so we could take off the top.

As we opened it, the first thing to meet my eyes was a shabby old brown blanket folded neatly and placed across the top as a cover. Immediately, I felt ashamed of myself as if I had intruded upon someone's private belongings. Feeling like a trespasser, I wanted to close the chest and bury it once again. Then the sun's rays caught a piece of something shiny in a corner that the blanket had not quite covered. I pulled the cloth back and recognized Papa's beautiful fine leather saddle, the special one he used only for fiestas and bullfights. The saddle had once belonged to a Grand Duke and there was not another one as fine in New Spain. It was adorned with a border of rubies and silver bells, and the stirrups were cones of solid silver decorated with the Maldonado crest.

"Jaime, it's Papa's saddle!" I gasped, still leaning over the chest.

Jaime pulled the blanket completely off. "That's not all. I see Mama's silver chalice and something that looks like her pearl rosary."

The chest was full of valuable things, some of which we recognized as coming from our house. We thought we saw Papa's blue silk doublet folded up near the bottom.

"Jaime, how do you suppose he acquired all these things?" I asked as I replaced the blanket on top. "He hasn't been allowed near the house for two years."

"We don't know who comes around when we aren't

here, Marta. Maybe the overseer is not so watchful then."
He shook his head as he stared down at the chest. "Come,
Marta, let's each take as much as we can carry. We can
send someone to get the rest." He knelt down to grab
Papa's saddle.

"Wait, Jaime. The saddle is heavy and many of these
things are cumbersome. Why don't we send some men
down to carry the whole lot back?"

"What if Pedro comes to check on it and finds it sitting here like this?"

We'll have to rebury it and leave it just as we found
it," I said as I closed the top and buckled the leather strap.
"It won't take long."

"No, let's leave it like this. It's too much trouble to
bury it again. He won't be back before we send the men."

"It would be safer to bury it."

"Well then, do it yourself, I'm going back to the
house." Jaime sprinted down the beach toward the path
that would take us back to the cane fields. I looked once
again at the exposed chest and turned and ran after him.
He disappeared into the shady bushes before I could catch
up with him. As I arrived at the spot where the path led
up from the beach, I noticed that Jaime had forgotten his
shoes. There they lay beside mine. I quickly slipped mine
on and grabbed his and hurried after him along the shady
path. It was then I heard a scream ahead of me.

"Aye! Marta, help me!"

I ran to where he knelt on the dirt path between
the rows of cane. As I approached I glimpsed the tail of
a large brown snake slither into the sugar cane. By the
diamond-shaped pattern on its back, I knew it was a
barba amarilla, the deadliest serpent in New Spain. Jaime
was clasping his right leg just above the ankle. When he
removed his hand, the blood flowed freely from the wound.

"I've been bitten!" he exclaimed in a shaky voice.

"Lie down!" I cried, "You shouldn't move."

"Is it gone?" Jaime asked shuddering and looking around. His hands shook and his face had lost all trace of color.

"I think so. Lie still. I'll go for help." I tore some long green leaves from the cane, wrapped them around Jaime's wound and tied them as best I could. I hoped they would stop the bleeding. Then I propped his injured leg on a pile of rocks and instructed him once again to lie still. I ran toward the house as fast as I have ever run.

Rosa, I fear that you will be annoyed with me for ending my letter at this distressing point, but a courier is leaving now with mail to send on the fleet sailing for Cadiz. They have told me that I must give this letter to him immediately. I promise I will write again as soon as possible and not keep you too long in suspense.

Your loving friend,
Marta

Edward's Journal

LATE DECEMBER 1670, ISLE OF ST. CATHERINE

The Governor's plan worked and by midnight we took over the island. Then the wild time started. A thousand starving men ran loose on that small island raiding the huts and gardens and forts. Nothing that walked on four legs—not dog, cat, or horse—was safe from their knives. The tastier animals like cows, pigs, and goats were gone before the dawn. Once somebody spied one of those unlucky beasts he slaughtered and cleaned it in a wink, then threw it on the fire with patches of hair still stuck to the flesh. It stayed on the fire only long enough to singe the outside; then it was snatched from the flames, torn into pieces, and passed around. The starving eaters, like ogres in a story, stood around chewing the raw meat, the animal's blood running down their chins onto their chests. I was as hungry as the rest, but I felt sick to my stomach at the smell of all that blood and undercooked flesh. When the rib meat off a horse was offered me, I turned it down.

After they broke into the stores of wine and rum in

the fort San Mateo, the celebrating got noisier and wilder. Men ran around firing their flintlocks at the moon and stars. They hollered and drank and ate and set fires to the houses on the island just for entertainment. Nobody, not Captain Morgan nor Blackwort nor Mr. Potts came to stop them. They just got drunker and drunker, wilder and wilder, and did what they pleased.

Flames from all those huts on fire lit my way when I started down a lane that ran from one end of the island to the other. I wanted to get off by myself because I felt kind of uneasy with all that drinking and carrying on. It seemed to me that it wasn't going to be long before somebody turned real mean, and I would just as soon not be around for that. I walked along the road for awhile listening to the yelling and shooting behind me and hoping that I would come upon something to ease the pains in my belly. Then I happened on a wooden hut, all dark inside, with its outer wall built up against the edge of the road. In the moonlight I could just make out a path leading to the back of the place. I followed the path and found myself at the round stone walls of a well. I helped myself to a cool sweet drink from that well and looked around in the dark hoping to find something edible. But it was no use. It was too dark. I stumbled and tripped over some kind of greenery as I came up to the hut. Then I groped my way to an open doorway and stuck my head inside.

"Hello," I called. My voice sound peculiar, like it came from somebody else.

There was no answer. I tried again a trifle louder, not wanting to disturb anybody inside who might be sleeping there with a loaded musket on his chest. But again, no answer. Feeling nervous as a blind man around a beehive, I groped my way inside the house saying loud, "Can I come in?" so as to show anybody who might be in there that I meant no harm. There was still no answer, but I had the peculiar feeling I was being watched. I was uneasy about it, but I stepped inside anyway and it was darker in there than outside, and there was no hope of seeing anything. I turned to my right and my arm brushed against what I recognized from the rough pliant material to be a hammock. Then I nearly jumped out of my skin. A screech filled the air and something leaped out of that hammock and tore out of the hut like shot out of a cannon. I started to laugh. It was a cat. Nothing but a cat.

Since it was too dark to find food, I took the cat's bed instead. There would sure be at least a bag of flour around the place in the morning light. I spread the hammock and crawled in letting it fold around me like the skin on a banana. It smelt smoky from the vapors of cooking fires and the smell made my empty stomach ache. The last thing I remember as I fell asleep was hoping that nobody would set fire to the hut. But I was too tired to let that worry me long.

I woke up the next morning feeling hot and sweaty. The sun was shining on me through a window and I guessed it must be about eight o'clock. I lay there in the hammock for awhile looking around me. The dirt floor was freshly swept and there were shelves on each side of the door which held neat rows of boxes and jugs. My hammock hung in the corner to the back of the hut next to the road and in the opposite corner hung another hammock. Sometime during the night, the cat had come back, and he sat in the other hammock staring at me with a mean expression as if to say I didn't belong there.

When I glanced through the doorway I shot out of that hammock like a cannonball, for right there where I stood in the dark the night before not suspecting a thing, was the prettiest garden you ever did see. There were beans, potatoes, chayote vines, and corn, and off to one side, two rows of pineapples standing straight and stiff like lines of fat soldiers. I knew for certain that fortune was smiling on me when I discovered four chickens pecking and clucking under a calabash tree to the right of the hut.

I ate two pineapples and a handful of unripe beans, and I considered capturing one of the chickens and making a stew, but I was afraid the Captain might be looking for me, and the last thing I wanted was to get on his bad side. So I set off to find him, telling myself I would be back later for the chicken soup, and hoping nobody else would beat me to it.

I headed back the way I had come the night before. As I went along the coarse sand road, I saw thin lines of smoke rising from smoldering fires. Men slept along the way in the shade of palm trees and bushes. I went over to a group of fellows who were playing cards under a bohío, a sun shelter made with four poles and a thatched roof. I had planned to ask them where the Captain was, but two of them were arguing so fiercely over the game that I figured it best if I didn't make myself noticed. Finally I met a man who was sober enough to tell me that the Captain was quartered in the fort, San Geronimo, up the road a bit further. It was the fort we tried to take in the rainstorm the day before.

When I came to San Geronimo, I crossed over a narrow moat on a rotten wood plank and went through a tunnel in the thick stone wall which led to a courtyard. Right in front of me, in the shady half of the area, lay a couple dozen sleeping bodies. Some were spread out on their back or stomachs using their arms for pillows, others were all hunched up like kittens with their knees almost touching their chins. Over in the corner lay two fellows dressed in what looked to me like women's costumes, one green, the other violet.

I recognized Higgins lying there on his back with his mouth open. A fly kept landing on the side of his nose and Higgins, still sleeping, brushed it away again and again.

A door opened on the far side of the courtyard and Mr. Potts came out.

"So there ye are, Ed," he said. "We was wonderin' what happened to ye." He grinned, so I figured he wasn't mad at me for not showing up sooner.

"I guess I got lost in the confusion."

"And confusion there's been." He walked over to me and stood so close, I smelled the rum and tobacco on his breath. "And funnin' and carryin' on too." He laughed and pounded me on the back. "Ho, Ed, ye should have been here about sunup when some fellers came upon a trunk full o' ladies' clothes. They dressed up real pretty and paraded around—had some of the men believin' they were real señoritas." Mr. Potts laughed so hard his eyes watered.

"I'm sorry I missed that," I said, grinning. "Were you fooled Mr. Potts?"

"Aye, I confess I was for awhile there until I got close up and saw the whiskers on their faces. But some of the boys was too drunk to notice details like that. They still don't know the truth. That drunkard over in the corner there danced with the same one three times and he still didn't get it."

"Mr. Potts, I came thinking there'd be work for me."

"No work now." He eased his body down to the ground and sat leaning against the stone wall. "Captain's out visiting a lady friend."

"You mean he has friends on this island?" I asked.

Mr. Potts found something funny about what I said,

because he began to laugh all over again. Somehow, between hoots he managed to say, "Ed, my lad, you are a rich one." But he didn't answer my question and I felt foolish.

"Mr. Potts," I said, wanting to turn his mind to something else, "where are the folks who live here? I haven't seen anybody save our men since we landed."

He put his head against the wall, placed his hand on his forehead and shut his eyes like he had a headache. "They're all caged up in that San Mateo fort at the other end o' the island. Captain's got Blackwort down there making sure they behave themselves."

A door opened to one side and Ned stepped out carrying his boots under his arm. He squinted in the bright light and put the palm of his free hand to his face, shading his eyes. Then he saw me. "Ed, I was just thinking about you." He sat on the stone floor and began to pull on his boots. "Come with me to find some breakfast."

"Well, I don't know if I can." I looked at Mr. Potts.

"Go on, lad," he said. "It's my guess that Captain's gone for a good part o' the day, and there ain't nothing for ye to do around here now." He put his head back against the wall and closed his eyes. "I think I'll just catch a little shut eye."

I led Ned out of the fortress and back to the hut where I spent the night. He was happier than a crow in a corn patch to see all the provisions. When we had our fill of chicken and beans and pineapple, we went inside and lay in the hammocks after shooing the cat away. It was cooler in there away from the midday sun. I felt lazy and happy to just lie there listening to the clucking of the chickens in the yard and the buzzing of the flies that flew in and out the windows.

"Merry Christmas, Ned," I said, remembering what day it was.

"Christmas? So it is."

Off in the distance I heard more gunfire and the wild hoots of fellows still celebrating from the night before or just waking up to start in all over again.

"It doesn't seem like Christmas, does it?"

All of a sudden I wanted to see Mother and Father and sit at the table with them and hear Father say the blessing. I felt a lump grow in my throat and I told myself I had better think of something else quick.

"Doesn't matter to me." Ned put his foot on the floor and swung the hammock. "I can't remember it ever seeming very much like Christmas. I guess I don't know what Christmas is supposed to seem like."

I put my foot down and gave my hammock a swing. "Oh, you know, lots of food and drink and relations and friends visiting and merrymaking and good feeling. At least that's what it's like at home. Wasn't it the same in England?"

"Maybe for some. Not for me."

"What was it like for you?" I suspected his family might be Puritans who wouldn't believe in merrymaking.

"There was just my mother and me," he said as he swayed gently back and forth, "and she worked every Christmas, every day for that matter, until they took her away."

"Took her away?"

"Yes, they took my mother away."

I stopped swinging, sat up, put both feet on the floor, and looked straight at him. What was he talking about? "You mean the Spanish?"

"No, the sheriff."

"But you told me your mother and father drowned."

He looked at me real serious and said, "I invented that. Truth is, I never had a father, and my mother knew nothing but London all her life."

I didn't know what to think. It might have been a joke, but he didn't look like he was joking. "And your sister?"

"I don't have one. Never did."

I felt myself getting angry at him. "Why did you lie to me before?" I demanded, "Or are you lying now?"

"What I've told you just now is the truth." He put his hands behind his head and smiled at me. I didn't know whether to believe him or not.

"Ed, believe me, you put yourself at a disadvantage if you let a person know everything about you the first time you meet. Leave him wondering, maybe a little afraid. Then you'll have the upper hand next time." That was too much.

"Upper hand?" I almost shouted, "Who cares about the upper hand? What about trust? What about friendship?"

"That'll come in time, if it's to be."

I turned my head away. Something was sinking inside me. "I could never be a friend of someone who lied to me."

"Ed, you have my word that I'm your friend. I can't promise I'll never lie to you. Where I come from it's common practice. But I'll do my best to be truthful with you." I wanted to believe him, but it wasn't going to be easy.

I looked him in the face again. "Why did the sheriff take your mother away?"

He pushed off extra hard with his foot and the hammock swung back and forth violently. "They say she was clipping coins."

"You mean cutting them down and making new ones out of the shavings?"

He nodded.

"Did they send her to Newgate?"

"Aye. Before they hanged her and two women they said helped her."

I didn't know what to say. Ned looking at me as if he

expected me to say something, so finally, although I knew it sounded kind of feeble, I blurted out, "I'm sorry about your mother, Ned."

"It was a long time ago. I don't think about it much now."

"How old were you?"

"Ten."

"What did you do? How did you live?

"A magistrate gave me a job as a messenger and I ran between the court and his offices all day long. He let me sleep in a corner of the office and he gave me enough coin to keep me in food and clothes. When days were slow, I looked through volumes of laws on the shelves in the office and taught myself how to read."

"Is that where you learned to speak so fine? From the way you talk, I thought for sure you had a duke somewhere in your family."

"All ye 'ave to do is talk right and ye can fool anybody," he said in a thick London accent.

"And you never had an uncle in Jamaica?"

"No. One night I took a short cut through a tough part of London and before I knew it, they jumped me, threw me in a sack, and pressed me aboard a ship bound for the West Indies. Then off the coast of Cuba, a Spanish privateer captured us and I was indentured to that sugar planter I told you about. That part of my story was true." Ned sat up, put his feet on the floor and said, "I'm hungry. Come on Ed, let's find some mangoes."

I crawled out of the hammock not knowing whether I should believe him or not, but thinking what an unusual fellow this Ned Green was.

We left the hut and headed down the lane away from San Geronimo, passing men lying beside the way in whatever position they happened to fall when drink finally got the best of them. There were a few strong ones still celebrating. We came upon seven of them grouped around a mango tree in the middle of a garden. Moon, his bald head covered by a blue handkerchief, was there looking up at the tree and pointing at one of the higher branches.

"There's a beauty, pink as a piglet, right out on the very end o' that there branch," he yelled. "Get that one for us, Monkey."

I looked through the leaves of the tree and spotted Monkey straddling a limb up near the top. "First, ye 'ave to catch these ye rummies," he cried as he began to pelt us with a store of mangoes he held in the front of his shirt. I caught one and took a bite,

Moon, ignoring the fruit falling around him, called, "I got me heart set on that one up there at the top I told ye about." He pointed again toward the top of the tree. "Be a good chap and get it for me, Monkey." His voice had a whine to it and he stumbled forward a little as if he was having a hard time standing up.

"For you, Moonie, I'll do it." Monkey answered as he climbed up to the branch and slid slowly out toward the end where it was so thin it was nothing but a twig. We watched, amused, wondering if Monkey would be able to pick the fruit hanging there by its long stem like a pink heart on a cord. He inched closer and closer to the end of the branch until it gave way under his weight and it started to bend toward the ground. Quick as you can swat a fly, Monkey grabbed the branch and held on so that when it was bent as far as it would go, he was hanging there by his two hands like a shirt on a clothesline.

As he swooped toward the ground, everybody yelled, "Thar he goes!" and they all hooted and hollered and carried on, Monkey right along with them. Then he made a grab for that mango, got it, tossed it down to Moon, and worked his way arm over arm back to the trunk of the tree and the thicker branches.

"Get me that one up there," yelled another chap who lolled on the ground in front of me. He pointed to the very top of the tree. Then he took a swig from a goatskin full of rum and passed it to Moon.

"Ye think I can't?" answered Monkey as he started climbing to the top. "Well, watch this."

Showing no fear of falling, he went through the trick again making his way out to the end of the limb and swinging down toward the ground with everybody yelling and hollering.

Moon took a drink from the goatskin, threw it on the ground, and bellowed. "I got the urge for a fight. Who'll take me on? Think afore ye come for'ard, 'cause I'm feeling mighty mean."

"That ain't the way you look, Moonie," yelled Monkey from the tree. "You look like you belong in church givin' sermons." Then quicker than you could say, "go," Monkey leaped out of the tree onto Moon's back. The blow knocked Moon to the ground and the two of them rolled over and over trying to pin one another down. The men yelled encouragement first to one, then to the other. Moon, being the bigger man, finally pinned Monkey to the ground and boxed his ears from side to side, saying. "This is the kind o' sermons I give, Monkey." Then he climbed off him and turned his back. "Where's that goatskin? I'm thirsty."

Monkey leaped to his feet; the shiny blade of a knife sparkled in his hand.

"Look out behind you, Moon," came a shout, "He's got a knife."

Moon spun around while he pulled a dirk from his trousers. The two faced each other and danced in a circle slashing out with their knives. Monkey, quick and light on his feet, had the advantage over Moon who moved slow and heavy and Moon's stomach was soon lined with two scratches where Monkey's knife had sliced his skin. Suddenly Monkey stuck his foot out and tripped Moon who stumbled to the ground. Monkey was on him in an instant, straddling his back. He pressed the tip of his dirk hard enough against Moon's neck to make it bleed a little.

"Give in Moonie, or I'll carve my mark in yer back."

Moon tried hard to throw him off, but Monkey had him pinned too tight. "I give," he said in a thick voice. Grinning, Monkey hopped off and Moon, looking sheepish got up real slow.

"Ye bested me this time, Monkey, but ye ain't yet seen the end o' this."

"Aw, Moonie, ye ain't gonna hold a little funnin' against yer old pal, are ye now?" Monkey said while he put his arm around Moon. "I've always been quicker'n you and you know it. Come on, let's go fishin'."

I think Moon would have taken him up on his offer if he hadn't looked around him and seen all the other fellows laughing at what happened to him. He looked at everybody one at a time, and when he came to me, he stopped and fixed his eyes on me. His shamed expression changed to a mean glare and he said, looking at me all the time, "Wait up there, Monkey. I got a better idea."

Monkey looked at me too. "Now, what kind o' scheme just might be rollin' around inside o' that shiny dome o' yours, Moonie?"

Moon put two fingers in his mouth, licked them and ran them over the scratches on his stomach. Then he said, "This here lad, Ed, he's been in the crew for a good long time now, and I don't recall him receivin' the initiation. It ain't like us to be so forgetful."

I took a step backwards before Ned touched me on the arm and whispered, "Don't let them think you're afraid."

Monkey circled me saying, "I'll be damned if you ain't right, Moonie. It's my feelin' that we ought to get it over with right now." He stepped behind me and a chill ran up my back while I wondered what he was going to do to me. "What do you say, boys?"

"Aye!" came the answer from the men.

"Then let's get on with it!" Monkey grabbed my arms from behind. I tried to twist away, but he held me while somebody took a handkerchief and tied my hands behind my back. The handkerchief was twisted, and it cut into my wrists. "Now take it easy, Ed, we ain't going to do ye no harm," Monkey said leaning toward me, his mouth close to my ear. He smelled like rum and dirt and animal fat. "We're just going to take ye for a little walk down to the beach." He grabbed my elbow and led me through the garden away from the road and down toward the water. "Moonie, why don't ye run on ahead and see if the owner o' this here garden might have some kind o' vessel down there on the beach that'd be useful."

I looked back over my shoulder at Ned who was following close behind. Without making a sound, he formed the words, "Don't act afraid," with his mouth. That was hard for me to do, but I tried my best because I knew he was right. If they had the slightest notion that I was afraid, they'd make it that much worse for me.

Monkey pushed me by the elbow through the garden and through a stand of bushes until we came to the beach. There, down where the sand met the water, Moon was standing beside a dugout sized to hold two or three men at the most.

When we reached the boat, Monkey gave me a shove and said, "Sit down there in the sand for a minute, Ed." I eased my way to the sand and he flopped down beside me. "Where's the drink? I need me some more fuel."

A man handed him the goatskin and he took a long drink; some of it seeped out from the corner of his mouth and down onto his chin. He turned his face and wiped his chin on his shoulder.

I wished they would get on with whatever they had planned for me. I knew there was nothing I could do but go along with it and I wanted to get it over with because I hated being so nervous and trying to act calm at the same time. Since I can't swim I was hoping real hard that their plans didn't include taking me out in that boat.

Moon sat down in the sand and held his hand out for the goatskin. Then the rest of the men, save Ned, sat down too, making a sort of loose circle. Ned leaned against the boat a little way from me.

"What are you going to do to me, Moon," I asked trying to sound no more than curious.

He took a long drink and passed the skin on. Then he turned to me and said, "It's just a little somethin' we usually do aboard ship, but since we ain't on the ship, we'll make do with what we have here. Ye ain't afeared now, are ye, Ed?" He reached out and nudged me. Since my hands were still tied behind my back, I couldn't catch myself and I fell over on the sand like a sack of grain. Moon thought it was funny and he laughed deep from his belly while he crawled to his feet. "Give me another swig o' that rum and let's be on with it." While he stood above me teetering back and forth like a chamber pot on a railing, he pulled the handkerchief off his head, grabbed me by the shirt, and yanked me to my feet.

"Hold still now, Ed, while I put this here blinder on ye." He fumbled around and tied the sweaty handkerchief over my eyes. I was thankful that he had a hard time managing the knot. The cloth was so loose that I could see underneath it, but I wasn't going to let on.

"Moonie, ye've done a scummy job o' the blindfold. If it weren't for the nose on the lad's face, the thing would be hanging down around his shoulders by now." Monkey retied the handkerchief so tight that my ears pressed flat against my head and my eyes were pushed into the sockets so hard I saw diamonds of light flash in the dark.

They put me into the little boat and made me sit on the bottom. Then they pushed it over the sand into the water until it floated. It nearly tipped over when they climbed in, They started to row, one in front and one behind and it felt like we were going in a circle. The one in the back had the hiccoughs.

"Damn yer eyes, Moonie," growled Monkey from the front. "Yer makin' us go in circles! There was no answer, just the sound of hiccoughs and the rough splash of oars hitting the water at different times. I had learned enough about boats to know that it was bad rowing. I could feel the boat go first to the left and then sharp to the right like a dog with distemper.

"Lay off, ye drunken scumbag. I'll do the rowin'."

I heard Moon pull his oar in and the boat began to glide straight across the water. I was thinking all the time about what I was going to do when they threw me over. I was pretty sure that was what they had in mind.

The rowing stopped. I felt the boat sway, and then Monkey grabbed me by the shoulder and forced me to stand. "It's time fer you to take a little swim, Ed." He said. I panicked, but I couldn't move. "Moonie, let's help the lad into the water."

I heard loud snoring behind me.

"Damn his drunken carcass. Looks like I'll be doin' the job alone. Come on now, Ed, it's over the side with ye."

I stood there stiff with fear. "But I can't swim."

"Well, well, ye can't swim," Monkey said in a mocking tone like he didn't believe me. "Then I'll untie your hands and let your learn. I don't want to drown ye, just initiate ye. And he untied me with one quick motion, knocked my legs out from under me, and shoved me overboard.

I took a big breath just before the water covered my head and I went down, down, down, I tore the blindfold off and batted my arms and legs trying to get back to the top before I had to breathe again. After what seemed like a day and a night, my head came out and I gasped for air. I took three or four gulps and swatted the water with my arms, trying to keep my head from going under again. I could feel real panic setting in, and I thrashed around harder. I thought that if I tried hard enough I could jump right out of that water like a fish. But it didn't work. I could feel myself going under again. While I gulped a last breath, Monkey jumped out of the boat and grabbed me on the shoulders from behind. I took some water into my windpipe and I felt the urge to cough, but my head was under water and I knew if I coughed, it would be all over for me, so I held it.

I fought like a jaguar to get away from Monkey, but he held on tight and we went deeper and deeper. I tried to bite his hands so he would let me go, but I couldn't. Just when I was sure I had to cough or burst my lungs, he let go of me and gave me a hard shove. I watched the surface get closer and closer and I wondered if I could hold my breath long enough. Just as my head broke through, I couldn't hold it anymore; I had to cough. I sucked in half water and half air, and I coughed and sputtered trying hard to stay on top. Then Monkey swam up underneath me and grabbed me by the feet and pulled me under again. I was still coughing as I went down, and I took in water through my mouth and nose. I could feel it sting as it went up my nose and down into my lungs. The last thing I remember was looking up and seeing the boat right above me like it was floating in air, I blinked and saw Mother's face on the bottom of that boat. She smiled at me like she didn't know I was drowning. Then everything was dark.

I woke up lying on my belly over a barrel on the sand. My throat and the inside of my nose stung and my chest ached.

"Oh ho!" shouted one of the men who was holding me on the barrel. "He's comin' around. I guessed he would when he spit out that last bit o' water. "How ye feelin' lad?"

"Not so good." My head stung on the inside and I couldn't stop coughing.

"Not so good, huh?" He helped me off and eased me down onto the sand. "You're lucky ye can feel anything. We thought we'd lost ye for awhile there. Monkey didn't know ye was in trouble until that fellow Ned over there swum out and pulled ye into the boat. Ye've got him to thank for yer life."

I looked around and saw Ned coming my way. Behind him I could make out the shape of Moon lying flat on his back in the sand, his arms and legs spread out like spokes on a windmill. The sun was down close to the horizon, and I figured it must have been an hour or so since I took my swim. I eased onto my side on the sand and coughed and coughed until I ached all over.

Ned sat down beside me, smiled and said, "Want to go swimming?"

I shook my head.

"That damned Monkey ought to be flogged," Ned said with clenched teeth. "He nearly killed you."

"He was just having some fun. I sat up and coughed as if I was trying to force my lungs out through my mouth.

Ned piled some sand up for a pillow and I lay back down propping my head against it.

"If that's fun, what's he do when he's feeling mean?"

Then Monkey himself came up to us, looking sad, without the usual spring in his walk.

"Ed, honest, I thought ye was jesting when ye told me ye couldn't swim. "He made circles in the sand with his bare toes. "If you're goin' to be a sailor, ye better get Ned here, to learn ye. Otherwise one o' these times ye'll end up a meal for a shark."

"Monkey," Ned said frowning at him like he was poison, "with you around, who needs sharks?"

"Watch yer tongue, there lad, or I'll have another initiation." Monkey glared at Ned in a real unfriendly way. Ned stood up, looking like he wanted to hit Monkey, but he only spit at his feet and walked away.

"That high talkin' guttersnipe'd better watch his tongue," Monkey sneered.

I didn't say anything. I just shut my eyes and went to sleep.

—Edward

Edward's Journal

EARLY JANUARY 1671, ISLE OF ST. CATHERINE

Tomorrow we sail for the mouth of the River Chagres. Some ships went ahead to capture the fort, San Felipe, and clear the water route to Panama. We heard today that they did it and they're waiting for us. I'll be glad to get off this island and have an excuse not to take any more swimming lessons for awhile. Ned's trying his best to teach me, but I don't like it much.

—Edward

Marta's Letter to Rosa

16 JANUARY 1672, FINCA LAS BRISAS

Dear Rosa,

I promised myself that I would not delay in writing you and I will write each day until the whole story is told. Because you will most likely receive a bundle of letters at one time, I am numbering the envelopes. Please read them in order so they will make better sense.

After Jaime was bitten by the *barba amarilla* I ran to the house and summoned Mama and the overseer. We carried Jaime to the house where he was put to bed and watched over. At first he felt no effects from the venom, and teased us for the concern we were showing, but it was not long before his leg began to swell. It turned red, and then black. The skin stretched so tight over the swelling that it looked like his leg would burst, and it became so painful that he could not keep himself from crying out. He spent a sleepless night moaning and tossing in his bed. There was little we could do for him except pray to the Lord for his salvation. Mama sent the maid to make a poultice of plantain leaves, which we wrapped around the wound and changed every few hours. We also made him drink the juice from the plantain leaves. The Indians use it as a cure for snakebite.

The next morning Jaime developed a fever and a nose bleed that could not be stopped. When I went in to see him, the first thing to catch my eye was a pile of blood-soaked rags on the floor beside his bed. Grandma sat beside him holding yet another cloth against his nose.

"Marta, come help me," she called as I entered the room. "I need you to hold one nostril closed with this cloth while I put a piece of lint in the other."

I did what she asked. Jaime stared up at me in discomfort, but he didn't cry or complain. In fact, he tried to smile. His face was hot. His lips were parted so he could breathe through his mouth.

"There now, let me get to the other nostril."

Grandma took another bit of lint between her fingers. When I removed the cloth, the blood gushed from his nose and ran down his cheek. Grandma plugged his nostril at last, and we cleaned him up and changed his bedding. Finally he fell into a feverish sleep. "Will he be all right, Grandma?"

"Perhaps. In time. If God wills." She brushed back some strands of white hair which had fallen in her face and I noticed that she looked old and tired.

"Please, Grandma, let me sit with him. You need to rest."

"Thank you, Marta. He is peaceful now, but if the lint doesn't stop the bleeding, call me."

"Yes, Grandma."

"Don't disturb your mother, she was up all night. If you need anything, come to me."

"I will, Grandma."

She left the room. As I sat there, I missed the usual lively morning sounds in the house. Eulalia was not singing while she mopped the floors; this morning she worked in silence. There was no clanking of dishes and flatware; the table was quietly set for breakfast. Even the birds on the patio seemed to squawk at one another in hushed tones. It was a quiet, cheerless morning.

I looked at Jaime sleeping. He could not die. God would not allow it. If he were able to see himself lying there with his nostrils stuffed full, he would make a joke about it. He was that kind of boy—using humor where others used anger or sorrow. I wiped my watery eyes, got up, and bathed his forehead with a cool damp cloth.

It was afternoon before I remembered the buried chest down on the beach. I had just come from sitting with Jaime who slept fitfully, when a cabinet along the wall filled with silver tableware caught my eye and brought to mind Mama's silver chalice which was in the chest. I decided not to bother Mama and Grandma with the matter since they were burdened enough already. Instead, I went to the overseer and told him where to find the chest. He gathered several men and led a party to the beach to retrieve it.

A while later I was in the chapel when I heard the men return. I went to the patio expecting to see the chest and its contents ready for inspection but I was disappointed to find only the overseer.

"Did you get it?" I asked.

"No, Señorita Marta," he said wiping his brow with a handkerchief. "We were too late. We arrived at the place you described only to find an empty hole in the sand. Judging from the dryness of the sand beside the hole, I would say that the chest had been gone for some time. Perhaps since last night."

"*Dios mio!* Then he knows we found the chest. He must have taken it somewhere."

"My men are looking for him now," said the overseer. "They will find the scoundrel, Señorita, I assure you."

"Don't mention this to the others. They shouldn't have to worry about it now," I said, motioning with my arm toward Jaime's room. "Bring any news of Pedro or the chest to me."

"Yes, Señorita." He bowed and left only to return later with word that Pedro Garabito was nowhere to be found. I was angry with myself for not bringing some of the contents of the trunk back when we discovered it. At least we might have saved Papa's saddle or his silk doublet. Perhaps Jaime would not have been in the snake's path if we had taken the time to rebury the chest.

Jaime's fever ran high, and he was delirious for three more days. Then, by the grace of God, on the fourth day his fever lessened and the swelling in his leg seemed to decrease a bit. For the first time, he was able to sit up in bed. He even ate some boiled chayote and a small morsel of bread. His nose bled sporadically for those four days. When the bleeding was gentle and slow, Grandma was pleased, saying that he was ridding his body of the poisons that way. But when it flowed fast and was difficult to stop, Grandma became worried that it would weaken him too much. We said prayers of thanks to Santa Maria when on the fourth day he had but one small bleed. It appeared that he might survive his ordeal, and at last we dared to think so.

On the evening of that fourth day, Mama and I were sitting alone in the dining room finishing supper when she asked me to tell her what Jaime and I had been doing just before he was bitten. I told her about everything including Pedro Garabito and his trunk full of stolen things. I knew she would be angry at me, and she was.

"That filthy man and the stolen things don't matter,"

she said scornfully. "But Jaime does matter and he nearly died. If that snake had killed him, Marta, I don't think I could have ever forgiven you."

My cheeks grew hot. She was not being fair.

"Mama!" I cried, "It wasn't my fault. It was his idea to go to the beach!"

She made her hand into a fist and said, "You know he wouldn't have gone without you." Then she pounded the table. "Marta, why must you always defy me? You are stubborn and headstrong and someday you will pay for it."

At that moment I hated her. Whey did she always find fault with me? Wasn't there anything about me she liked?

"You're just like...." She never finished her sentence because we heard the sounds of a horse and rider moving swiftly up the road toward the house. Mama called for Eulalia to go see who was approaching. Then we heard Don Gaspar's voice at the door.

"Eulalia, I must see your mistress at once!" A tone of alarm had replaced his usual dull way of speaking. The sharp noise of his heavy boots on the patio told us he was coming our way, and then he stepped into the dining room and stood before us without waiting for Eulalia to announce him. His face flushed, he blinked furiously as he stood there in his traveling clothes, which were covered with a layer of dirt from the road. In his hand he held a riding crop.

"Doña Carmen, Marta," he said, not bothering to bow. "Henry Morgan has captured San Felipe and he is on his way up the Chagres, with nearly two thousand men. You must return to the city."

"Don Gaspar, what are you saying?" Mama was on her feet. "I cannot believe such a thing."

"Listen, I have just now come from Panama where a near dead soldier who escaped from San Felipe staggered into the city warning that the devils are on their way."

"What *is* the disturbance here?" Grandma called from the hall. "Jaime needs to rest and you people, who should know better, are making enough noise to wake the dead." When she appeared in the doorway, she was startled to discover Don Gaspar.

"What a surprise! You heard about poor Jaime, no doubt." She went over to him and offered her hand. "You look weary."

"Doña Ana," interrupted Mama, her face ashen, "Henry Morgan is on the Rio Chagres."

Grandma looked sharply at Don Gaspar, "But you must be mistaken. How could he get past our soldiers at San Felipe?"

"They were caught by surprise and outnumbered as well. I wish I were mistaken, Doña Ana, but I heard it from a soldier who was there.

Grandma sat down. Her hands trembled as she put them on the table. "What are we to do?" she asked.

"Well, it is certain that we cannot stay here in the country, unprotected," said Mama. "We will have to go back to the city." She looked around her at the silver tableware and the chests full of dishes and linens. "The servants will begin packing tonight and we will leave tomorrow as soon as everything is ready."

"No, Doña Carmen," replied Don Gaspar, "you must leave on horseback tonight. There is no time to be encumbered with a carriage and wagons."

"Tonight! Without wagons!" Mama nearly screamed. "What about Cimarrónes? We are too few to defend ourselves. Surely they will rob us and who knows what else?"

Cimarrónes are escaped slaves who live in small villages deep in the jungle. They hide along the roads waiting to rob travelers who go unprotected.

"We must leave tonight in spite of Cimarrónes," said

Don Gaspar. "I have just come along the road, and I saw no sign of them. Morgan gets closer every hour. You cannot risk staying here another night. As it is, it will take a day and a half on fast horses to reach the city." He sat down at the table. "I'm thirsty. Would it be possible to have something to drink?"

Mama ordered Eulalia to bring him food and drink. Then she turned to him and said, "But we have to take one carriage. Jaime is too ill to ride, and Doña Ana has not been on a horse in years. The ordeal would kill her."

"If I had to, I could ride. But Carmen is right. Jaime is too ill to travel. He should not be moved." Grandma put her hand over Mama's, "Carmen, you and Marta go on with Don Gaspar. Jaime and I will stay here."

Mama and I both opened our mouths to object when Don Gaspar, who had been eating, boomed out, "Nonsense! Those men are vicious and immoral. If they found you and Jaime here alone, do you think they would take pity on you? Do you remember the pity they had for the nuns and priests at Portobelo?" He pushed his plate away from him and stood up nearly knocking over his chair. "No, Doña Ana, we all go into the city together. I would not leave you here to wait like chickens for the fox." He said it all with passion and with his eyes wide open. He looked like a different man. Then, as if he suddenly remembered, he started blinking again.

"What ails Jaime? It isn't fever season."

"Ah, Don Gaspar," answered Mama smoothing her hair with her hand. "Jaime ran into a *barba amarllla* in the cane fields and he was bitten." She fixed her eyes on me. "He has been near death for days, and only today the Lord has given us hope that he may recover."

"Aye. *Madre mia!*" Don Gaspar shook his head. "You think he can be moved?"

"It will be painful for him, but we have no choice. I most certainly will not leave him here at the mercy of that band of evildoers."

"Then we can't waste time. Ladies, will you prepare the household and the sick child while I arrange the carriage and horses?"

"Yes, of course," said Mama standing up. "We shall be ready in an hour's time. Come, Marta, you can help me pack a few things."

Speaking only about what to take, and avoiding each other's glance, we filled two valises with some jewelry, a gold candelabra and some silverware. Then Grandma and I gathered the precious tableware, jewelry, and household items that we could not take with us and we put them into several cloth bags and lowered them into the well where they rested on a ledge just a few feet above the level of the water. The ledge was concealed by an overhang so a person looking down the well would not see it.

Mama called the servants together and told them about the approach of the pirates. She gave them their choice to stay at the finca or to go with us into the city. Most chose to seek safety with us in the city, and they were given horses and sent on ahead to prepare the house for our arrival. Two decided to remain at Las Brisas with the overseer and the slaves who would care for the rice and cane fields. Mama thanked them and told them that their bravery would not be forgotten.

It was near midnight when we finally departed. The carriage had room for four persons inside, but Jaime lay across one of the seats and Mama and Grandma sat on the other, so I rode outside next to the driver. Don Gaspar trotted beside us on his grey horse. He wore a cutlass at his side and in a holster on his saddle I saw the handle of a pistol. Sitting on his horse, he didn't seem so unattractive.

Although I realized that we were in great danger, his presence made me feel a little safer.

The night was calm. There wasn't even a breeze. The sound of the horses' hooves pounding the dirt and the creaks of the carriage wheels broke the stillness, while the stars sparkled above us unknowing and uncaring. We all rode in silence with our own worries and fears. We were traveling faster than normal; the bumps and holes in the road were especially jarring when we hit them at such speed. A hard jolt sent me off the bench into the air. The coach lurched to the left and tipped menacingly. A moan came from inside. Mama parted the curtain, stuck her head out, and asked the driver to be more careful for the sake of Jaime, who was in great pain.

We jolted along for what felt like a night and a day. But it was only a few hours. The first light was just beginning to appear in the east. My legs were stiff. I wished we could stop so I could stand up and stretch, but I knew we must hurry on. I sat there, unable to sleep, thinking that we had at least another day ahead of us before we could see the spires of the Cathedral of Panama.

It was the beginning of the dry season. There hadn't been much rain for three weeks or so, which made the road dusty. The dust was thrown up by the horses' hooves and the wheels of the carriage, and it seemed to form a cloud around my head. There was dust in my eyes, ears, and nose despite the shawl I wore over my head. I hesitated to speak, because when I did, I could taste the dust particles which landed on my tongue.

I envied Don Gaspar his place high in the saddle above most of the dust, and I was considering asking him if I might take a turn riding his horse, when he raised his arm and motioned the driver to stop. As we slowed, I looked up the road in the direction of Don Gaspar's gaze.

There in the distance was a large, uneven dark shape. A pile of rocks was blocking our way.

"How puzzling," I thought. "It can't be a rockslide; the land is flat on both sides of the road." Don Gaspar turned quickly in his saddle and looked back the way we had come. I stood up on the seat and turned to look in the same direction.

"What is it? Why have we stopped?" Mama called as her head appeared at the window.

"Stay inside and leave this to me," Don Gaspar said turning his horse around. Coming toward us at a slow trot were five horsemen.

"Cimarrónes," I whispered, suddenly afraid.

"Marta, turn around, sit down, and be quiet!"

I obeyed. He rode away from me toward the oncoming horses, but I heard him stop only a few feet behind the carriage. He waited until the riders drew near and stopped in front of him. Their horses pawed the ground and snorted.

"What is it you want?" Don Gaspar asked,

"Idiot!" said a low voice with a thick accent.

"I don't understand," Don Gaspar answered giving no sign that he noticed the insult.

I peeked around the side of the carriage. Don Gaspar sat on his horse facing the five men. Four of them were black men; the fifth was a white man who sat upon Papa's silver saddle. I recognized him at once. It was Pedro Garabito.

"Do you understand this?" The leader, a fat man whose clothes were too tight, pulled a pistol from his belt and fired it at the feet of Don Gaspar's horse. The horse reared up and whinnied in terror. Don Gaspar struggled with it and finally brought it under control.

"Who's in there?" The man said pointing at the carriage with his gun.

"Two women and a sick child."

"What's the matter with your eyes, Señor? They blink so. Are you afraid of some poor old slaves?" The fat man pointed his gun at Don Gaspar. Then he snarled, "Get off your horse and clear everybody out."

Don Gaspar dismounted and came over to the carriage. He opened the door and helped Mama and Grandma down, then he and the coachman lifted Jaime out and laid him on the ground. Jaime sat up painfully and watched me as I climbed down off my seat. Once we were all gathered at the side of the road, the horsemen approached us and encircled us as if they suspected that we might try to run away,

"Well, well, Tino, we caught us a real prize," said Pedro Garabito, drawing his horse near the fat man. "It seems we have here the ladies of the house of Maldonado." He bowed from the waist, mocking the motions of a gentleman and leering at Mama with an obscene toothless smile.

Mama drew herself up tall, arched her eyebrows and said, "So you have come to this, Pedro Garabito." Then she recognized Papa's saddle and her expression turned to one of anger. "How dare you ride upon my husband's saddle?" She stood there in front of him unafraid, like a goddess ready to strike him dead with a bolt of lightening.

"Your husband is a rich man. He can get another." Pedro's eyes traveled slowly from the tip of Mama's head to her toes and back to her face.

Mama's lip parted as if she meant to reply, but Grandma caught her arm and tugged gently to quiet her. The man named Tino ordered the other riders to search the coach. They threw everything that was loose out onto the ground. Then they ripped the lining from the inside to see if we had concealed anything. They ransacked the two valises with the treasures we had brought from the finca. Then they ordered Mama, Grandma, and me to give

them the jewelry we wore. They searched Don Gaspar and
Jaime, whom they ordered to stand up although he had
barely enough strength to do so. When they were satisfied that we carried nothing more of worth, they forced
us to lie down on our stomachs in the road with our faces
pressed into the dirt.

"We going to shoot them, Tino?" one of them asked.

"Shoot them, Tino," growled Pedro Garabito, "they
tell the Señor it was me that robbed them and it won't be
safe for me anywhere but the hills."

"I ain't thinking of your hide, hombre," said the fat
one, "I'm thinking if we kill them, the whole army will
come after us. This family's too important."

One of the Negroes said, "Let them go. I hear they
don't treat their slaves too bad."

"Bah. They kicked me out with nothing," snarled
Pedro.

"There ain't a master nowhere that don't treat his
slaves bad," said one, "I say kill them."

"No, it'd be suicide. The army would comb these hills
'til they found us and gave us the slowest, agonizing death
they could cook up." The fat one spoke convincingly.
"We'll leave them here. Load the swag on the Señor's
horse and let's go."

Pedro Garabito snarled "If I had my way, you'd all
be dead." Then he drew his horse near Mama, its hooves
nearly stepped on her head, which was pressed to the
ground. "Here is a message for your husband, Señora,"
and he spit on her

The spittle, a blob of brown slime, hit her cheek, and
she began to spring up until Grandma and I reached for
her and pulled her back down.

"Stay calm, Carmen," whispered Grandma. The
Cimarrónes laughed wickedly at what Pedro Garabito

had done. Then the fat leader said with mock courtesy, "I hope we shall meet along this road again, someday, señores. Until then, *adios*." And the five of them rode off, their horses kicking a cloud of dust over us.

We waited until we were certain they were gone, and then we picked ourselves up and brushed off our clothes. Everyone was weak and shaky, but we had to continue the journey. There was no time to waste. Mama, Grandma, and Jaime got back into the carriage. Don Gaspar climbed up onto the driver's seat and sat next to me, squeezing me tight between him and the driver. We started on our way once again only to have to stop when we arrived at the pile of rocks that blocked our passage along the road. Don Gaspar and the driver, with some exertion, managed to clear a way wide enough for the carriage to pass and we continued on. I heard Mama and Grandma talking from inside the carriage about the Cimarrónes and how they were worse than pirates and that they ought to be burned with no mercy when they were captured.

After some time, we stopped at the inn where we usually spent the night on our way to and from the city. It was here that we usually rested and ate and got fresh horses. Our driver's family owned the inn. When we arrived, we were dismayed to find only his sister there. She explained that her sons and husband had left for Panama to fight the pirates and they had taken all the fresh horses with them. Don Gaspar was vexed to hear this, but he urged us to continue the journey with the tired horses. Our driver chose to stay behind with his sister. It was good that he did, for it gave Don Gaspar and me more room on the seat at the front of the coach. Our traveling was slower now because the horses were so fatigued. It seemed that we barely crept along the dusty road. The midday sun scorched us and made the horses' job much harder.

We rode for some distance in silence. Don Gaspar seemed lost in thought. He even forgot to blink. He had been brave in front of the Cimarrónes, and I was ashamed that I had thought him a fool. He was really not such a bad man. He certainly had courage. When his face was at rest and he forgot to blink, I noticed that he was rather handsome with high cheekbones and a straight, noble nose.

"Don Caspar," I said as I stood up to stretch my back and legs which felt very weary from sitting for such a long time.

He was still lost in his own thoughts and paid no attention.

"Don Gaspar," I said again a bit louder.

He turned to me and I saw worry in his eyes, "Yes, Marta?" He said, the beginnings of a smile coming to his lips.

"The horses, will they be able to carry us all the way to Panama? They look so tired."

"It is my hope they will if we don't ask them to go any faster than they go now. It is unfortunate that your brother is ill. If we did not have this carriage to pull, we would be in the city by now." He gently flicked his whip on the flank of the right rear horse, who paid no heed and plodded on at her accustomed pace.

"How much danger is there for us?" I asked sitting down and feeling the aches return to my legs and back.

"If we can make it to Panama before Morgan, we will be safe. The city is well protected. It is getting caught out here on the road that I worry about."

I must have looked frightened because he suddenly touched my hand and said, "Ah, Marta, do not fret. We will reach the city in time." Then he quickly drew his hand away and gazed down the road. He began to blink once again. I too looked straight down the road. My face felt flushed. I could tell I was blushing. I felt uneasy that his touch should make me blush. As we rode in silence, I sensed that Don Gaspar turned his face toward me several times as if to speak, then changed his mind and turned away again.

We rode in embarrassed silence for a few minutes. I tried to think of something to say, but everything I thought of seemed silly.

Suddenly, Don Gaspar looked at me and said, "Marta perhaps this is not the right time to speak to you, but I have to know. When we have vanquished Morgan and Panama is once again a safe place, may I ask your father for your hand?"

I felt myself blush deeper. My mind became confused with thoughts and feelings. I wished he had not asked me that question. If he had spoken to me of marriage a few days earlier, I would quickly have refused him even though Mama would have been furious. But now, with us fleeing for our lives, with Jaime still weak, and with Don Gaspar becoming our savior, I was not certain I could say no. All these thoughts were crowing my mind while Don Gaspar sat on the seat looking at me timidly but hopefully, "You seem surprised, Marta. Surely you must have suspected the reason for my visits."

I nodded, but could find no words to answer him.

"Then you must have been considering what you would say to me when I asked for your hand." He leaned toward me peering into my eyes. I looked down at my hands clasped tightly together in my lap.

"Is it my age? Do you think I am too old for you?"

"Oh no," I said looking at him once again. How could I hurt this man who was risking his life to see us safely back to the city?

"You know, Marta, I am a wealthy man with excellent family. If you marry me, you will want for nothing. I will build you a house and furnish it with the finest Spain has to give. It would be the greatest house in all of

Panama. And if you liked, and it was safe, we could travel to Spain where you could choose the things to go inside it." He blinked furiously. "I know that I am a great deal older than you, but you are a sensible girl, not given to youthful frippery. I could make you happy. What will you say, Marta? Shall I speak to your father?"

It wouldn't be such a bad life, I thought, I certainly would have everything I wanted—as long as it wasn't something Don Gaspar considered "frippery." I supposed I could learn to be fond of him. Perhaps Mama was right that I should not let this chance slip by. Perhaps Don Gaspar was the best match a plain girl like me could hope for. He was a brave, kind, steady man. What more could I want? It wouldn't be like Grandma's marriage surrounded by music and poetry and ideas, but it would be comfortable.

"Well?" he questioned.

"Yes," I said softly as the tears pooled in my eyes. The minute that word escaped from my mouth I knew I had made a grave mistake. I didn't want to marry him.

He put his hands over mine and squeezed. They were moist, almost cold. I felt like snatching my hands away, but I knew it would be impolite.

"You make me a happy man, little lady." He took the reins in his hands and pulled on them urging the horses on. "When your father returns from Peru, I will waste no time in speaking to him. In the meantime, tell your mother and grandmother if you wish." He smiled at me in a new way. It was a special smile that I had not seen before. It was as if suddenly there was a bond between us which hadn't been there a few minutes before. I could not return that smile. I tried with great difficulty not to let him see the tears in my eyes.

I spent the rest of the long ride into the city feeling panic. I was filled not with fear of the pirates capturing us, but with a terrible feeling that I had made a grave mistake. There I sat beside the man whom I had just told I would marry, feeling no joy or excitement. Now and then he turned and gave me that special smile that I was growing to hate. I wanted to tell him it was all a mistake; that I had changed my mind; but I couldn't hurt him. He was a good man even if he looked foolish. I would make myself grow fond of him.

Rosa, it is time to end my writing for this day. My hand is tired and remembering once again that frightful trip back to Panama, my back aches in sympathy. I will take a walk in the garden.

Until tomorrow,
Marta

Edward's Journal

JANUARY 1671

RIVER CHAGRES, DAY TWO

It is near dark and I sit here cross-legged on the riverbank.
I wish I had some dinner. Yesterday we started up the
River Chagres with canoes each carrying eight men and
some boats big enough to hold cannons. There's not much
food because we need space for weapons and ammunition. We hope to catch our food as we go along, but so
far we've had little luck. In my pockets are some chips of
dried turtle meat; now and then I eat one, but it doesn't
satisfy my hunger.

The river runs slow here. For as far as I can see up and
down, small groups of men are camped beside the grey
water in clearings only big enough for a dozen men to lie in.

Trees, vines, and bushes are thick on both banks, and
they grow down to the edge of the water where the roots
make a tangle so dense it's nearly impossible to climb
through them to dry ground. We keep our eyes open for
camping places that have been cleared by the Spanish,
who use the river for travel to and from Panama. If we

had to clear spots for ourselves, it would take the good part of a day just making room for everybody to lie down. Rowing against the current is easy when you think of the work it would be to clear the jungle. There aren't only trees and roots to cut away; some vines that wrap around the tree trunks are thicker than fence posts, and a dozen hard chops with a machete won't cut through one of them.

I ride in the canoe with the Captain, Ned, Higgins, Monkey, Moon, and two fellows I hadn't seen much of before, Martin, a smith out of Port Royal, and Tigurt, a skinny sort who is missing two fingers on his left hand. Now on land, we're spread out as far apart as we can get. We're all feeling cranky after two days rowing against the Chagres' current.

Before we started out yesterday, I was glad that I would row. I like the feeling of pulling on those oars and making the boat glide over the water so swift and smooth. But I soon found out that rowing upstream isn't much fun. Nothing I have ever done has been so hard, not plowing, not planting, not building fences. You sit there in that boat with seven other bodies each one straining and pulling on an oar, and you strain and pull too 'til your shoulders feel like there's a big rock sitting between them and you think your arms are going to break. And after a good while, you glance at the shore to see how far you've come and your heart falls when the familiar rocks and bushes show that you've hardly gone forward at all; you've used up a bushel of energy just to keep the boat from drifting back down the river.

From the sounds at night, you can tell there are animals around, but we haven't seen any; just a few birds in flight. Most of the animals stay hidden in the day and come out after dark. That doesn't help us much; we need the light of day to see what we're hunting. But I know

food is out there. Last night the monkeys set up such a
howling and screaming that you would have thought there
was a massacre going on in the tree tops. It was worse
than the night we captured St. Catherine. Those monkeys
make more noise than a thousand drunk pirates.

We have night watches here like we do onboard ship.
The Captain says it's to watch for the enemy, but Higgins told me it is mostly to guard against crocodiles. They
come out at night along with the monkeys, and they have
been known to attack a sleeping man. Higgins told me
something else about them. If you're ever chased by one,
he said, you should run like the devil, but not straight
ahead. If you do that, the croc can catch you sure as a
hawk catches a chick. If you run first to one side and then
to the other, zigging and zagging, the croc finds it hard to
turn. Every time he does, it slows him down enough to let
you get away. That sounds reasonable to me.

So far, in two days we have seen no sign of the Spaniards except for their deserted camps. But I swear they
must have left the bugs here to torture us. We have bugs
in Jamaica, but nothing like these. The mosquitoes are
always around, and just before dark their cousins, the
gnats, and some invisible little devils that bite with fire,
show up. They attack through your shirt and pants and
fly up your nose and into your mouth and ears. I have
bites all over, even between my fingers and on my eyelids.
They drive me wild with their itching. Higgins says I'll
get used to it.

March to Panama, Day Four

Our progress is slow. I don't think we made more than a
league or two today. The river is hard going here because it
runs shallow and the Spaniards have chopped down trees

and piled them in the water to block our way. The Captain decided tonight to take most of the men and travel on foot along the edge of the river. He'll let a few canoes keep going upriver however they can. The rest of the canoes and the five boats with artillery will be left here with a small crew until we come back. The Captain said it's folly to take the heavy guns any further. The only way we'll make it to Panama is to lighten our loads. So we'll carry the swords and flintlocks and shot and powder and stonebows. The cannon stay behind. I will travel with the Captain tomorrow on foot. Ned goes with us. Blackwort and Higgins and Moon and Monkey come along with us too, while Mr. Potts will be in charge of the men in the canoes.

Our hunger gets worse and worse. What little food we brought with us is gone, and we chase after any motion in the jungle, hoping it is a bird or animal that will make us dinner. But fortune has frowned on us. The creatures in this forest are wary. They tease us with a fluttering branch or a rustling bush. When we rush at the moving spot, they are gone. There we stand, empty-handed and hungry, with dirt and scratches all over from the thorns and vines we rubbed against in our mad dash toward the promise of food.

Earlier today I was so hungry that I was ready to eat most anything. We pulled ashore and set our camp in a clearing that, judging from the warm fire pit, had been used by the Spaniards a day before. We looked all over for signs of food but there was nothing. The Captain took a musket and two men and headed into the jungle. Most of the rest of us lay around on the ground in a weakened condition due to hunger and long hours of rowing. Ned lay on his stomach beside me, his head pillowed by his arms. I was busy scratching the bites on my ankles that itch so they near drive me mad.

"Ed, remember that little house with the garden and the chickens on St. Catherine? What wouldn't you give now for one bite of the chicken soup?" He closed his eyes as if he was dreaming about it.

I thought about it, too. "Remember the mangoes," I said, "all pink and juicy and sweet? I'd even settle for a piece of hardtack."

Ned propped himself up on an elbow and reached into his pocket.

"Your humble servant at your service," he said and grinned at me as he produced a piece of dry biscuit about the size of the lens in a pair of eye-glasses. It was just enough for two medium bites. "I've been saving it for us," he said breaking it in half. "Let's eat it slow. I've a feeling it may be all we get for awhile."

We sat there nibbling the biscuit as slowly as we could. I broke off a piece not much bigger than a grain of sand and held it on my tongue, letting it get soft and trying to enjoy the bit of salty flavor. Then I swallowed and waited a little before I took another piece. Even stopping as long as I could between bites, it seemed like no time before the water was gone and I was left just as hungry as if I hadn't had any at all.

Feeling sad about finishing off my last morsel of food until who knew when, I looked across the clearing and saw the hulking form of Blackwort come out of the dark jungle. Instead of the usual scowl on his face, he was as close to smiling as I guessed he could manage. In his arms he carried a pile of leather bags. He took two or three steps toward the fire pit and threw them on the ground. The bags were deep and round, made to hold flour or maize. Those of us who were watching, jumped to our feet and ran over to see what they held. I opened one of the bags and felt around inside, but I found nothing but a few grains of rice and some white powder that tasted like flour. I sunk to the ground disappointed; but Ned stood there by the pile of leather looking at it as if it still might have some possibilities.

Blackwort picked up one of the bags and tried to take a bite out of the handle. I saw his jaws strain and his teeth grind, but even his iron strength couldn't break the tough hide. He tried again harder, until you could see the veins on his neck stand out. Finally he bit off a piece and tried to chew it. He chewed and chewed and rolled that hide around in his mouth trying to soften it up, but he didn't have much luck. He almost looked funny putting his face through all those contortions. After awhile he gave up and spit that piece of saddlebag through the air like a stone out of a slingshot. It hit Moon on the back of his bald head with a smack.

Moon whirled around ready to fight, bellowing, "What the...." But when he saw who it was who'd hit him, he calmed down real quick and just stood there rubbing his sore spot.

Blackwort's one eye glinted with rage and it seemed to me that the scar on his cheek grew redder. Then he turned his back and went to the edge of the river where he sat alone glaring at the muddy water flowing past.

Ned touched me on the arm and pointed to the leather bags that still lay in the pile by the fire. "Those hides came from cows and horses, right?

"I imagine so," I said wondering why he asked me something that he knew the answer to already.

"And a man can eat cows and horses, right?"

"Right," I said.

"Well then, let's figure a way to fix those so we can eat them. There must be some nourishment still in them." He pulled a machete from the trunk of a tree where it had

been stuck, and he lay one of the bags across a fallen log,
Then he chopped the handle of it into small strips about
as big as your little finger.

I was beginning to see what he had in mind and I
found some stones down by the river and the two of us
beat those leather strips between the rocks until they were
as thin as the leaves of the trees above us. Soon we were
surrounded by curious faces. When the fellows saw what
we were up to, they pitched in with the chopping and the
pounding until we had enough scraps to take down to
the river where we soaked them. The soaking made the
leather soft and ready to boil. When it was cooked, I ate
a piece. I must say that if I had my pick, I wouldn't order
leather for dinner, but it did have a little flavor like roast
meat. It was still tough and hard to chew, but we learned
to hold it in our mouths, chew it real good to get any
juices out of it, then swallow it fast.

One man, seeing how it was possible to get some nourishment out of plain old leather, offered his boots, and
another gave his powder bag, and boots and bag soon met
the same fate as the leather Blackwort found in the jungle.
Blackwort didn't help us prepare the hides, but he chewed
on some of the boiled pieces that they took to him in
his spot down on the river bank where he sat still as a
post, not even moving to swat the mosquitoes that buzzed
around him.

In the middle of all the activity, the Captain came
back, having had no luck at catching anything to eat.
He laughed when he saw what we were dining on, but he
helped himself to some scraps. He promised us a real feast
once we get to Panama.

MARCH TO PANAMA, DAY FIVE

We made camp early today. Some of the men are sick with aches and fever. They were too weak to go on, so we stopped. It's hard making our way along the river bank, chopping through the vines and brush. But I like it better than riding for hours in the canoe, where your back aches so and your feet and legs go to sleep. Parts of the river's edge are swampy; more than once today I had to wade waist deep in muck, hoping that I wouldn't meet up with any crocodiles or snakes. I'm used to breathing in insects now. I hardly even notice. But I can't get used to the itching on my legs and arms. Sometimes I think I'm going to cry, they itch so bad.

About midday we came upon this spot where some of the Spanish camped not too long ago. Like the other places we found, they took everything edible with them, but fortune gave us a small present. Captain Morgan went out into the jungle to hunt and came upon a cave that contained two sacks of maize, two jars of wine, and a stalk of plantains. He brought the food into camp and divided it among us all; the weakest ones got the biggest share.

MARCH TO PANAMA, DAY SIX

I woke at daybreak this morning to the moaning of a fellow, one of the sick ones from yesterday, who groaned and tossed on the ground. He was calling for water, so I got up and fetched him some from the muddy river. He sat up to take the water, but his eyes didn't see me. They were all fuzzed over and misty looking. His face was hot to my touch; the poor fellow was burning up with the fever. His skin had turned yellowish-brown like an overripe banana

"Poor old Tigurt, he's got the yellow death," Higgins said, looking over my shoulder at the chap. He shook his head and his sagging cheeks jiggled. "And it don't look so good for Frenchie over there either." He signaled to another man who lay still and stiff a few yards away. His skin was yellow too.

We stood there looking at the two sick fellows and swatted away some mosquitoes and gnats. Higgins slapped two fat mosquitoes that sat on Tigurt's cheek and the blood in them smeared across the sick man s face. "Them damn bugs should have a little mercy for a dying fellow. He's suffering enough without them mosquitoes sticking him full of holes."

"Water," moaned the sick man. I knelt down and gave him a drink.

By this time most everyone in the camp was awake and stirring. Captain Morgan came over to inspect the two fellows. He sank to one knee, put his hand on Tigurt's brow, while he cursed and shook his head. "Damn that swamp of a river. It's the vapors in this hellhole that gets the weak ones." He looked at Higgins and me and growled, "Leave them be. We have to head out."

"But Captain, they'll die sure if we leave them," Higgins said.

The Captain shook his head. "They'll die anyway. Get moving. We'll leave the sick ones here and come for whoever's still alive on our way back."

So we started the slow hike up the river's edge leaving behind close to a dozen men who were too sick and weak to go on. Our stomachs were empty, and hoping to find something to fill them, we sampled the leaves and grasses that grew along the way. Most of the ones I tried were tough or bitter, and I spit them out after one bite, but once, I found a low growing bush with tender, sweet-tasting leaves and I grabbed a handful to eat as I went along. Ned who was behind me grabbed my shoulder, turned me around and snatched the leaves from my hand.

"You fool!" He said, "Are you trying to poison yourself?"

His acting so rude made me mad and I shoved him so hard he fell back and landed in the bushes. "Don't push me around!" I shouted at him. "I'll eat what I want." Then I turned my back on him and marched on. He must have picked himself up real fast because I heard him close behind me. We walked along not talking to one another for awhile. Then he spoke.

"Ed."

"What?"

"I guess I acted like an ass back there."

I didn't answer, but I turned around and looked at him.

"I'm sorry, Ed. It's just that I was afraid you'd poison yourself. It's bad enough here in the swamp with the bugs and crocs, but at least there's you to talk to." He stuck his head in front of my face and knitted his brows. "We're still friends, aren't we?"

I felt my anger leaving. "Yes, we're friends," I said.

We shook hands and trudged along beside the dirty River Chagres. High overhead in the cloudless sky flew the dark form of a large bird, probably a buzzard. We looked at it with the hope that it might come low enough to shoot, but the bird had wit and kept its distance.

"You know," said Ned who walked just far enough behind me so he wouldn't step on my heels. "I keep thinking it's peculiar we haven't met up with any Spaniards or Indians. They know we're coming. Why haven't they tried to fight us? Now that we re all spread out along the river like this, you'd think they would try an attack. Do you suppose they're scared of us?"

"It wouldn't surprise me. Mr. Potts says that the name Henry Morgan strikes fear in every Spanish settlement

in the New World. He hit them once bad in Portobelo.
I think they're afraid to fight us." Hungry and tired as I
was, I suddenly felt happy and sure that I was going to get
home with a bag or two of gold.

"I don't know, Ed," Ned said. "The Spanish are crafty.
I'll wager they have something planned. Probably when
we get closer to Panama. You know, they say the city is
impossible to attack. With all those warehouses full of
gold and silver, they're not going to make it easy for us.
It's sure they have a plan but I don't think they'll do anything out here in the jungle."

How did he know they wouldn't attack us out here in
the jungle? His words made me feel uneasy and I looked
around me. But there was only the still, dark jungle on
one side and the slow river on the other. If the Spanish
did have something for us, it wasn't going to happen right
there. Just then a thought came to me. "Ned?"

"What?"

"Do you ever get the feeling that what we're doing is
stealing?"

"Stealing?"

"Yes. I know we have the King's permission and all,
but somehow it just doesn't seem right—going in there
and taking what we never did anything honest to earn."

"Look at it this way, Ed, we're Englishmen and anything
we can do to weaken Spain's hold on the New World is good
for England. We're helping our country open up trade routes."
He grinned, "And we're helping ourselves a little, too."

I never thought about it that way before.

About midday, we spied shapes moving up ahead in
the river. When we got closer we saw some people standing
waist-deep in the water. Five or six brown-skinned Indians
with straight black hair that hung to their shoulders were
bathing close to the opposite shore. The first thing that

came to mind was that they must have food somewhere, so we charged ahead, trying to reach them. When we got to within shouting distance, we yelled and motioned with our hands—putting them to our mouths and rubbing our stomachs—hoping the Indians would understand that we wanted something to eat.

At first they just stood on the opposite bank of the river, staring at us. When they made no move to cross the river, five of the men dove in, meaning to swim across. Monkey was in the lead, moving with a fast easy stroke. Seeing the men swim toward them the Indians turned and rushed from the river shouting strange noises which came from deep inside their throats.

Monkey was halfway across the river when the arrows started flying. Out of the jungle came twenty Indians who stood at the edge of the greenery, shielded by bushes and trees, and pelted the swimmers with arrows. The air was heavy with the sound of arrows leaving bows. A few came so far that they landed close to us. When the swimmers realized their danger, they turned and started back to our side, the arrows falling around them like rain in a hurricane. I heard a scream and saw one of our men sink below the water. Then Monkey disappeared under the water and I heard two more men scream and saw them go limp before the current dragged their bodies downstream.

We took cover in the jungle and watched as the one fellow who was left made it back to shore. Just before he climbed out of the water, Monkey's head broke the surface close to him and the two of them crawled out together, arrows still falling all around. They made it to safety and waited with us for the Indians to stop firing. Once we were all hidden in the jungle, the arrows stopped and the Indians disappeared into the green of the opposite shore. After a safe time, we came out to the riverbank again.

"If only there was some way to get the guns across that river, I'd go after them savages," Moon said. "There's sure to be eats over there. What do ye say, Captain, do we go after them naked hellhounds?"

"No, Moon. Who knows if we'd ever catch up to them? We're here to get to Panama, and that's what we'll do. It isn't much farther to the head of the river, and then it's an easy walk to the city of gold." He reached into a bag he carried over one shoulder and pulled out twenty or so hard biscuits. "I've been saving this last bit of food to get us by. It's time we ate it."

He gave Moon the biscuits. "Here Moon, see that everybody gets his share."

Monkey helped his friend cut the biscuits into quarters with his dagger. Then he passed a bit to each man. The last man to take his was Moon. I watched while Monkey handed him his bit; if my eyes weren't playing tricks on me, I swear I saw Monkey pass him two whole biscuits along with the bit that was his rightful share. Moon, quick as lightening, slipped the booty into his trousers pocket.

I looked around to see who else saw it, but nobody was paying attention. Ned had gone off into the woods. When he came back, I pulled him aside and told him what I'd seen.

"The greedy hogs!" he growled while he glared at the two men standing off by themselves with their backs to us. "I'll wager they're eating them right now!"

That was my guess, too. It was no use telling anybody. The evidence was gone. I would just have to watch them more carefully from now on, so they wouldn't have a chance to do anything like that again.

I followed them and listened to their talk about what they were going to do when they got to Panama.

"Me," said Moon looking up at the sky, "first I'm going to help myself to a chunk o' that solid gold altar."

"Sounds good, Moonie," said Monkey while he looked over his shoulder. "But I been thinking. Morgan's goin' to be sure that we hit the warehouses and the churches. Then all that swag'll have to be divided up according to the Articles."

Moon shook his head, "Yep, it will."

"But who's to know if you and I find us some swag of our own. While the rest of them are out raiding the warehouses, we'll pay a visit to some of the prosperous citizens of ol' Panama. There's bound to be coin and jewels there. I hear there's lots of rich men in that city."

"More than Maracaibo?"

"Aye. A hundred times more."

Moon chuckled. "Monkey, ol' friend, I like yer idea. We might even find us some women in them rich men's houses."

Monkey said, "Yeah. Now you're using that shiny noggin o' yours."

I was beginning to hate those two. There was no trust in them. It didn't seem to bother either one of them that men had been dropping along the trail all that day. Some got up and stumbled on only to drop again a little later. I didn't know if it was hunger or fever that dragged them down. I guess it didn't matter. They were too weak to go on, and we had to leave them lying there. I kept track of the bodies I passed on the trail and I counted twelve. Since I walk toward the front of the line, I'll wager thrice that many fell behind me. Three of the ones I saw were already dead. The others just lay there, some moaning, some quiet. It seems a shame there's no preacher to say some words over them. Higgins says it's the fever causing this, and it's bound to get worse.

March to Panama, Day Seven

We had a bad time of it today. It's hard to think of words to describe how downhearted I feel. It seems a long time since this morning, when we reached the village of Santa Cruz, which marks the farthest point that boats can travel up the Chagres. When we heard we were close to the village, our spirits lifted; we knew from Santa Cruz on, we wouldn't have to make trail. There was a mule trail from there to Panama. Before we saw the village, we smelled smoke, and knowing that smoke meant cooking fires, and best of all, food, we hurried along the riverbank. About an hour later, when we finally got there, we found buildings smoldering in ashes, not cook fires. The people who lived there had set fire to every building around—houses, two *bohíos*, and a little warehouse. By the time we got there, everything was near burnt to the ground. We searched around in the ashes for food, but we found only charcoal and some iron nails.

I fell to the ground so disappointed I felt like crying. Then I just lay there and thought about the night before and the men that died between sundown and dawn. We must have left fifty bodies at the camp. I didn't sleep all night for the moaning and suffering going on around me. The fever was what was doing it to them. It was horrible! I saw men that were healthy in the morning dying that night. I don't know who it's going to hit next. Anyhow, fear of the fever and disappointment at not finding food at Santa Cruz made us all feel like condemned men whose pardons were taken away.

"God," a fellow fell to his knees and prayed, "get me out of here alive, and I'll never do anything bad again." He was barefoot and his feet were cut and bloody from walking all this way with no boots. There were open sores on the bottoms of his feet.

Another fellow hit the trunk of a tree with his fist and sobbed, "We're all good as dead!" He wailed and cried like he was out of his head, "Nobody'll ever know what happened to us! We'll die and the buzzards'll eat us."

It went on like that for a while with hardly anybody having enough energy to do anything but lie around feeling bad. Then some hearty fellows discovered a cache of wine and maize, and that cheered us up.

The maize made tasty bread after it was mixed with salt and water and baked. The wine smelled funny, so I didn't drink any. Neither did Ned or the Captain, I noticed. But there weren't very many others that didn't partake, and that wine was finished off in no time.

No more than a quarter of an hour later, just like a rainstorm where first there's a drop, then there's two, and pretty soon there are so many you lose count and run for shelter, the first man grabbed his belly, complained of cramps, and vomited. He was still retching when a couple more got sick and before I knew it, the village plaza was crowded with men rolling around on the ground sicker than dogs.

There was only a handful of us that didn't seem to be bothered. "Ned, what do you suppose is wrong with 'em," I asked. "The fever?"

"No, the fever wouldn't work on everybody at once like that."

"Something they ate?"

"Must be."

"Ned, how do you feel?"

"All right."

"Me too. And the Captain isn't sick," I said while I watched him walk among the men talking to the ones that could talk.

"Either of you drink wine?" he asked us.

We shook our heads.

He picked up a gourd cup that some of the men had used and he sniffed it. Then he stuck a finger into the cup and licked it with the tip of his tongue. He scowled at the taste and wiped his tongue on the shoulder of his shirt.

"The jackasses poisoned the wine!" He bellowed. Then he hurled the cup against a rock where it splintered into a thousand little pieces. "Poison!" he yelled again. There were only a few of us paying heed to him. Most of the fellows were rolling around on the ground retching and heaving too sick to care.

"They're in no condition to move on today," he said when he'd calmed down some. "We'll wait here and see if the others can catch up with us by morning. We have to wait for them somewhere anyhow. Might as well be here." Then he looked at Ned and me and pointed a finger at us, saying, "Green and Leach, find yourselves a pair of guns and a couple men and go hunt us up some food." We turned to obey him when he added, "And mind you, don't come back here empty-handed."

We nodded and found two others who weren't sick—a tall skinny chap named Martins and his friend, Peters, who was quiet and prayed every night before he went to sleep. We were about to set out into the jungle with two flintlocks among the four of us when the Captain stood in our path and said, "Green, you're in charge. Remember, the Spaniards aren't stupid. Be on the lookout for ambush. Go through that jungle like there's one of them snakes behind every bush."

"Sir," answered Ned while he hoisted one of the guns over his shoulder "I'll wager we don't find a Spaniard between here and Panama."

The four of us started down the trail that led into the

thick green of the jungle when all of a sudden, the Captain charged Ned from behind. He ran at him full force with his head bent and he butted Ned right off his feet. The flintlock flew out of his arms and landed in some grass at the side of the path while Ned sprawled on his stomach with the wind knocked out of him.

"You're too sure of yourself, Greene," said the Captain standing over him. "The minute a man gets too cocksure of himself, he's headed for trouble."

Ned just lay there trying to catch his breath,

"That jungle out there's full of Spaniards waiting to get us. Just don't get feeling too cocksure."

Then he turned his back on us and walked away.

Ned got up real slow and I handed him his gun. "Damn him," he said glaring after the Captain. "Damn him."

Watchful for signs of the enemy, we followed the path away from the river into the jungle. Ned walked ahead carrying the flintlock. He still smarted from the Captain's rebuke, but he put on a casual air like nothing had happened.

I was nervous though, and I looked from side to side examining every branch or twig that was bent or pushed down in an unnatural way. After we walked for some time, we came to a clearing about the size of a corn patch. There was a cold fire pit in the middle but nothing for us to eat anywhere, so we walked on. In a little while we came upon another clearing the same size as the first. But in this one, the fire pit was still warm, and ashes glowed red when I blew on them. Better still, to one side we discovered a *bohío* where three clay jugs full of flour were stored.

But our good fortune did not last long. While Ned and Martins and Peters were checking the flour for signs of poison, I discovered a trail behind the *bohío* that looked like it hadn't been used for some time. There were vines growing over it, and the bushes hid it in spots.

I turned to call to Ned and the others, who were still looking over the flour, that I was going to see where the trail led. I thought I saw some movement in the bushes behind them at the other side of the clearing, but when I looked hard, there was nothing. I told myself I was just too jumpy.

"I'm going down this trail a ways," I called. Then I left them. I guess it was lucky that I did.

I thought maybe I would find something more to eat hidden along the old trail. It looked so overgrown and unused. It seemed to me that if I was a Spaniard, I would choose a place like that to hide stores. I made my way along what was left of the path for a while but I didn't see much of anything except more bushes and vines and trees and some butterflies and a stinging centipede. When I was just making up my mind to turn around and go back, I heard a commotion back at the clearing. At the sound of shouts and a gun shot, I turned and ran back toward my friends. When I got to where I could see the clearing, I stopped and threw myself to the ground. There, right in front of me, not more than a stone's throw away, were Ned and Peters and Martins surrounded by Spaniards who shouted at them in words that were quick and sharp and unfriendly. Then the Spaniards shoved my friends ahead of them, and the whole group moved down the trail away from our camp.

I lay there hidden in the bushes. After a few minutes I heard some gunshots in the distance and then silence. When I thought it was safe to move, I made my way to the clearing and ran as fast as I could back to the camp to get help.

The Captain was madder than a hurricane when I told him what happened. He cursed the Spaniards for being swine and he cursed Ned for being careless. Then, still cursing, he had me lead him and ten men who were feeling better, along the path in the direction the Spaniards had gone. We traveled carefully, not wanting to fall into another ambush. There wasn't any sign of Ned or Martins or Peters, and before long we had to turn back because it was getting dark.

It is with heavy heart and hand that I write this tonight by the firelight. Where are you Ned? Are you alive?

—Edward

18 JANUARY 1672, FINCA LAS BRISAS

Dear Rosa,

In my last letter I told you about us being robbed by the Cimarrónes and our mad flight to reach Panama before the pirates. Somehow during that frightful trip into the city we managed to secure fresh horses from a farmer to whom Don Gaspar paid a handsome sum. It was a blessing that the farmer still had horses, because when we came upon him that afternoon, ours were near death from heat and exhaustion. With the new horses we were able to make better time, and we arrived at the house in Panama early next morning. The house had been freshly painted in our absence, and it looked clean and inviting. The walls were newly whitewashed, and the doors had a new coat of black paint.

We awakened the servants who prepared a meal for us and gave us the news that Morgan was at least five days away. Then we fell into bed, and in spite of the danger, we slept all that day and most of the next.

When I awoke around two or three o'clock, I dressed and went in search of Mama, whom I found in the pantry directing the servants in the packing of the silver and dishes. They loaded them into large chests which were to be taken by horse cart down to the docks to be stowed aboard one of Papa's ships. The Governor ordered all ships in port to be packed with valuables and important citizens, after which they would sail to the island of Taboga which lies a few leagues off the coast. There, everyone would be safe from the greedy hands of the pirates.

Mama and I talked about how terrible it was that the Golden Altar was too big and heavy to be moved. It was the pride of everybody in Panama. People came from Lima and Mexico to see it. What a shame that there wasn't a way to keep it out of Henry Morgan's reach. I couldn't stop myself from thinking about it in spite of all the activity going on around me. My thoughts kept returning to the Golden Altar with its figures of the Saints and the flowers and animals all delicately worked together in a piece that covered the front of the church and nearly reached the ceiling. When the sun hit it, the shine was so brilliant, it seemed to have come from Heaven.

The man who created the altar was not a great artist. In fact, the altar is the only thing of note he ever did. It seems that he was a poor wood-carver who worked for our most important architect. One night, when this great architect was in the process of building the Cathedral, the Virgin visited the poor wood-carver in a dream, and she told him exactly how she wanted the altar. He woke up in the middle of the night and drew a picture of her request on the wall of his hut with a piece of charcoal. Everyone who knew this man swore that he was not good at drawing pictures, and yet on the wall of his tiny house he had drawn a perfect plan of the Golden Altar. It was a true miracle. The great architect made this man head of the crew that built the altar and the result was a beautiful, sacred masterpiece. I am sorry to report that the poor wood-carver died of the fever a few days before the altar was finished, and he never saw it completed.

Eulalia and Luz hastily went about pulling things from the shelves and drawers, wrapping them in rags, and stowing them away in the wooden chests.

"Be careful not to set anything heavy on top of that platter, Eulalia," said Mama as she handed a silver bowl to Luz. Her voice was tense, and her usually smooth forehead was wrinkled into a frown. She moved around the room finding things to pack and placing them on the round table which stood in the center of the room.

"How's Jaime, Mama?" I asked.

"I don't know. He is sleeping. Grandma's with him. Why don't you go see how they are?"

"And Don Gaspar?" I asked, watching her face for any sign that he had told her anything.

"Oh, he left some time ago," she said not looking up from a tray of things he had taken from a drawer.

"When will he be back?" I asked watching her expression closely.

"Oh, Marta, I don't know." She sounded exasperated. "That's not important right now. Come, help me with these things. We've got to hurry."

I guessed that she knew nothing and I felt relieved. Even though it would make her happy to learn that I had agreed to marry Don Gaspar, I could not bring myself to tell her. I had a bleak feeling knowing that I was in a horrible situation and it was nobody's fault but my own.

I reached for a mirror which hung on the wall when Mama cried, "Marta, find me some more rags."

"Yes, Mama," I said as I started for the laundry.

"No, no, it's better that you check on your brother. "

I turned in the direction of Jaime's room. "Yes, Mama."

It was just like Mama when she was doing something important like preparing for a fiesta or company to give us an order and to follow it with another before we had time to carry out the first.

I ran for Jaime's room before she could change her mind. Jaime was sitting up in bed. He smiled when he saw me. Grandma was still fast asleep on a cot against the wall. She lay on her back with her mouth slightly open. Her long grey hair had come unpinned during the night and it lay loose across her pillow.

"She's afraid," whispered Jaime. "She's been talking and moaning in her sleep."

"Aren't we all afraid?" I asked. I could hear the sounds from the street outside Jaime's shuttered window. Horses and carts passed with people calling to one another. It sounded like all of Panama was on its way to the docks.

"How do you feel, Jaime?" I whispered as I walked over to his bed. A bruise, black and swollen covered one side of his face.

"Better." He carefully touched his bruise. "Yesterday I felt like a herd of bulls gored and trampled me and dragged me all the way to Panama. Today I don't feel the gored part anymore, only the dragged." He winced when he moved his arm toward a glass of juice on the table beside his bed. Jaime's illness had left him with large bruises all over his body and every one of them was sore.

"Well, at least you're getting your sense of humor back. I want you to know, Jaime, that for a few days you were not very funny."

"What's the news of Morgan?"

"Only that he's at least five days away. Mama is packing and sending everything down to the docks. The plan is to put out to sea and take everything with us. That should disappoint the pirates."

"Disappoint the pirates, ha!" He yelled. Then he winced again because it hurt his mouth to open it so wide. "I want to see that they get what they deserve. Every one of them should be drawn and quartered. We shouldn't run from them, we should fight them."

"Oh, we're going to fight them, but the Governor wants to be prepared just in case our lines don't hold."

"Well, I'm not running," Jaime said clenching his fists on top of the sheet. "I'm fighting!"

"Be serious. In your condition you couldn't fight a cockroach."

I left him and went into the *sala* to help pack the pictures and furniture. After a few minutes Mama rushed in holding a miniature in a tiny gold frame.

"Marta, I found this at the bottom of a drawer and I want you to have it." She handed me the picture of a small girl of seven or eight who looked at me with blue eyes the color of china plates. The miniature was of Mama as a child in Seville. It had been painted by a student of Velásquez, the court painter. She told me how hard it was to sit still while the young man painted her.

"My nose itched so I thought I would perish if I couldn't scratch it, but I didn't dare for fear I would ruin the painting," she said, taking it from me and holding it in the palm of her hand. The gold frame was as lovely as the picture. It circled Mama's face with three rows of ruby beads and loops of gold.

"My mother, may she rest in peace," Mama, crossed herself, "presented this to me when your father and I left Spain. She wanted me to give it to my own daughter someday." She frowned at me. "I wonder if she ever suspected she would have such a headstrong, disobedient grandchild." Then she placed the miniature in my hand. "Put it somewhere safe, Marta," and she turned and hurried away. I slipped the miniature into pocket of my green dress meaning to put it in the small wooden box with my rosary when I went to my room.

I continued to help the maids pack the pictures and furnishings. Everything was done in such haste it was a miracle that we didn't break anything. When I turned to fetch a book from a table which was soon to be taken away, I was surprised to see Jaime come into the *sala*. His walk was slow and a bit unsteady as you might expect of someone who has been ill, but I was elated to discover him up and about. He was dressed in his usual white shirt and trousers, and except for the bruises on him, he looked quite good.

"Oh, Jaime, you don't know how happy I am to see you up and around."

"How could I stay in bed at a time like this? Just give me a musket and a saber and I'll fight Morgan, himself." He made an unsteady swipe with an imaginary sword and collapsed into a chair.

We heard some voices at the door and then Mama came in followed by Don Diego Seron, one of the Governor's aides, and by a young man, about my age.

"Marta, Jaime," said Mama, "I want you to meet Miguel Antonio Munoz de Madriaga. Miguel is the son of my cousin, Geraldo, the planter in Cuba." She locked her arm in his and said to him, "1 haven't seen Geraldo since I was a child, and I haven't heard about him in years. How wonderful to have you here, but under these circumstances it is not the best of times for you to have come. I'm afraid our hospitality will be somewhat unusual."

The newcomer bowed. "Doña Carmen, after what I have been through, the slightest kindness is hospitality enough."

His Spanish had an accent to it I had never heard before. It was a little too informal, as if he had learned it from field hands. But, I thought to myself, perhaps that is the way they speak in Cuba. He was taller than any of us in the room by four or five centimeters, and he stood erect, pulling his slim body up to its full height, which gave him an air of dignity despite his speech. His face was handsome. It was framed by wavy dark hair, and his thick eyebrows set off his dark eyes. They were the first thing I looked at when I saw him. They were beautiful. I tried not to stare at him, but I couldn't help it. His nose and cheeks were covered by light brown freckles. Except for the clothes he wore, which were in tatters, he was very attractive.

"1 will leave Miguel here with you," Don Diego said, "and I will be off to the Palace. There is much to do in preparation. The Governor sends you his greetings and asks that you make Miguel as comfortable as possible." He bowed and hurried away.

Mama left the rest of the packing to the servants and led us out onto the patio where there were some wooden chairs which were not to be sent away. We all sat down. I made myself sit on the other side of Mama from Miguel. Mama said, "Tell us, Miguel, what brings you to Panama at such a time as this, and why did you not write us and tell us you were coming? I am ashamed that we cannot greet you in a better fashion."

Miguel looked at Mama and shook his head slowly as he replied, "You see, Doña Carmen, it was not my intention to come to Panama. I was not aware that I had family here. My father is so occupied with his sugar cane that he finds time to talk of little else. Mother died when I was only a baby, so you see, there has been no one to tell me about family."

Jaime was becoming more and more impatient to hear Miguel's story and he said rather rudely, "Then what are you doing here?"

Miguel looked directly at Jaime and said, "I am here because of Henry Morgan."

"Morgan?"

"I was traveling for my father in Maracaibo, looking over a new kind of cane a planter was growing there, when we were attacked by Morgan and his outlaws and I was taken prisoner. Morgan's design was to ransom me to my father whom he assumed to be wealthy, but he decided to invade Panama before he had time to get word to my father. He brought me along as an interpreter." Miguel leaned forward, placing his hands on his knees. "Fortunately, I was captured by some Spanish soldiers while I was hunting for food in the jungle with some of the pirates. They nearly killed me before I could convince them that I was indeed Spanish and not an English dog. When at last they believed me, they brought me to Panama to tell my story to the Governor. Lucky for me, the Governor remembered that Doña Carmen was related to the Munoz' of Seville, which is also my family. He sent Don Diego here with me to hear her give her assurance that my father is in fact her cousin and that I am who I say I am." He looked at Mama and smiled.

"Tell us about the pirates," said Jaime. "Do they really think they can capture Panama?"

"Yes they do," Miguel replied. "But they are no match for the Spanish army." He looked around at the things being packed away. "You are wise, though, to take precautions."

"And Henry Morgan," I asked, "is he as fiendish as they say?"

"Worse. He is a man who lets nothing stand in the way of what he wants, and he commands the worst cut-throats in the Caribbean. One of his chief men is a giant with only one eye who is so mean he can squeeze ransom from a beggar."

Miguel caught the look of alarm on my face, and he smiled in a reassuring way. "But don't worry Cousin Marta, these men won't see the inside of Panama. After all, this is the invincible city."

I don't think anybody really believed him.

"How long do you judge it will be before...,"Mama hesitated.

"With all of those men and the equipment, two days at least."

"Two days?" she cried, "1 was told it would be longer! Children, we must rush!" She arose biting her lower lip. Then she sighed, "If only Papa were here. What a dreadful time for him to be gone." She whirled around and hurried from the patio, nearly knocking down Grandma who was coming in.

"Excuse me, Doña Ana," she apologized and went on.

Grandma saw Jaime first, and said, "Well, my young man, I see you're up and around. That's good, but don't try to convince yourself that you are as strong as you were before. Not yet." She walked up to Jaime and put her hand on his brow, checking for fever. Then she noticed Miguel.

I introduced Miguel to her, and he once again told how he came to be in our house. When he began to speak, I saw Grandma raise her eyebrows in surprise at his accent, but she soon forgot her surprise as Miguel related his story. After he had finished, she said, "Well, that doesn't give us much time, does it?" She looked around the room and said, "I must find Carmen and see what I can do to help."

We spent much of the rest of that day packing things away and loading the carts that waited in the outer court-yard. We hurried but there was an unreal sort of calmness over everyone. There was not much talk; when anyone did speak, it was about the things being stowed away. Never did I hear anyone speak of what might be in store for us in the next few days. Everyone, even the servants put his mind to the immediate task and did not let himself think much beyond that.

Miguel was given a shirt and pants belonging to my brother, Roberto, since the two of them were about the same size. In the new clothes he looked better than Roberto ever did. Although he was quiet and somewhat reserved in his conversation with me I liked him almost immediately. He seemed to have a silent strength, which in a person his age, is very rare. I had seen it in only a few people, and they were always older. I have seen it in Grandma, and in Papa. It is a kind of strength that suggests honor and dignity but also suggests the person can see below the surface of things and find the deeper meaning which sometimes lies hidden. He would never let things happen to him. He would make things happen. That was my first impression of Miguel.

We planned to sleep one more night in the house, and then leave early next morning in order to sail with the tide. I went to bed that night anxious and frightened. It was impossible to sleep. I lay there imagining the worst that could happen to us. I could see in my mind the pirates gaining entrance to the city and robbing it of every precious thing. I could see us watching from the ships near Taboga as the city burned. Then I remembered the Golden Altar. I had visions of those filthy infidels chopping it into pieces and carrying it back with them to wherever they had come from. I could see the head of the Blessed Virgin being severed from the altar and melted down into bullion by some villainous creature who smiled a toothless smile as he deposited the gold in his pouch. I thought to myself that there must be some way to prevent such desecration. But what?

We gathered for breakfast the next morning. Everyone looked tired. When the meal was over, Mama asked me to go through the kitchen, pantry, and outbuildings to make sure that everything was secure and that we had not forgotten to pack anything of value. The kitchen and pantry were nearly bare, and I found nothing there that had been overlooked. The outbuildings were still nearly full. One shed held casks of wine and barrels of grain and sugar. Another held tools and harness for the carts and horses.

"Those pirates will be disappointed when they come here looking for gold," I mused as I looked around me.

I saw a bucket with the remains of the black paint, which had been used to paint the trim on the house and I nearly laughed to think of them breaking in here and getting a bucket of paint for their efforts. Mama called me to hurry, so I left the shed and went into the courtyard and climbed into a cart with Mama and Jaime. Grandma and Miguel followed us in the other cart.

"Goodbye, house," I said as we pulled out into the street. "See you again soon, I hope."

"Mama, I feel fine. Why do I have to go with you?" Jamie argued.

"Jaime, I've told you before, you've been sick. You're still weak."

"Not any more, Mama. I'm over that. Can't I go, Mama, please?"

"No, Jaime. I won't have you making yourself sick again. You don't seem to realize that you nearly died."

"But Mama, I'll take care of myself. I'll be alright."

"I said no. I mean it. And I won't discuss it any further."

"All my friends will be fighting. Where will I be? Off with the women like a coward."

Mama ignored him and looked straight ahead. We rode in sullen silence. The horses' hooves clopped on the cobblestone street, and the cart bumped along. All around us, people were coming from houses built close to the edge of the street. Some were friends in carts like ours headed to the docks; others were servants, loaded down with sacks full of belongings, also headed toward the docks. The going was slow because of all the people, carts, and animals moving along in one direction. An occasional poor soul tried to go against the stream and was pushed back three steps for every two he took forward.

As we passed the Cathedral, I thought about the lovely altar waiting to be plundered. "If only…" I said to to myself. Then the idea came to me. I jumped from the cart, almost catching my skirt in the wheel. "Marta, where are you going?" Mama screamed. "I just remembered something important. I've got to go back to the house. I'll meet you at the docks," I shouted as I disappeared into an oncoming crowd. From the corner of my eye, I could see Jaime stand to come after me, but Mama caught his arm and he remained on the cart.

I had been fighting against the crowd for a while when I felt a hand on my shoulder, and I turned to discover Miguel. I could feel my face turning red.

"Let me lead the way," he said. Then he stepped in front of me and cleared a space in the crowd for us to pass through. Moving through the crowd together seemed natural, and I soon forgot to feel self-conscious.

As we went along, I shouted my idea to him. The noises of people calling to one another, of mothers yelling for lost children, of horses whinnying, of mule feet clopping, of the creaking of carts laden with precious possessions all made normal speech impossible to hear. When Miguel finally understood what I shouted to him, he smiled his approval and said he would help.

When we reached the house, I led Miguel to the out-building where the paint was stored, It was lucky that he had come because I would never have been able to carry the heavy bucket by myself. We were deciding how to carry the heavy thing without spilling any paint when Eulalia came in.

"Ah, Señorita Marta, *gracias a díos*," she made the sign of the cross, "I was afraid I might find a thief here. Why aren't you with the others?"

"Because we're going to save the Golden Altar." I smiled, pointing at the bucket. "Eulalia, are there any carts or wagons left? We need something for this bucket."

"Si, there is one small handcart behind the kitchen."

"Bring it here, and hurry!"

"Yes, Señorita."

She left to fetch the cart. Miguel took the lid from the bucket of paint and looked in. "You know," he said, "I don't think you will fool anyone if you merely paint the altar black. Some of those pirates are very quick-witted. They'll take one look at that altar and say, 'I thought them Spaniards fixed up their churches real fancy. Now why do ye suppose they would have an ugly black altar in a church this fine?' And then one of them would go over and scratch part with his fingernail and the black would peel like skin off an avocado and the gold underneath would shine back at him as if to say, 'Here I am. Come and get me.'"

He was right. We would have to think of some way to make the altar look pretty, as if it was meant to be black. I thought for a minute and then I had an idea.

"Miguel, there must be some things still in the house that we could decorate the altar with. Come, let's go look."

We ran from the outbuilding across the courtyard and into the house. Then we went from room to room looking for anything that might be used to decorate the Golden Altar. I grabbed the gold braid that tied back the draperies in the sala and threw it in a pile on the floor, while Miguel began to take down handfuls of silver beads which hung from the chandeliers.

Then I went to my bedroom and searched my wardrobe for any jewelry that I had not packed. In my haste, I threw dresses and petticoats to the floor, but I found a glass rosary and three pairs of earrings, each with a different colored stone. I grabbed them and hurried back to the sala. There I found Miguel explaining our plan to Eulalia.

She looked at me through her dark, timid eyes and asked, "Senorita, may I help you? May I go with you to the Cathedral?"

"Of course, Eulalia, come along"

"One moment, please." She hurried from the room.

We threw all of our decorations into a bed sheet and gathered it up to put into the cart along with the paint, Eulalia returned as we were leaving the house. "I too have something for the altar," she said as she handed me four ropes of brightly colored glass beads. They were the beads that Mama had given her on her saint's day, and I knew that they were the only fine things that Eulalia owned. She wore them proudly on fiesta days and took great pleasure in showing them off before the other maids.

"You have pleased God with this gift," I said and kissed her on the cheek. "Come, we had better go now."

When we arrived at the Cathedral, I entered first carrying the paint brushes, knelt, crossed myself, and proceeded toward the front of the church where the Golden Altar gleamed in the morning sun. I looked around just as Miguel came in carrying the bucket. He hesitated and seemed confused before he knelt and haltingly made the sign of the cross. Eulalia waited behind him, then she too performed the ritual and came to the front holding the bundle of beads and braid.

It gave me a very strange feeling to transform that beautiful shining altar into an ugly black object on which you could barely make out the intricate carving. Miguel was smart to think of decorating it, because when we finished with the painting, it certainly looked like nothing anyone would put in a church to glorify God. We draped beads here and we hung braid there, and when we were finished, it had improved somewhat. There was no hint of its former beauty, but it looked respectable.

We said goodbye to Eulalia in the street outside the Cathedral. She returned to the house to wait. Miguel and I hurried toward the docks where I would board the ship with the rest of my family. By this time the crowds had lessened somewhat. In fact, there were some people and wagons coming toward us. I saw a friend, Señora Espinoza, riding atop a loaded wagon. She wore a frown and did not see me. When we reached the spot where we could see all the way to the water my heart sank. The docks reached far out into the bay, but there was not one boat tied up to them. I looked out into the bay where usually at least one or two ships would be anchored. Nothing. Far in the distance I saw sails traveling toward the island of Taboga off the coast. The ships had to sail with the tide. I was too late. I had forgotten about the time.

I grabbed Miguel by the arm. "There is no need to hurry now," I said.

"The ships have left you," he replied, "will they be back?"

"Not today. The tide won't allow it. Maybe tomorrow."

I looked around me at the craftsmen closing their shops along the street. The silversmith was boarding his windows while the printer next door secured the entrance to his shop with an iron bar, which was fastened with a large chain. The candle maker and the tailor had already closed up. There was no sign of activity around those places. The owners must already have secured everything and sent their apprentices away to fight.

A soldier on a brown horse approached us rapidly. He was shouting something that we strained to hear, "Morgan at Las Cruces! Morgan at Las Cruces!" he cried, his voice hoarse, as he rushed past us. His horse's hooves sent dust flying from the street up into our faces.

People in the street called to one another, "Las Cruces. Can it be true? Is he really that close?" There was a rush of activity as they ran in many directions to spread the news.

"Las Cruces?" said Miguel. "Is that close?"

"Papa easily goes from here to there in a day with heavily laden mules," I answered, and although it wasn't cold, I shivered.

I saw the silversmith put a final nail into a board. Then he threw down his hammer and he, too, hurried off.

"Well, I guess there is nothing to do but go back to the house," I said with a sigh. "The ships won't come back tomorrow with the pirates so close."

"I will see you home. Then I'm going to join the army."

I looked at his handsome face, his beautiful dark eyes. "Yes, I suppose you must."

Miguel was a quick and confident young man and I could imagine him leading ranks of soldiers against the pirates. I could see him atop his horse, his sword drawn and ready. Miguel had a strange invincible air about him that told me not to worry. I knew somehow that whatever happened, he would be all right.

It is odd, but as we walked home, we didn't talk of the danger. Instead, it seemed we were out for a peaceful afternoon stroll. A phrase from Cicero about war and glory, came to my mind, and I said it out loud. Miguel was surprised, and said, "Where did you learn to speak Latin?"

"We once had a tutor who taught me. He didn't like it here, and went back to Cadiz."

"There aren't many girls who know Latin," said Miguel.

At the Cathedral we looked in to see our handiwork. The altar loomed dark and unappealing. It gave no hint of the golden brilliance which lay beneath the paint. Then I remembered how awkward Miguel had looked when he first entered the Cathedral, and I said, "You are Catholic, aren't you?"

"Of course, why do you ask?"

"You seemed uneasy when you carried the paint into the Cathedral."

"I did?"

"It was as if you didn't know how to kneel."

"It's been so long. I guess I'd forgotten. My father didn't take me to church as much as he should have."

We continued along the street toward the house while I told Miguel about our finca, Las Brisas, and how I thought he would love it there. I made him promise to come with us to the country after the city was quiet and safe once again.

A short way from the house, we spied Don Gaspar coming toward us. He was relieved to see me, and explained with furiously blinking eyes that Mama was at the house. She had refused to sail on the ship without me. I introduced Miguel, but Don Gaspar was not at all friendly.

"May I ask why you aren't in the army like the other young men?" He looked suspiciously at Miguel. Miguel ignored his rudeness and replied, "I want to see that Marta gets home safely, and then I plan to volunteer."

Don Gaspar took my arm and bowed stiffly to Miguel. "I will see her home. There is no need for you to come further."

Miguel raised his eyebrows and parted his lips as if to speak, but he said nothing. Instead he bowed to Don Gaspar, "As you wish." He bowed to me, smiled, and said, "Cousin Marta, we shall meet again soon." Then he turned and walked briskly back toward the center of the city.

"Where have you been?" snapped Don Gaspar.

I was irritated, but I made myself be polite, "I left the carts and ran back home after something I had forgotten. By the time I reached the docks, the ships had sailed."

"Foolish girl!" he cried. "What could have been so precious that you would put yourself and your family in such jeopardy?"

I tried to think of something to say when he exclaimed, "And this cousin Miguel, what is he doing here?"

"He's the son of Mama's cousin in Havana. Chance brings him here at this time," I replied, not caring to tell him anymore.

"I am suspicious of him, Marta. His speech is common. He's not what he seems."

I was tempted to say that he was worth two of my present company, but I held my tongue.

"Marita," he said, squeezing my arm gently, "you haven't told your mother about us, have you?"

"No," I didn't look at him. "Would it be better if I told her?"

"Oh no! Please let me do it."

"You should tell her now. If I'm not mistaken, it would please her." He smiled, and I could feel the dislike rise in me.

"Perhaps we should wait until Papa returns," I said, suddenly hopeful of putting him off. "It is customary for you to speak to him first."

"That is the case in ordinary times," said he, "but these are not ordinary times. Your father may not return for a fortnight, and if I'm not mistaken, the news of our betrothal would do much to cheer your mother." He looked at me, expecting a reply.

"Perhaps," I managed to choke out.

He patted my hand and said, "Marta, my dear, I am confident that it will please your father to learn that his daughter has won the heart of an old friend.

I thought, "How could I have said yes to him?" But I was caught. I would have to do the honorable thing.

"I will tell Mama," I said.

I end this letter now, Rosa. More will come tomorrow.

> Your friend,
> Marta

Edward's Journal

OUTSIDE OF PANAMA, DAY TEN

The long trek is near done. We are camped on a plain just far enough outside the city so their cannon balls can't hit us. I can't get Ned out of my head. We found the bodies of Martins and Peters lying in a heap on the trail all shot up, but Ned wasn't there. I wonder if there's a chance he's still alive, hiding somewhere in the jungle.

Aside from the day we lost Ned, yesterday ranked as the most miserable yet. I was in the Captain's party in the lead looking out for ambush. Blackwort commanded the men in the rear. We didn't move very fast since we were all so weak, not having had much to eat. Actually, I was past the point of feeling hungry. I didn't even think much about food anymore, but I sure did feel tired. The only thing I could concentrate on was putting one boot in front of the other and trying to stay on my feet. My legs felt so heavy it was all I could do to lift them up and set them down again. I couldn't have felt any worse if someone had tied a cannonball to each foot and told me I had to walk like that forever. Most of the other fellows were having the same trouble, and there was more tripping and falling than moving forward.

A little after noon we were tripping and trudging along the road, which was cut through the jungle, just wide enough for six men to march abreast, when we had to pass through an opening between two rocky cliffs covered with a thick growth of greenery. We'd seen no sign of the enemy since we'd begun our march early that morning, and we weren't looking out for them as keen as we should have. All of a sudden, from out of nowhere, it seemed, arrows showered us. We took cover along the edge of the road and looked for the source of the arrows. I should say that most of us took cover. Three fellows lay in the road, dead. Another three lay there twisting and moaning with pain. The storm of arrows stopped as fast as it had started. We still didn't know where it had come from, but we knew our attackers were Indians. The Spaniards never use bows and arrows.

We pulled the dead and wounded into the bushes and waited to see if there would be another attack. Everything was silent, except for the buzzing of the bugs around us. After some time, the Captain figured it was safe to continue. We left the wounded there to be cared for by those who followed us, and cautiously started down the road again.

That attack of arrows from nowhere scared me enough to make me wary and alert. This time as I followed the Captain down the road, I looked around me for signs of another attack. But everything was as calm as if we were the only people in the jungle. All at once there came a shout from behind us, then another shout, and another, as if someone was calling to us. The Captain wheeled around and I did the same. There on top of a rocky cliff just out of range of our guns, stood ten Indians, naked except for cloth skirts around their middles. They seemed to be chanting something. We listened harder.

"A la savanna! A la savanna! Perros ingleses!"

"Let's get those devils!" The Captain shouted. He grabbed a gun, loaded it, and fired. The Indians were too far away for the shot to hit them, but when some of the other fellows fired at them too, they turned and fled back into the jungle. The Indians scared us into forgetting how tired and weak we were, and the whole army seemed to perk up. We started to march in rows of six across, looking all around for signs of Indians. There wasn't time to march more than a quarter of a mile when we heard more shouting and saw the same Indians standing on a rise close up ahead.

"A la savanna! A la savanna! Perros ingleses!" They shouted again. This time we were ready for them and we charged. But they were fast and knew where to hide, and when we got to the rise, they were gone. All we found was a few broken twigs.

Late in the afternoon we stopped to camp in a clearing where three small huts stood. There was no food in the huts. I flopped on the ground to rest, but the hardship of that day was not over. Just a little after dark, it started to rain, and we had had to run around making sure that the guns and shot and powder were all stored inside those three small shacks. There was only room left inside for a few men to get out of the wet, so we took turns. It rained all night, and there was nobody who didn't suffer from the wet and cold. Feelings were running low. Even the sun when it came out didn't cheer us any.

Even Moon was downhearted. He sat on a rock with his elbows on his knees and his head in his hands. Monkey sat on the ground leaning his back against Moon's rock.

"It ain't no use, Moonie. There's no turning back now."
Monkey was saying.

"Maybe so, but there ain't no use going on either."
Moon lowered his hands from his face. He had lost the
bandana that he wore over his bald head. The skin was
covered with scratches and bites, and the sun had colored
it a dark reddish brown. "I'm so tired and sore, I just want
to sit here and die. Let them others go after the so-called
gold. I want the Lord to come take me." And he buried his
head in his hands again.

"Moonie, it ain't the Lord's goin' to take you. It's the
other fellow." Monkey stood up and put an arm around
his friend. "And if you think you got it bad now, you just
wait till they get you down in them lower regions," he
said patting him on the back. "Cheer up, Moonie. Panama
ain't much farther. I swear it ain't."

Just then the Captain gave the call for us to start
marching again, so we fell into starving, bedraggled ranks
of six men across and stumbled down the road. After we
had gone a mile or two, the road led up a steep hill. The
air was full of groans and cries as we trudged up the slope.
It seemed like our spirits got lower with every step that
took us up that long, hot hill.

Moon tripped on a rock and fell. He started to cry
when the fellow behind him came near to tripping on
him. "Get up! Ye sniveling scum sucker!" he bawled. And
he kicked Moon in the ribs. "Get up or get out o' the way."

Moon picked himself up and stumbled on. But there
were others who couldn't get up. They just lay in the road
to be stepped on and kicked by the ones behind them. We
have lots worse hills than that in Jamaica, and they're no
trouble to climb. But with me not having eaten much in
over a week, going up that hill was the hardest thing I've
ever had to do. I never knew my legs could be so heavy.

When the first ranks of men got to the top, they started to shout. I couldn't hear what they were yelling, but I saw them waving their hands above their heads and jumping up and down, like they'd won the lottery. Soon the word was passed down through the ranks that they'd sighted the South Sea and the city of Panama. On hearing the news, spirits picked up and we moved faster. I tried to run, but I was too weak.

When I finally got to the top, I couldn't see anything but men slapping each other on the back and hugging one another. Some were even trying to do a jig. When I got clear of the crowd, I saw below me a broad plain, maybe three leagues wide. There were some trees growing on it, but most of it was grassy. Way across on the other side, where the sea met the land, I could make out Panama. It was too far away to catch many details, but I could see ships dotting the coastline just offshore. I squinted, checking to see if the ships were coming or going, but I couldn't tell.

In high spirits, we quickened our pace as we marched down that hill. You wouldn't have recognized us as the same men who were near dead a few minutes before on the way up. By later afternoon we could make out the spires on the cathedral. When we were close enough to see the separate buildings of the city, the Captain gave orders to stop and pitch camp. He said we would wait and attack in the morning. The minute we stopped and made ready the camp, the big guns from the city began to fire and they haven't stopped. We are camped just beyond their reach, but the noise they make is real unfriendly. It sounds like they have an awful lot of guns inside that city.

About an hour ago a band of twenty horsemen rode out here and stopped a little way from us. They were dressed in mail and metal breast plates and helmets and they carried lances and muskets. They sat there for a long time yelling at us in words I couldn't understand.

Blackwort wanted the men to shoot them, but the Captain wouldn't hear it, saying that we needed to save our ammunition for the morning. When the Spaniards got tired of yelling at us and saw they couldn't tease us into fighting, they rode away to the city.

I'm trying not to think too much about tomorrow. Those Spaniards looked ready to fight. Their uniforms were clean and shiny, and their horses were handsome. They looked to me like they could hardly wait for the chance to come at us. There were two thousand or so of us when we started out, but now there can't be more than six hundred. Sickness and hunger and enemy arrows have taken most of us. And what of me? Will this be the last time I write in my diary?

—Edward

Edward's Journal

PANAMA, DAY TWELVE

Yesterday morning we woke a little before sunrise and readied ourselves for battle. The men who still had their flintlocks after the long trek through the jungle divided up the powder and shot. The Captain loaded me down with two extra guns and a big, heavy bag of ammunition. My knees near buckled under the weight, but I wouldn't let myself fall.

The road was wider here, so we lined up in rows of twenty across. We hadn't gone more than half a mile when the Captain stopped us and ordered us to turn from the main road leading into the city to the other side where the Spanish might not be expecting us. We left the road and traveled overland, always keeping the city in sight and never getting away from the noise of the cannon. The ground was uneven and hard to walk on. I was staggering under my load, worried that I was going to drop something, when I felt someone grab the two extra guns and take them from me. It was Higgins. "There, lad, let me help you," he said, and we walked along together.

We were heading for the side of the city south of the

main gate, and we had to climb over another hill to get there. When we reached the top, we stopped to look down on Panama. What a sorry sight it was. The plain between us and the city was full of rows of horse soldiers waiting to charge. Behind the horses were three times as many foot soldiers lined up and ready to go, and off to one side a large herd of bulls, kept together by some riders on horseback, snorted and pawed the ground.

The sight put fear into the heart of every man among us, except maybe the Captain. There was talk of us being so outnumbered we wouldn't stand a chance. I heard more than one man say we should turn back. When the Captain heard such talk, he came to the front.

"Men," he said, climbing onto a boulder, "I'm hearing cowardly, faint-hearted talk in this group.

He paused and looked many of those in the front row straight in the eyes. His look was mocking and the expression in his eyes was cold and mean as if he'd just as soon run a sword through you as you look at you.

"I'd have thought the faint-hearted would have been cleaned out long ago. But no. There's still some among us who aren't quick enough to see that what we suffered hell for this past fortnight is all right before us for the taking." He thrust his arm toward the city below. Then he pointed to a sickly, ragged-looking fellow in the front row.

"I heard Humphrey here saying how we didn't stand a chance against all those Spaniards. Well I ask you, Humphrey, why did you come along? Did you think you could just saunter right into the city and help yourself to whatever caught your eye? Hm? Did you?"

Humphrey looked at his feet and shook his head.

"Any of you who feel the same as Humphrey here is welcome to turn around and crawl for ten days back through that pest hole of a jungle. We'll burn your rotting corpse when we march back loaded with swag and fattened up on that rich Spanish cooking we'll be tasting tonight."

My stomach tightened with an ache, and I remembered how hungry I was.

"And remember what happened to our friends that fell captive to the Spanish devils?" He moved his finger across his throat with a slicing motion. "Well, that's what's waiting, or worse, for any of us who is coward enough to be taken alive."

He was silent for a moment, then he yelled, "Tonight Henry Morgan will sleep in the Governor's bed, or Henry Morgan will be dead!" He leaped from the boulder and picked up his gun. "Come! Let's make that Spanish blood flow."

After that, things happened so fast that I didn't even have time to think about being scared. We formed up into files and moved back down the hill and around to the other side, staying out of sight as long as possible. When we came into view of the Spanish, we were only a quarter mile from them across a flat, grassy field. We lined up. The men who had guns took the front, and the rest stood behind them with swords, cudgels, stonebows, and plain bare hands. I positioned myself behind Captain Morgan, who was in the front line. I thought to myself, "Well, this is it." I swallowed real hard and followed the Captain as best I could under the weight of the guns and ammunition.

We hadn't marched far when a line of horse soldiers charged us, shouting, *"Viva el rey!"*

The ground was soggy from the rain and the Spanish horses couldn't run very well on it. It took them a horrible long time before they got close enough for us to fire. Their motion was so slow they made good targets, and our front line shot a number of them before they had a chance to shoot us. At the Captain's yell, the front line dropped to its knees on the soggy ground and the next line stepped forward and fired. Then I lost track of what happened next. The whole plain was a mixture of us and the horsemen shooting and stabbing at one another. Our lines and theirs disappeared. There was just a stew of horses, foot soldiers, and us. Guns fired and metal clanked as swords hit swords. Humans groaned and horses whinnied. There were cries of pain and yells of triumph. With everybody mixed together so, it was hard to tell who was getting the worst of the fight. Bodies of men and horses lay everywhere.

I looked to one side just in time to see a fellow come at me with a sword. Quick, I dropped the shot bag and empty gun and pulled my knife wondering how I was going to fight that sword with my little blade. I was lucky. Somebody to one side of me sent a piece of shot through the fellow before he got to me. Then I saw Blackwort ahead of me taking a swing at a Spaniard with his cutlass and cutting the fellow's head clean off, helmet and all. The body just stood there for awhile, headless, before it crumpled to the ground.

The Captain fought like three. He was a sure shot and his targets were all dead men. He took a shot and then threw his gun at me to reload while he grabbed the other one to shoot again. When the fighting got so heavy that I couldn't keep the guns loaded fast enough, he took his cutlass in one hand and a sword in the other and did those Spaniards as much damage that way. He raged and yelled, swearing like a demon out of Hades, more beast than man.

The sun was near three-quarters across the sky before the fighting quieted down some. I breathed the heavy smell of gunpowder and looked around me. The field was scattered with dead men and horses, and the horsemen were retreating toward the city. There weren't a lot of them left.

We didn't retreat. We regrouped where we stood in the middle of that field, over half the distance to the first buildings of Panama. We had lost many men, but we had done real damage to the Spanish horse soldiers. Off in the distance I saw riderless horses running away into the hills.

Captain Morgan grabbed a spyglass from his shot bag and looked long and carefully at our enemy across the plain. Then he threw the glass to Blackwort who put it to his good eye and studied the Spanish army too.

"It looks to me like our Spanish friends are in a state of confusion over there," shouted the Captain. "They'll send those bulls at us next."

Blackwort nodded, but said nothing.

"I say we don't give those bastards a chance to regroup," shouted the Captain. "Men, there's a herd of fat beef over there. What do you say, we go get some."

Every man among us that could cheered, and we set out at a good pace across that field. As soon as we got close, they fired on us with fury and we lost a number of men, but that didn't last long. We had time to fire only three or four volleys before their reports got less and less and then stopped altogether save a single shot here and there. "They're out of ammunition!" yelled someone. "They're out of shot."

A cheer went up from our side and we rushed on the Spanish with hope of victory, But they weren't through with us yet. They stampeded that herd of bulls at us meaning them to break our ranks and trample us. But fortune smiled on us: those beasts hit the soggy ground and floundered. The few bulls that made it to our side were dispatched quickly, while we shouted and sang that there was beef for dinner. Seeing that the cattle didn't do

us the harm they hoped, the Spaniards retreated into the
city, leaving us to feast on the good, fresh meat.

Most of the Spaniards who could still run, escaped
into the city, but we captured ten unlucky ones who
weren't fast enough to get away. The Captain said we
couldn't spend the effort to care for prisoners. He ordered
the captives to be shot, but not before they told us all they
knew about the defenses of Panama. Blackwort dragged
each man before the Captain and held his arms behind
his back at such an angle that it must have hurt real bad.
Then the Captain called for a Spanish-speaking man from
St. Catherine who had come all the way with us. That
man asked the prisoners if there was an armed fort inside
the city and where most of the cannon were. Some of the
prisoners were proud and refused to pay heed to what the
Captain said. One fellow spat in the Captain's face and
Blackwort dispatched him with a sword blow like he was
swatting a fly.

The Captain was down to the last couple prisoners
before he finally came on one who was willing to give him
some answers. The man said the fort standing at the main
entrance to Panama was armed with many big cannon.
Most of the batteries with their cannon were pointed
toward the main entrance to the city, which was the route
the Spanish expected us to take. The Captain knew how
hard it would be to change the aim of those heavy guns,
so he decided to take another way into the city. We would
go in the back way. It lay up against a hill and was hard to
reach, but the Spanish wouldn't expect us to come that way.

Blackwort wanted to kill the prisoner, but the Captain
said to spare him and use him as a guide. So they tied
him up and threw him on the ground to spend the night,
while we feasted around him on the roasted beef.

The next morning we all felt victory in our hearts as

we marched into Panama through the back door. Somebody had carried a flute and a drum all the way from the North Sea, and for the first time since we left the ships, they were played. The music made it hard not to sing and before you knew it, every man was singing his lungs out on the way into the city. We expected to be shot at or ambushed even though we'd be escaping the big guns, but nothing happened. The streets were deserted. The buildings were boarded up. Except for a stray dog or cat, we didn't see a sign of life. Our prisoner said the Spanish had retreated to the Governor's palace, where they would make their last stand. The Captain ordered him to lead us there, and we followed him through empty quiet streets lined with wooden houses and shops. Were people hiding behind those boarded-up windows and doors, I wondered.

The quiet ended when we came in sight of the Governor's palace, a two-story stone building with arched doorways and many windows facing the sea. All of a sudden, the Spanish were shooting at us from every window and door. Men were dropping all around me like cane at harvest time. I just kept running after the Captain. Somehow we made it over the wall and into the building, where we weren't such good targets. We could hide around corners and behind doorways, and fighting was man against man.

As soon as we got through the door into a courtyard, we met a horde of Spanish with swords and pistols. The fighting was heavy. Foes and friends kept bumping into each other, and it was hard to tell who was who. I lost the Captain in that mess and ran into a narrow passageway, hoping to reload the pistol I held in my hand. The passageway started filling up with English and Spanish chasing each other, so I ducked into a small, dark storeroom. Outside, where I had been a moment before, I heard swords hitting each other and the grunts and cries of struggling men. I was putting the last bit of powder into my gun when a panting Spanish soldier holding a sword stumbled in and leaned against the wall near the door. He hunched there trying to get his breath. By the dim light, I saw that he was a stout fellow with a big belly. I held my breath and pointed the pistol at him, hoping he wouldn't see me. But he must have sensed I was there, because suddenly he straightened up giving a startled yell, and in one motion, lifted his sword over his head with both arms and came at me. Before I had time to think, I pulled the trigger. The explosion threw me back a step or two, but not far enough. He stopped for an instant and then staggered at me still gripping his sword. Then he toppled forward on me, and we both struck the ground. I heard a crack when my head hit the wall as I went down. Then I felt the pain.

I was sandwiched between the damp floor and the man I shot. He lay on top of me heavy as a horse. I could tell he was breathing, because his chest moved in and out against mine. His weight was making it hard for me to breathe, and I tried to push him off. I couldn't. I tried to wriggle out from under him, but we were wedged into the corner of the little room, so I couldn't go anywhere. The hard stone of the wall on my left was too close for me to move that way. On my right was a row of barrels that were too heavy to push with the one arm I had to work with.

I felt the Spaniard's breathing slow down, then stop altogether. I whispered to him, but it was like talking to myself. He lay there like a rock. I guessed he was dead.

For a while, I heard the sounds of the heavy fight in the passage, the swords striking each other, the shouts, the explosions of flintlocks, and the groans. Then they got farther and father away, as if the fight was continuing in other parts.

I thought about calling out for help, but I didn't lest I was heard by a Spaniard. Once the fighting moved away, the stillness in that room was horrible. The dead man lay on top of me, his cheek next to mine. I tried to move my face away from his, but I could only manage an inch or so. He smelled like sweat and smoke and blood. We lay there for some time, me trying hard to breathe while he pressed so hard on my chest that it ached.

Then I felt his chest move, and he started to breathe again. I whispered to him again, but like before, there was no answer. Then he began to moan softly making a low whining sound like a wounded animal or maybe the devil.

I was scared, I wanted more than anything to get out from under the heavy fellow, but try as I would, I couldn't budge. It seemed forever I lay like that, my body aching under the man's weight. He finally stopped that awful moaning and a little while later he stopped breathing again. I wondered if he was really dead this time. Then, just as I was thinking about that, the fellow let out a long, hard sigh that nearly scared me right out from under him. I was sure the devil was in him and he was out to get me. My throat grew tight and I started to shake so hard that I made the heavy body jiggle on top of me. After a while, when there were no more sounds from the body, I calmed down, but I half expected him to do something else.

It was quiet except for the muffled sounds of battle in the distance, and I let my mind drift almost like I was dreaming. I awoke suddenly to the sounds of a metal door slamming and boots hitting the stone corridor outside.

"Please be friends," I thought as I lay there waiting for English voices. My hope died when I heard two men call to each other in Spanish. They spoke in sharp, quick

tones like they were real excited. I got the feeling they
were arguing with each other. I heard them get closer
and closer, and my heart almost stopped when one of
them stepped into my room and called to the other one.
I thought for sure I was good as dead. But lucky for me,
right then a metal door clanked open again and somebody
shouted, "Search everywhere. Clean 'em out of every nook
and cranny! We don't want none left to surprise us with
a shot in the back."

From where I lay between the sacks and the wall, I
could just see one of the Spaniards with his back to me,
move closer and closer as he tried to find a hiding place
out of the light from the corridor. Slowly, he kept coming
in my direction, and I prayed he would stop before he
stumbled over the legs of the dead man. But he didn't
stop. He backed right into the legs, stopped with a jerk,
and let out a quiet cry.

"*Que?*" whispered the other man to the fellow, who
was now on his knees feeling the dead man's feet.

"*Muerto,*" he whispered back. Fortune was on my side
because he stood up and moved away to hide on the other
side of the barrels with his comrade. He no sooner did that
than I heard Moon and Monkey outside in the corridor.

"Let's take a look in here," Moon's voice boomed.

"Righto, Moonie," came Monkey's answer.

As soon as I sensed them in the doorway, I yelled to
them, "Watch out! Two of 'em are in here!" My voice was
weak from so little air in my lungs, but it was enough to
warn them.

The two Spaniards whispered something, but they
stayed hidden.

"Who's in there?" shouted Moon.

"It's me, Edward," I called, "and two Spaniards on the
other side of the barrel."

Just then a torch lit up the room and Moon and Monkey charged in and quick dispatched the Spaniards with a few sword blows. I felt sick listening to the screams and groans, but Monkey and Moon were enjoying it, going after the two trapped soldiers like hog butchers. When the slaughter was over, Monkey yelled at me, "Ho! Ed, ye got yerself stuck in there real good, haven't ye?"

He and Moon grabbed hold of the dead man's ankles and slid him off me. It sure felt good to have that weight off my chest. It felt almost like I was floating on air. My body felt light as a leaf on the wind. That is, it felt like that until I sat up. Then 1 discovered how stiff I was from lying there on the cold floor for so long. My head ached real bad.

"We got the palace," said Moon. "And the Governor's dead."

"And right now," said Monkey, "Henry Morgan and some of the boys are up there in the council chamber convincing the Governor's men they'd better give us what we came for."

"And there's some of us out in the cookhouse seeing to the making of a feast," said Moon. "Come on, Ed, let's clean this place out o' any loose Spaniards and then get us something to eat."

I was stiff, but I tried to keep up with them, thinking all the while about a feast. We checked the rest of the rooms along the corridor without finding anything much. Then we hurried into a courtyard toward the back of the palace, where I smelled meat cooking and bread baking. I thought about how long it had been since I had a piece of fresh, warm bread in my mouth. That reminded me of Mother and Father and how safe and simple life had been on the plantation.

—Edward

Marta's Letter to Rosa

19 January 1672, Finca Las Brisas

Dear Rosa,

The Governor's messenger was waiting at my house for Don Gaspar when we got there. Henry Morgan and his men had been sighted near the gates of the city, and Don Gaspar was going to join the horse soldiers.

Mama was anxious to chide me for running off like I did, but she held her tongue while Don Gaspar took leave of us.

"Doña Carmen, I shall look in on you and Marta at the first opportunity. Be calm, I'm certain there's nothing to fear. We'll have those hellions in prison by sundown," he said bowing and blinking furiously. Turning to me, smiling and squeezing my arm, he whispered just loud enough so Mama could hear, "Will you give your mother the good news while I'm gone?" Then, to my relief, he left without waiting for my answer.

Mama saw him out. Then she bolted the door and came back to me in the *sala* with its bare walls and only the furniture we hadn't been able to pack.

"Marta, foolish girl, I want to know what possessed

you to run off like you did. Do you realize the jeopardy you have put us in?" she asked frowning at me. Mama had a way of frowning without wrinkling her brow, for she didn't want to cause lines on her face. Then her frown turned to a smile. "But first tell me of this good news."

I knew I didn't have to tell her. From her expression, she had already guessed. I could feel tears flooding my eyes. "Oh, Mama!" I said through trembling lips, "he asked me to marry him." And I started to sob.

"There, there, Marta, I'm surprised at you crying like this. Get control of yourself, daughter." Mama put her arm around me and led me to a chair. "To be sure, these aren't the best of times, but you've just been proposed to by a great man. Is this any way to act?" She sat next to me and took my hand.

"Great man, bosh! He's ignorant and silly and small."

"Child, how can you say that?" She let go of my hand and stood up to look down at me. "He is a man of courage. If it hadn't been for him, who knows what the Cimarrónes might have done with us. Remember how he stood up to them out there on the road? I doubt that your father could have done better. And remember how he risked his life to get us safely back here from the finca? How can you say such a man is silly?" She stuck her finger in my face, "You are the silly one."

"But I don't like him. How can I live for the rest of my life with someone I don't like?" I wailed.

"Marta, think who he is, his name, his family, his wealth. That will all be yours. Don't lightly cast off those things." She sat down next to me again. "You have many good qualities, but you are a plain girl. You will not have such a chance again."

"If I'm so plain, why does Don Gaspar want to marry me?" I snapped.

"He sees beyond appearances. He sees your virtues. He sees the you that many younger men would overlook. Believe me, Marta, this is not Spain. There isn't an abundance of suitable men here. You must take care not to make a spinster of yourself." She reached for my arm, but I pushed her aside and jumped up.

"You want me to be miserable, don't you? You don't love me. You want me to marry that old man so our family will be connected with royalty. You want the marriage for yourself, not for me!" I found myself screaming at her. "I hate you and your hypocrisy!"

"Marta, how dare you speak to me like that!" She rose as if to strike me, but she let her hand drop to her side. "You don't mean it, and I will forget that you said it. These are hard times for us all. It is not easy to be calm and reasonable. But for your own good, you will marry Don Gaspar. Now, go wash your face. We won't discuss this again."

Mama and I spent the rest of the day and evening sitting in the *sala*, not speaking. We jumped every time we heard cannon fire, I sat there resenting her and telling myself that when Papa returned, I would go to him and tell him my feelings, He wouldn't make me marry Don Gaspar. I went to bed that night and slept fitfully, waking up at any little noise: a dog barking in the street, the wind blowing a branch against the roof. Toward morning I woke in terror to the sound of cannon fire in the distance and voices and footsteps close by in the street. From the sounds I knew the pirates were not yet in prison as Don Gaspar had said they would be. I got up and ran into the *sala*, where I found Mama sitting in the dark looking out. She must have caught a cold for she was coughing.

"Mama, what is the noise in the street?"

"It's men from the country who've come to fight the pirates."

My anger at her had not yet left me when I sat down beside her to watch the dawn come, but that feeling gradually softened as daylight arrived. With daylight came the heaviest cannon fire yet.

A servant brought us word that the pirates had attacked the side of the city across the marshy plain that separates Panama from the hills to the north. All morning we checked windows and doors to make certain they were secure, and waited for word of the battle. In early afternoon we received the bad news that our soldiers had been destroyed, and our remaining men were fighting hand to hand with the pirates. We still had some hope the city wouldn't fall, Mama, her cough getting worse, rushed off to the hospital to help with the wounded. When I pleaded to go with her, she wouldn't hear of it. She ordered me to stay behind in the locked house until she came for me.

It was horrible being left alone in the house. Any noise sent fear through me. The windows were boarded so I couldn't look out onto the street to check the activity. I kept thinking that the pirates were at my door. From what I could hear, it was quiet out there; everyone who wasn't fighting was hiding. I found myself wondering if Miguel and Don Gaspar were safe. In spite of the danger, I felt sick when I thought of Don Gaspar. And Rosa, I have never admitted this to anyone, but it occurred to me that if Don Gaspar were killed, I might not be too grieved. I was ashamed to have such thoughts, but nevertheless they came. I prayed to the Lord for forgiveness.

Eulalia was company for me while I fretted away the afternoon and early evening. The cannons fired constantly, I tried playing the harpsichord, but I couldn't concentrate, so we spent the interminable time pacing the house and checking the windows and doors over and over again. I thought about following Mama to the hospital, but I had already disobeyed her once that day. It was better to do as she ordered.

The time passed more slowly for me than for a child waiting for his saint's day. At nightfall the cannons stopped firing and I watched through the peephole as the first of the wounded moved through the street to the hospital. When I could stand it no longer, I unbolted the door and ran into the street to ask for news of the battle.

Men and boys of all ranks streamed past me, tired and tattered. Many limped or clutched wounds on their arms. Those who couldn't walk alone were aided by others. The badly hurt and mortally wounded lay on horse-drawn carts. The procession moved toward the hospital slowly and sadly. Hardly a word passed among the men.

"Can I help?" I called out.

A man who hobbled along supporting another man wounded worse than he was looked at me with surprise and said, "No, Señorita. Go back into your house and lock the door."

"But what has happened?" I shouted at him, "Did we win the battle?"

He paid me no heed, and hobbled away.

I was about to accost another soldier when someone called my name.

"Marta!"

Coming toward me was Felipe, a friend of my brother, Roberto. His arm hung limply at his side, and there was a bloody gash across his forehead.

"Felipe, you're hurt! Let me help you."

"No. I'm all right," he said. "But what are you doing here? Why aren't you on the island with the rest of the women?"

"I missed the last ship."

He shook his head and nearly growled, "Girl, you are in terrible danger. Is there nobody here to protect you?"

"I'm alone. Mama's at the hospital."

"*Dios mio!* Get inside. Bolt the door. And don't come out again until this is finished. You should be on the island with the other women," he accused as if I had purposefully stayed behind.

"Felipe...," I wanted to explain, but he interrupted.

"Go now. Get in the house and secure it. The pirates will soon be here." He pushed me toward the door; then he turned and was gone.

I went into the house and bolted the door behind me, filled with fear. The pirates would soon be here: Felipe's words made it clear that things weren't going well.

I passed the night and most of the next day in suspense. At daybreak, the guns started again, but soon, to my surprise, the heavy gunfire lessened and most of the noise came from the direction of the Palace. That was a horrible sign. It meant the pirates must have invaded the city. I knew then that my only hope was to stay in the house and wait to be rescued. It would be suicide to go out into the streets.

Late in the evening my heart nearly stopped when a loud pounding came from the outer door to the street. Cautiously, I peeked through the peephole, not knowing whether I would find friend or foe. It was Miguel. My fear quickly turned to joy. Miguel and a servant supported a body on a blanket. I let them in at once, and embraced Miguel.

"Miguel, is it over?" I asked, hoping to see victory in his eyes. Then I looked down at the man on the blanket. It was Don Gaspar. He lay there, his face grey as ash. He looked at me through hazy eyes.

I took his hand and said, "Shouldn't you be in the hospital? All the doctors are at the hospital."

"He won't go," answered Miguel. "He insisted on coming here."

"What happened?"

"Shot in the chest," Miguel's eyes told me the wound was bad. "He's lost a good amount of blood and he needs a better dressing."

"We'll put him in Roberto's room."

Miguel and the servant put him to bed, and the servant left. I changed Don Gaspar's dressing, which had been nothing more than a man's shirt wadded into a ball and secured to his chest with a belt. He did not seem to be in pain, but he was very weak. His breathing came hard, and he could barely speak.

"Leave my pistol on the table," he whispered when Miguel took if from his holster.

After Miguel placed the gun on the table by the bed, the two of us stepped out onto the patio where we could talk.

"Will he die?"

Miguel shrugged. "I don't know. He needs a doctor."

"Are we lost?" I asked, certain that we were.

He nodded and said in his peculiar accent, "Marta, you are in danger, but I can help you if you will trust me."

"Of course I trust you, Miguel," I answered, thinking it strange of him to speak of trust. Why wouldn't I trust him?

"Marta," he said as he leaned against the wall, his hands behind his back. "I am not what I seem."

Before I could question him, he put his hand out and said, "Don't ask me to explain now. Just trust me."

We looked at each other. Then he said, "Marta, I am fond of you. Please remember that whatever happens, I am fond of you and I will do all I can to help you." His voice was almost pleading, "I have to go now," he said, squeezing my hand. "But I'll be back with a doctor. Keep the house locked. Don't let anyone in unless you know him. And whatever happens, don't leave the house."

"What about Mama? She's at the hospital."

"She's safe there." He pulled a pistol from his belt and handed it to me. "Keep this and use it if you have to." He left me and ran across the patio to the door before I had a chance to ask any of the questions that were starting to fill my head.

I stood there for a moment, pistol in hand, wondering at him with his strange accent and the words he had just said. Then I heard a moan from Don Gaspar, and I went to him. He followed me with his eyes as I placed my gun on the table next to his. In a quavering voice, he asked for water. I sat beside his bed and wiped his brow with a damp cloth, that being all I could do for him. He drifted in and out of consciousness, and when he slept, I anxiously put my hand under his nose hoping to feel his breath.

The gunfire that I had heard all day had ceased a few hours before, and now it was replaced by sporadic shots from muskets and pistols. I sat there worrying about Mama and hoping that Miguel would come back soon. It was lonely sitting in an empty house with a dying man and a frightened Eulalia. I had to fight off a desire to run to the hospital.

Several hours later, my fears came true. There came an impatient pounding on the door. I was sure it was Miguel returning with the doctor, but Eulalia came running in, a wild look in her eyes.

"Señorita, two foreigners!" she screamed. "God help us!" and she started to cry.

"Let me see." I ran to the door, which was shaking madly from all the pounding and kicking it was receiving. Through the peephole I glimpsed two dirty men who were hacking away at the door with a cutlass and a dagger. Both had several days' beard on their faces. One was clad in grey pants, dark shirt, and heavy boots, while the other wore only a pair of soiled, tattered pants and a green kerchief around his head. They shouted ugly foreign words as they kicked and chopped at the door. I closed the peephole and shivered.

"What will we do?" whined Eulalia. "They'll kill us! *Dios mio!*"

"Come with me!" I led her back into the room where Don Gaspar lay unconscious on the bed. I closed the door and bolted it. Then the two of us stood against the back wall and listened in terror to the two pirates destroying the outside door. Eulalia wept and made moaning sounds deep in her throat. Don Gaspar awoke and called for water. I gave him a drink wondering if he knew what was happening just a few paces away. He gave no sign of it, and soon fell back asleep.

Then with a crash, the front door broke open and flew against the wall. There came sounds of boots stomping along the patio floor, and the voices of the two pirates as they shouted to one another. They must have started going through all the cupboards and drawers, for I heard things crashing to the floor.

After a while they came along the veranda, trying the doors to the bedrooms. They rattled ours and when it did not open, they went on to the next. When Eulalia's moaning became louder I put my hand over her mouth and whispered to her to be quiet. She trembled and I shook her, urging her to get control of herself.

They threw things around and broke up the furniture. I was sick to hear the twang of the harpsichord strings as they chopped the instrument to pieces. Then they were back at our door, trying to get in. The two of us instinctively crouched on the floor against the wall. Only Don Gaspar's bed lay between us and the door. I took one of the pistols from the table and hid it in the folds of my skirt, and we watched in terror while the two pirates forced open the door. The one with the boots nearly fell into the room as the door gave way under his last blow. For a moment he looked surprise at finding us there, but surprise quickly changed to pleasure and he shouted to his companion in a loud, filthy voice. The two of them stood in the doorway leering at us across the unconscious Don Gaspar. I could only stare.

The booted one said something to me. Perhaps it was a question. I remained crouched on the floor next to Eulalia and didn't answer. He came around the bed toward me, a dagger in his hand, I didn't move. He bent down to grab me, and I grasped the pistol tighter. At the moment his hand touched my shoulder, I jumped aside, nearly falling over Eulalia who still cowered next to me. There was a shot, and the pirate fell forward. His head hit the wall against which I had just been leaning. Then he lay still, I was relieved but mystified, for I had not fired the gun I held. I heard a groan and turned to see Don Gaspar lying there with his pistol in his hand, its barrel smoking.

None too soon, I remembered the other pirate. As I leaped to my feet, he raised his cutlass to strike Don Gaspar who lay helpless on the bed like an animal ready for slaughter. I held the pistol out with both hands, steadied it as best I could, and pulled the trigger. The pirate dropped his sword and grabbed his throat. He staggered forward a few steps then sank to the floor. Blood trickled from his throat onto the white tile.

I dropped the gun and went to Don Gaspar who lay with his eyes open but unseeing. Over and over I called his name but his ears no longer heard. His last act had been to save me. I grew cold and then I started to shake. Every part of me trembled, and the harder I tried to stop, the worse I shook. I don't know how long I was that way, but I finally stopped when Eulalia ran screaming from the room. I stepped over the pirate's body and followed her outside, but she was gone.

Sinking into a chair, I tried to collect myself and to decide what I should do next. Miguel had said he would come back, but that had been hours ago. How did I know he hadn't been captured by the pirates? I had to leave the house. Now that the door had been destroyed, there was nothing to stop more intruders. I was certain there would be more.

Where would I go? I would go to the hospital and find Mama. Miguel had said she was safe there. Yes, that was where I would go. It would be safe there.

The two villains had emptied what was left in the cupboards and drawers onto the floors of the rooms they had ravaged. In a pile of clothes in Mama's room I found a black shawl, which I wrapped around my shoulders and head. I had the strange feeling that I might never return to the house where I had been born, where I had lived for sixteen years, and I went from room to room saying goodbye.

What I saw sickened me. The pictures we had left on the walls had been slashed so that they were unrecognizable. Pieces of canvas hung from the frames in tatters. Cushions in the deep chairs were slashed, the stuffing pulled out and thrown about. My harpsichord had been hacked to pieces. The madmen had left nothing untouched.

In the dining room I stood among the broken dishes and began to cry. Fortunately I am a quiet crier. I heard a noise from the patio. Quickly, I grabbed a carving knife from the floor. Its handle was bent, but its blade was sound. After hiding the knife in the folds of my skirt, I ran to the door and peeked out onto the patio. Since I saw nobody, I walked out to look around. Suddenly, from behind a door, the pirate with the heavy boots, his forehead and shoulders caked with dried blood, leaped out toward me. I tried to run, but he grabbed me with enormous hands. He held my left arm behind my back and gripped me tight around the waist with his other arm. His arm pressed me against him. I clutched the knife and pushed it deeper into the folds of my skirt.

He held me so tightly that I didn't try to move, and he made ugly sounds, a mixture of a whine and a demand. His odor was dreadful, as if he had swallowed in a sewer. The stench was nauseating. He loosened his grip a little, and began to shove me along the side of the patio towards the *sala*. I stumbled ahead, thinking furiously about how I could get away.

I began speaking to him in soft, friendly tones, trying not to let my voice betray me. I said things like, "I hate you, you swine, and you smell worse than a cesspool." But my tone sounded like I was inviting him to supper. My plan worked, for he let go of me and spun me around to better hear what I said. The moment I was free from his grasp, I drew the knife from my skirts and swung wildly at him. I hit his forearm, which was reaching for me. His cry told me I had sliced him, but he lunged at me anyway. I jumped away and ran for the door. I felt his fingers brush the back of my dress. As I left the patio, I pulled over an empty cupboard to block his path. I heard it crash behind me as I ran out of the house and into the street.

Still clutching the knife, I raced towards the hospital, which lay half a league away. I turned a corner and stepped behind an open gate to catch my breath. As I leaned against the wall gasping for air, I heard shouts in that foreign tongue and sounds of destruction from within the house. That was enough to make me run from that place still panting.

My progress toward the hospital was slow because I was afraid I might run into more of those hateful foreigners. It was a clear night; the moon lit the streets, and

I stayed close to walls to conceal myself in their shadows. Still, I had several close encounters with the pirates. When at last I reached the hospital, my heart sank. It had been taken over. I stood across the street among the shadows, and I watched pirates go in and out. One man guarded the entrance.

I heard loud, evil laughter coming from that place. Was Mama in there? Still gripping the knife I took from home, I slid back into the shadows and leaned against a wall, tears filling my eyes. Searching for a handkerchief in my pocket, I felt the miniature of Mama in the gold frame that she had given me only the day before. I pressed it into my hand and wept.

The sound of someone coming up the street made me dry my tears quickly. Then I crouched in a doorway and tried to conceal myself in the flowered vines which grew around it. They scratched my arms and face, but I hardly noticed. A man approached at a fast walk. He passed my hiding place quickly and kept on in the direction of the hospital. I watched him as he stopped abruptly in the same spot I had been a moment before and studied the movements of the pirates going in and out of the hospital. The light from the torches at the entrance framed his silhouette. There was something familiar about him.

I watched him cross the street toward the hospital, stop at the entrance, and speak with the guard. Then I gasped, for the torchlight illuminated the face of my cousin, Miguel, who spoke familiarly with the guard and embraced him as if they were friends. I grew suspicious. It was true that Miguel had been a prisoner of the pirates, but did they treat their prisoners, especially the escaped ones, in such a friendly way? Why had Miguel been so bold as to walk right up to the man without drawing a weapon? I felt sick. He must be one of them. Then I grew angry, I wanted to fly at him and scratch his eyes out. I hated him. He was a spy.

As he turned and came up the street toward me, I sank back into the shadows and tightened my grip on the knife which I still carried. I let him get far enough ahead so he would not hear me, and then I followed him, looking for a place where the two of us could hide, unnoticed. I prayed that the street we were on would stay deserted, for I didn't want anyone to hear his cries for help. I would dispatch the traitor quickly and then forget about him. A few feet ahead of him was a vacant lot where a house had burned down. As soon as I sensed that Miguel had reached the lot, I called to him. He turned at the sound of my voice and stopped, giving me time to catch up. I hurried to him, being careful that the knife was hidden from his view.

"Marta!" he exclaimed, "What a relief to find you. I've been searching the whole city." He spread his arms as if to embrace me, but I stopped short so he couldn't touch me.

"Have you?" I said icily as I stepped into the vacant lot which was concealed from the street by a stucco wall. Miguel followed me.

"Yes, I went to your house. What happened? Don Gaspar and the other dead fellow?"

"You don't care what happened," I snarled at him.

He tried to touch me again, but I jumped backwards.

"Marta, cousin, what is the matter? Why are you so angry?"

"You're not my cousin. My cousin would never be a traitor and a spy!"

Miguel drew himself erect and in a calm voice said, "What do you mean?"

"You swine! You filthy swine: You traitor!"

I screamed and lunged at him, intending to kill him. I

aimed for his throat, but he jumped to one side so that I hit the very edge of his shoulder instead.

"Marta! Stop it! What are you doing? Stop it!"

I went at him again, but he managed to dodge me. My skirts made it impossible for me to move as quickly as he, but I kept after him, determined to do him harm. I could see him try to get behind me to grab me, so I was careful to keep him at my front. All the time he shouted my name and tried coaxing me to drop the knife. We heard English voices in the street. "Marta," Miguel pleaded, "stop this or we'll be discovered!"

"What does it matter?" I made a stab for him. The men in the street came closer.

"Marta, I can help you if you will let me."

"Hah!"

Miguel gave my knife a hard kick sending it flying to the ground. Before I could cry out, he grabbed me and put his hand over my mouth. We stood there like that until the pirates in the street had passed out of hearing. Then he released me, keeping hold of my wrist.

"Marta, things are not what they seem," he whispered, "or maybe they are. But listen to me, you must let me explain."

"Explain what? That you are not better than a scoundrel, and a traitor?"

"Maybe so, but give me the chance to tell you my story."

I had no choice. Without my weapon, I was defenseless. And I was probably safer with him than with the rest of the cutthroats who were roaming the streets.

So we searched for a place to hide where he could talk. The Cathedral was empty, so we went inside. There seemed an unnatural stillness about it, a stillness of mourning what had happened to the city.

We hid ourselves in a small room used to store candles, robes, and vestments off the main part of the church.

Miguel lit a candle and we sat on the floor leaning against a soft bundle of cloth, I made a point of not sitting too close.

He told me the story of his life. How he, an Englishman, was bound for Jamaica when his ship was attacked by the Spanish. He was sold into slavery to my uncle who treated him badly, but from whom he learned to speak Spanish. He escaped from Cuba and found his way to Port Royal where he joined Morgan, the pirate, because he had no fortune and needed to keep himself somehow. When the pirates were nearly to the gates of Panama, Miguel was captured by some of our soldiers. His two companions were slain and he decided his only chance for survival was to pose as a Spaniard, which he did. That is how he was brought to Panama and how he came to our house.

I fingered the miniature in my pocket as I listened to him, and my anger drained away. His story seemed reasonable, and it explained his peculiar accent. I had to admire his wit in dangerous situations. I told myself I might have done the same thing. But I still resented him for deceiving me, and I told him so.

"I understand," he said, smiling at me. "I hated deceiving you. I didn't know that I would like you and your family so much. There were many times I wanted to tell you everything, but how could I with the pirates nearly on your doorstep? What would you have done with me if you had known? You would have turned me over to the Governor, and I am sure he would not have been merciful."

"Miguel, I will trust you. There's no other choice for me. Is it folly for me to trust you?"

"You have my word that as long as I have the power to do so, I will protect you and your family." Miguel put his hand out and I took it. It felt warm and steady. The expression in his dark eyes convinced me he was sincere.

There was a bond between this Englishman and me.

Why it was there, I don't know. I felt it first when he came to us those few days before. Then I thought it was because he was my cousin, and there is a strong bond in kinship. I was surprised to find after he had admitted deceiving me, the bond was still there. It had grown stronger. I tried not to like him, but it was impossible. What adventures he had had! How clever he was!

It must have been very late when I finally curled up on the floor and fell asleep. I slept fitfully and was awakened once by voices outside in the main part of the church. Miguel was awake also, and we listened to two men shouting at each other. They seemed to be examining the church. We heard them opening and closing doors. Quickly we hid ourselves behind some large bundles and blew out the candle. It was none too soon for the door opened and they peered into our little room. It must not have interested them, for they soon went back to the main chamber of the Cathedral. In a while they left the church altogether, and we came out of our hiding place.

"Miguel," asked, "what were they saying? Did they discover the Golden Altar?"

"They came close, but they didn't find it."

Dawn approached slowly, and the little room brightened as light poured through single windows above a wall of shelves. The smell of smoke filled the room, and from its intensity, I guessed a large fire must be nearby.

Miguel left me, promising to bring food when he returned. He made me vow I would stay hidden in that storeroom. After he had gone, I couldn't help doubting. Would he return? Was he really to be trusted? Was I foolish to believe him?

Rosa, I must finish this letter, for a courier leaves soon. I may have shocked you by telling you how I shot the pirate and how I nearly killed Miguel. Please remember, those were terrible times and people did things they would not normally do. As I sat in that room alone reflecting on what I had done, I smiled, confident that even if Miguel didn't return, I could take care of myself. I felt certain I would survive that terrible time.

I think of you fondly and will write to you soon.

Your loving cousin,
Marta

Edward's Journal

JANUARY 1671, PANAMA

Some days have gone by since I last wrote in my log. And what days! There's been fighting and frollicking, stealing and giving, laughing and crying. I guess there's been a little bit of just about everything a person could imagine.

The morning after we took the city, for the first time in a fortnight I woke up without the pangs from an empty stomach. But the first thing I thought about was breakfast, because who could be sure when I might have to go without again? So I got up off the floor, made my way down to the kitchen, and had a good meal. When I came back to my post outside the council chamber, the heavy doors were standing open, and Captain Morgan yelled from inside.

"Is that you, Ed, you slubbering noddy? Get in here!"

I went in quick but cautious, hoping I wasn't the reason for his ire. The Captain was leaning against a wooden desk as big as a four-man boat. It startled me to see him dressed so fine. His hair was combed and curled and his moustaches were oiled and he wore a fine yellow waistcoat over a white shirt with ruffles at the neck and wrists. His trousers were of the same yellow as the jacket and on his legs we wore white stockings that fit into a pair of shiny black shoes. He held a half-eaten mango in his hand.

Blackwort and Potts were there too. Mr. Potts, who sat in a chair across from the Captain, was dressed in clean clothes, but none so fancy as the Captain's. I wondered what gentleman's closet the two of them had robbed. Blackwort leaned against the wall to the side, arms crossed in front of him. He wore the same dirty pants and shirt he had worn when I first saw him. There couldn't be another man his size in all of Panama.

"It's here, and we'll get it all," the Captain was saying, "These muckworm Spaniards don't have wit enough to hide it from us for long." Then he saw me. "Edward, ye noddy, I've been calling for you. Where have you been?"

"Sir, I...." But he didn't give me a chance to answer.

"I want you to cover this town and spread the word to all the men that there's to be a meeting here when the sun's high. It seems the Spaniards are not inclined to tell us where they hid their precious treasure." He stood up and walked toward a window. Then he stopped and looked down into the courtyard below. Tell them that there are riches in it for every man that comes." He took a bite of the fruit he held in his hand and then he flung it out the window. "And Ed," he said, turning and looking at me, "warn them that these Spanish pigs fouled all the wine in the city. Any man who takes a drink is a dead man."

"Yes, sir."

"Get ye gone!"

"Yes, sir!"

"And Ed, one more thing, tell them that anybody caught hoarding any swag for himself will be thrown in prison to rot if we don't hang him first. We'll store everything we find in the room out in the hall there. Then we'll divide it up fair and square at the end."

I turned and headed out the door, but suddenly, I stopped and stared, thinking I had seen a ghost. There in front of me stood Ned, smiling like he'd just won a prize at the fair.

"Ned!" I shouted.

"Well, well," cried Mr. Potts. "Have ye risen from the dead?" He embraced him.

"No, no miracles," laughed Ned.

The Captain didn't seem surprised at all. He just shook Ned's hand and said, "Let's hear your story."

Blackwort didn't move from where he leaned against the wall. He didn't even smile. He looked mean as ever.

Ned told us how he and Martins and Peters were captured by the Spanish soldiers and how they shot the two men after torturing them.

"I knew I'd have to think of something fast if I didn't want to end up like those poor fellows, so I decided to pass myself off as Spanish." Ned smiled, spread his arms, and shrugged. "And it worked. I convinced them I was the son of the man I was indentured to in Havana and that you had captured me and were forcing me to be your guide."

"Yes, indeed, Ned my lad," said the Captain putting his arm around him, "you've got wit. It's a rare lad could pass himself off like that." Then he glowered at him and said, "But you're too cocksure. That's how you fell into their hands. Take care or it will ruin you." The Captain walked back and leaned against the big desk. "Sit down," he motioned Ned to a chair next to Mr. Potts. "Ned, were you in a position to know where the Spaniards hid their gold and silver?"

"Some of it, yes sir."

"Well? Did they send it off in ships like I think they did?"

"Yes, sir, they did, only a few hours before you marched in. A pity you couldn't get here sooner."

"And extra ships?"

"As far as I know, there are none. What couldn't be sent out to sea, they burned."

"Those scubbering rakeshell muckworms!" bawled the Captain. "Those scumbags!" He began to pace back and forth in front of the desk cursing loudly. "We'll burn the city down! We'll stay here and torment every living soul until those ships bring back every ounce of silver they left with!"

He stopped pacing and returned to his place leaning against the desk. He was quiet for awhile, and then said, "We took over the hospital last night, but we need a bigger place. I think that big Cathedral will do." He walked over and put his hand on Blackwort's shoulder. "My friend, will you go make the Cathedral a place for prisoners? Then start collecting everybody who looks even a little prosperous. Put them all in the church. We can persuade them it's good for their health to help us get what we came for."

Blackwort nodded and smiled a wicked smile that wrinkled the scar across his face. He left the chamber quick, stooping in the doorway so he wouldn't bump his head.

I noticed that while the Captain talked, Ned s expression changed. He stood up and said, "Captain…," but the Captain didn't hear him.

"Edward, get on with rounding fellows up for the meeting. It's close to noon already. You…"

"Captain," Ned interrupted. "Let me go with Ed. I haven't seen my friend for a long time." His voice sounded peculiar.

"No, the two of you'll waste time gabbing. There'll be a chance to talk after we pen up the locals." He motioned me to the door. "And I'm not finished with you here yet, Green. I have some more questions for you."

Before I left, I turned to Ned and said, "I'll hurry," He gave me a strong look like he was trying to tell me something with his eyes, but he changed expressions in an instant and looked then like he didn't have a care.

"Do that," he said.

As I left the chamber, I heard Mr. Potts ask, "Say, Neddy, you didn't happen to come across any Golden Altar, did ye?"

I didn't have time to hear his answer because I ran out of the Palace as fast as I could. I wanted to spread my message and get back to talk with my friend. I was sure he had plenty more to tell. What a crafty fellow he was! Imagine him getting the enemy to take him in as if he were one of their own!

Spreading the word of the meeting all over the city took longer than I thought. I was lucky to find a big group of fellows down in the eating part of the Palace, but I learned from them that many of the others were out in the city looking for booty. When I tried to get some of those fellows to help me spread the word, they all hooted at me. They shouted that they had just walked from one ocean to another, and they didn't care to walk another step. So I ran through the streets of Panama, shouting word of the meeting at noon.

When I passed the Cathedral, Blackwort and his men were already kicking and shoving the Spanish, mostly men but a few women and children, through the great wooden doors of the church. Some were being tugged by the hair. I discovered fires in two or three different spots. One fire was burning big, and I thought somebody should try to put it out. But there wasn't anyone around, except me, and I couldn't do it alone so I left.

It was close to noon by the time I covered the whole city, and started back towards the Governor's Palace. I was tired, so I took my time and walked slow. The Spanish had planted trees along the important streets, and I was happy for their shade because it was hot moving around at noon. My head ached and I was thirsty, so I headed for the fountain in the square in front of the Cathedral. After taking a long, satisfying drink, I glanced up to spot Ned coming out of the Cathedral. Although he was coming straight at me, he didn't see me.

"Ned!" I shouted, waving at him, "Ned! Hey!"

"Oh, Ed, hello." He looked sour.

"Are you going to the meeting?"

"Uh, yes."

We walked toward the Palace.

"What's bothering you Ned?" I asked, "What did they do? Try to pen you up in there too?" I motioned toward the Cathedral.

"Maybe they should have."

"What do you mean?"

He grabbed my arm and stopped me. Some fellows passed us on their way to the meeting and Ned pulled me away from them over against the Palace wall.

"There are a girl and her mother in there," he nodded toward the Cathedral. "Prisoners. They were good to me and they trusted me." His jaw tightened. "I've got to get them out before any harm comes to them."

"Ned, are you daft? They're the enemy."

"They're good people." His dark eyes shone and his look cut right through me. "But in their eyes, I'm worse than a worm. They think I've betrayed them." He looked again toward the Cathedral. "Marta wouldn't speak to me, and I could see the hate in her."

"Who's Marta?"

"The girl."

I pressed him until he told me about the girl, Marta, and her family who took him in, thinking he was a cousin. He took a liking to them all, the strong-willed grandmother, the beautiful mother, and the brother. He especially took a liking to the girl.

I smelled smoke and knew the fires were getting worse. A crowd of fifty men with Mr. Potts at the lead came from the Palace. They were in a foul mood.

"Damn Morgan!" one fellow said.

"I haven't had a good rest…."

"And he has us out fightin' a fire…."

"For all I care, ye can let the whole place burn."

"Not 'til we've cleaned it out o' swag."

Ned and I hid ourselves around the corner of the building not wanting to be spotted by that group and ordered to help.

"I've got to get them out of there," Ned said hitting the wall with his fist. "I've got to show her I didn't betray her."

"How are you going to get past Blackwort?"

"I don't know yet, but there must be some way."

"Why don't you just reason with him," I laughed. "Mr. Blackwort, sir, you can say, this beautiful lady and her daughter are nice kind Spanish women, and they are too delicate to be shut up here like prisoners. Would you please release them?"

Ned ignored me and slumped against the wall, pounding the palm of one hand with the fist of the other.

"Come, Ned, maybe we'll think of something later," I said. "I have to report back to the Captain or he'll have my hide. Are you coming with me?"

I started around the building toward the entrance and Ned followed, hardly paying heed to where we were going. The smell of smoke was getting stronger. To the north, thick, black clouds rose into blue noontime sky, a bad sign in a place where most of the buildings are wooden.

We were almost pushed from the doorway of the Palace by another gang of men coming out. They, too, were grumbling about having to go out in the hot sun and put out fires in the houses of Spanish swine.

Finally we found ourselves alone, walking along the gallery that led to the council chamber where the Captain was. I knocked on the closed doors.

"Who's there?" asked an angry voice.

"Edward and Ned, sir," I answered.

The doors opened and we stepped inside. This time, the Captain was sitting behind the high desk. His feet were propped up on it and he was cleaning his fingernails with a small knife.

"Why aren't you two out fighting fires?" He gave us an unfriendly look.

"Is that where all the men are?" I asked pretending I didn't know.

"Where've you been, lad? Don't you smell the smoke?"

I started to answer, but didn't have a chance to say anything because just then a fellow burst into the room all out of breath.

"Captain, them fires're gettin' worse. Unless we get more hands down there fast, the whole city is going to burn down."

The Captain yelled, "Damnation!" and shoved the blade of the knife he held into the top of the desk with such force that it went in an inch or so. "Who have you got down there now? Is everybody down there working?" He gave Ned and me a mean look.

"Aye, near everybody," the fellow looked at us too. "Except for Blackwort and his crew who're rounding up the local citizens," he added.

Captain Morgan got up and went to a window which looked out on the square below and the Cathedral off to the side.

"Have they collected a good number?" he asked still looking out the window.

"That I don't know. I seen them herding in quite a group when I ran by on my way here." The fellow wiped the sweat from his face with his bare hand and rubbed his hand on his pants. Then he smiled, "A fair number o' them looked real scared, too."

The Captain turned away from the window and walked back to his desk. "How many men would you say were in that group?" he asked.

"Oh, maybe a hundred," the fellow answered. "Then there were some women and children."

"I suspect the church is full of people who would be just too happy to help kill the fires that are threatening their homes," said the Captain as he leaned over and pulled the knife blade out of the top of the desk. Then, with his finger, he smoothed the scar it left. "Let's go get them," he said.

The four of us left the Palace and walked through the plaza to the Cathedral. It was a big church made of stone with a wide stairway leading up to three doors. The main doorway was wide, and its heavy wooden doors were carved real fancy. When we entered through the main door, I noticed that Ned didn't come inside with us, and I guessed why.

The inside of the church was real pretty. There were little coves in the walls down both sides where you could see statues of men from olden times. One caught my eye because it was of a poor man whose body was stuck full of arrows. He looked like he was suffering real bad. I wondered how he came to get so many arrows in him.

Down the wall a ways in another little cove was another statue of a man. Only this man looked real happy standing there with some baby animals at his feet and birds perched on his arms. Up at the front of the church was a big wooden thing so big it stretched all the way from one side to the other. It was black and had been decorated with jewels and fine cloth. At the center, I could make out the cross and the figure of a woman with a baby in her arms. Somehow, the black thing—an altar, I guess you would call it—didn't quite go with the rest of the church. I told myself I wouldn't try to understand the Catholic religion.

The prisoners were grouped around in different places. Some sat in the seats, talking. Others were on the floor. There seemed to be at least two hundred of them there.

I looked around to see if I could recognize the girl that Ned told me about. Up near the front of the church I saw a woman and a girl sitting apart from the rest. The woman was coughing into a handkerchief and the girl, who looked to be about fifteen, was patting her on the back. When the woman stopped coughing and raised her head, I was sure it must be the people Ned described. The woman was the prettiest female I had ever seen. I couldn't stop looking at her. She sat like a queen, straight and calm. Her dark hair was parted in the middle and flat on top, and it stuck out on the sides of her face in curls. Her dress was deep purple with a wide, white lace collar and cuffs. Rows of pearls ran from the collar to the point at her waist. She had pale skin and dark eyes and eyebrows so perfect you would think they were painted on. She was beautiful, but there was a cool air about her.

I could see something of the mother in the girl. Her eyes and her skin were just as pretty. But you wouldn't say she was a beauty. She sat there in a green dress, and she slumped a little in her seat. She looked worried and angry. There was something about her, maybe the fire in her eyes, that set her apart from the rest. Her mother coughed again and the girl, looking worried, leaned toward her.

"There must be a couple hundred men in here," said the Captain as he mounted the steps at the front of the church leading up to the black altar. "Let's get them out fighting fires." He looked around him. "Where's Ned Green?" he snapped. "Get him in here! Then his eye fell on the beautiful lady and her daughter, and he stared at them. He was still staring when a man came in followed by Ned who walked quick to the front of the church not looking to either side of him.

"Green's here, Captain."

Captain Morgan looked away from the woman and turned to Ned. "I want you to announce to all these slubbering souls that their city is up in flames and that if they want any part of it left by nightfall, they'd better get out there and help us put the fires out. He glanced again at the woman. And then I want you to go over to that woman over there and tell her I invite her to be my guest at the Palace. He pointed at the woman.

Ned stiffened. Then he turned to the crowd and made a short speech in Spanish. When the prisoners heard what he said, they became excited and there was some moaning and crying out. All this time, the woman and the girl remained seated and showed no reaction to what was going on around them. It was like they were deaf. The Captain waited for the prisoners to be led out before he poked Ned in the side with his elbow and said, "Now tell her."

"I can't do that," Ned answered.

"You what?"

"I can't tell her."

"And why in hell not?" bellowed the Captain,

Ned looked the Captain straight in the eyes and said, "Because I lived in her house and she was kind to me."

"Ah ha! All the better," laughed the Captain. "Then you can introduce me properly."

"No, I won't," Ned said through clenched teeth.

"You will, or you won't live to see sunset." The Captain slapped him hard across the face. The sound it made was loud enough to get the attention of everybody left in the church, including the lady and her daughter. The mother coughed hard. Her chest heaved with each cough. She took a handkerchief and wiped her forehead.

Ned didn't flinch from the Captain's blow. If anything, he stood straighter than before, and looked angrily back at the Captain, not saying anything.

Captain Morgan raised his hand to strike again, but then he lowered it and said, "Remember who that woman is, Green. She's Spanish, and she and her kind will kill you the first chance they get. They're enemy."

Ned didn't answer, but he looked at the two women.

"Now, take me over there and introduce me," ordered the Captain.

"No."

The Captain grabbed Ned by the shoulder and spun him around so they both faced the women. "You do what I say," he said fiercely, "or those two will end up in the men's quarters if you get my meaning."

There was hate in Ned's eyes. "You can't do that! They are women of quality."

"I will do it," snapped the Captain, "unless you introduce me."

"You'll pay for this!" Ned snarled at him.

"Mind who you threaten, Green," answered the Captain. Then he hauled off and slapped Ned across the face again so hard it knocked him down. "Now get up and do what I tell you."

The woman was coughing loud now, and she bent over holding the handkerchief to her mouth.

"She's sick," muttered Ned while he picked himself up.

"All the more reason for her to join me at the Palace," smiled the Captain.

I watched the two of them walk over to the women. The Captain bowed low. He was all smiles, but the women sat straight in their seats and looked right through him. If they knew Ned, they sure did a good job of hiding it. The Captain's smile died when the women paid him no heed.

"Tell her that I don't ask her to come to the Palace, I order her to come," he said, bowing once again. "I'll send her an escort." He made a sharp turn and left the church. A minute later, he came back in and shouted at Ned, "You and Edward get out here and fight the fires like everybody else." Then he was gone.

Ned stayed at the side of the two ladies talking to them. They ignored him. He seemed to be pleading with them to answer, but they stared straight ahead like statues.

It wasn't more than five minutes when two dirty men came into the church. Their arms and faces were covered with soot and ash from the fires. They went over to Blackwort who stood by the main door and asked him something. When he pointed to the beautiful lady, they came her way. They nodded to her and then they reached for her, trying to grab her arm and pull her out of her seat. She still didn't look at them, but Ned said, "Stop! This is a woman of quality." He stepped between her and the men. "You can't treat her like a slattern."

"They're all the same to me," muttered one fellow trying to push Ned out of the way. "Move. We got orders to take her to the Captain."

"I won't move until you understand that she is a lady and you must treat her like one."

"Oh ho! Who've we got here? The Queen?" and he stuck his nose up in the air like someone who thinks they're better than the rest.

Ned spoke real soft to the lady and her daughter. After that, she whispered something to the girl and they hugged each other. Then she rose and gave Ned and the two other fellows a look that could have frozen them. Before anybody moved, she turned and walked to the door, leaving the two fellows to hurry after her.

The girl, Marta, madder than a hornet leaped up and screamed at Ned who was trying to talk to her. I heard the sharp smack when her hand hit him, and the blow forced him back a pace. Then she ran past him to a group of women who had been watching from the other side of the church.

Ned looked at me. "Let's go," he said. I followed him as he walked quickly out of the church, rubbing his sore cheek and not looking back.

—Edward

FEBRUARY 1672, FINCA LAS BRISAS

Dear Rosa,

They brought me your letter this morning. I am so happy to know that my story is reaching you. It pleases me that your father finds my letters interesting enough to put in the cloth merchants' journal. I am nearing the end of my account. When I have finished, I trust you won't find my letters too dull to read.

At the end of my last letter, I was hiding in the closet of the Cathedral, waiting for Miguel to come back. He hadn't been gone long before I heard a lot of noise outside in the church. I put my ear to the door, and learned that the church was filling with townspeople who had been taken prisoner by the pirates. Once again I was sure that Miguel had betrayed me, and I shook with rage, I was such a fool. Why had I trusted him?

Suddenly, the door opened, and a dirty pirate stood there grinning at me, his mouth full of blackened teeth. He yelled something in his filthy tongue, grabbed me roughly, and pulled me from the room, making my shoulder ache where he clutched me. Finally he released my sore shoulder and grabbed my upper arm in a hold just as tight. I bit my lips to keep myself from crying out.

I was dragged and pulled to the back of the church, which was nearly full of my countrymen. An enormous man stood inside. The top of my head couldn't have reached higher than his breast. His face was cruel and evil looking. He had an ugly scar, which ran from his mouth across his cheek to his ear, and he wore a blue handkerchief at a slant over one side of his head, covering one eye. His shoulder-length hair hung straight down in stiff, filthy hanks as if it hadn't seen soap and water for months. This monster looked me over, and ordered my captor to search me. I shivered as the filthy man ran his hands over my dress, squeezing the folds, pressing the cloth tight against me, finally groping in my pockets, where he found the golden miniature Mama had given me. Without looking at it, he snatched it from my pocket and quickly tucked it into the folds of his shirt. But the one-eyed giant saw him and pushed him down, demanding the picture. Sprawled on the floor, snarling at the giant, the pirate reached for the miniature and flung it at the big man. It fell on the floor with a clatter and the gold frame bent. The big one smiled wickedly, stooped down, picked it up, and looked at the picture. Then he put it in a pocket of his filthy shirt. He pushed me toward a group of women who sat in pews off to one side. In my terror at having been caught, I didn't notice that Mama was in the church. As soon as the horrible giant pushed me away, she came running to me and we embraced.

I was so happy to see her that I couldn't help myself. I just stood there in her arms and cried. She cried too, telling me over and over how good it was that I was safe and how silly it was of her to have left me alone in the house.

We moved to the front of the church, as far away from

the pirates as we could go. When Mama broke into a fit of coughing that seemed to come from her very center, I put my hand to her brow and discovered that she was feverish.

"Mama, you're sick."

"It will pass." Her body shook with another siege of coughing. I told her about hiding in the storeroom and about all that had happened to me since I saw her last: Don Gaspar's death, the pirates attacking me, hiding with Miguel. She was shocked when I told her who Miguel really was. "I thought there was something not quite right about him," she said, "but I couldn't decide just what it was."

Suddenly, I don't know why, I felt like I wanted to defend him.

"But Mama," I said, "he was sincere when he told me that he didn't want any harm to come to us. He wants to help us. If I hadn't been caught, he would have rescued me from that storeroom." I had forgotten how angry I was at him just a few moments before.

"Nonsense!"

"Really, Mama, I believe him."

"Listen, child, he's English." She coughed again from deep in her chest. "The English are scoundrels who will kill us as soon as they find any valuables we have."

"But Miguel's not a scoundrel. You saw yourself how courteous and kind he was to us."

"They say Henry Morgan is courteous too, if that's the way to get what he wants."

"But Mama…"

"How can you think well of any English after what they did to your *novio*?"

"But Mama…"

"Let me tell you how I was captured and then defend that boy and his kind if you can." She paused to cough. "I was tending the wounded at the hospital when the pirates took it over. First they robbed us. Then they kept us there all night taunting us and trying to scare us. We had to plead with them to let us care for the wounded men." She placed her hand at the neck of her gown. "They took my gold rosary," she held up both hands for me to see. "And my rings." Then she put her hands in her lap on top of her lace handkerchief. "Then this morning they herded all of us who could walk over here to the Cathedral."

I saw her stiffen as she looked past me down the row of seats to the central aisle of the church. I looked in the same direction to see Ned enter the church. He went up to the giant and talked with him for a moment, then he began to look around for someone. I was sure it was me

"If he comes this way, don't speak to him," said Mama.

"But Mama…"

"Marta, if you say one word to him, you are a traitor and God will damn you forever."

He found us.

"Señora, Marta," he said, holding his hands out to us. He looked truly unhappy. "Forgive me for all of this. I am trying to get you out of here."

I wanted to speak to him, but I couldn't with Mama there. The two of us looked through him as if he were nothing but air.

"Marta," he said kneeling in front of me so that our eyes were at the same level. "I meant everything I said to you last night. Nothing has changed. I will help you and your mother escape from here."

It was hard for me not to look at him. I managed by staring at the collar of his shirt. We sat there for awhile, he trying to catch my eye, I not daring to let him do it, and Mama coughing into her handkerchief. Finally he rose and said, "You will see that I am your friend. I will be back." And he left the Cathedral.

"That swine!" said Mama between clenched teeth. I said nothing. Her cough was worsening, and tiny beads of perspiration formed on her forehead.

"Mama, you should be lying down."

"I'll be all right, child. It's just a cold. I've had them before."

After an hour or so, the Cathedral doors opened, and I saw a man coming down the aisle followed by a young lad about my age. The man wore an elegant coat that fit him loosely. He strode to the front of the church and mounted the stairs in front of the blackened altar. I wondered if Miguel would tell them about the altar. Perhaps that would be a test of his loyalty.

The stranger was a person of medium height and slender build. He was dressed quite handsomely in a yellow coat and breeches. His dark hair was curled and wavy, and he had the air more of a gentleman than of a common pirate. I watched him as he looked us over and talked to the boy at his side. It appeared that he was somebody in command. Could it be Henry Morgan, himself?

It wasn't long before the Cathedral doors opened once again and two more men entered. One was Miguel. I quickly looked back to the man on the stairs, who stared at Mama. Miguel approached the man, and they talked. All of a sudden they both looked our way and the man pointed at Mama. Out of the corner of my eye, I think I saw Miguel turn white, but he quickly looked away and shouted to the men and boys that Henry Morgan ordered them outside to fight the fires that threatened the city. Our men marched out, leaving only the women and children in the church.

Trying not to show that I was paying any attention to them, I saw Miguel shake his head fiercely and shout something at the man, Then suddenly, Morgan—it had to be he—slapped Miguel across the face so hard that it made a red mark on his cheek. There was more angry talk, and Henry Morgan knocked Miguel to the floor. When he got up, they argued some more. Then the two of them started toward us. I quickly anchored my gaze on a crack in the wall, so I could only sense that they were getting closer. I nearly jumped as Miguel stepped directly in front of me. The other man stood in front of Mama. Dread filled my heart. What did Morgan want with us that would make Miguel defy him so?

"Señora," Miguel began shakily, "forgive me but this pig of a man beside me has forced me to introduce him to you. He says that if I don't do it, he will harm you and Marta in the most degrading way." The man grinned at us and bowed. It was evident that he did not understand a word of what Miguel said. "This is the captain of our group, Henry Morgan. He wishes you to be his guest at the Palace where you will be more comfortable, Señora."

"Señora, this man is cruel and will do anything to get what he wants. If you refuse him, it will be very bad for you and Marta. Please save yourselves. Go with him. It will be better for you."

Mama made no reply. Henry Morgan lost his smile. His expression turned mean. Then he snapped at Miguel and strode out of the church without looking at us again.

Miguel pleaded with Mama to do as Morgan ordered. He promised to rescue her from the Palace and he told us that a far worse end would await us if she refused. All this time, Mama stared straight ahead as if she didn't hear or see. Two vile-looking men came to take Mama to the Palace. Without a word, she rose and went out with them, coughing loudly as the Cathedral doors closed behind her.

I leaped to my feet. "You godless insect!" I yelled and I slapped Miguel across the face with such a blow that he nearly fell backwards. "How could you let them take Mama away?" Then I ran from him to a group of my countrywomen who watched nearby.

Miguel stood and looked at me for a moment, but he didn't try to come close. After he left the church, the women tried to comfort me, but their words did no good. I could think of nothing but Mama, sick, in the hands of that monster, Henry Morgan.

A few hours later, tired and dirty men, their faces blackened with soot and smoke from the fires, straggled into the church. Some houses and shops had burned, but all the fires were out. One of the biggest fires was along our street. Our house escaped the flames although the three homes to the north were burned.

Somehow, I got through the rest of that day and night. The pirates left us alone to do as we wished, as long as we didn't try to leave the church. In fact they left us so much alone that they didn't even bring us food or drink. But I hardly cared. Mama was constantly on my mind, and I felt no hunger or thirst. Dawn was approaching by the time I lay down on a church bench and fell asleep.

The next morning, the Cathedral doors flew open and two pirates entered dragging a ladino between them. There was something familiar about the fellow and I went closer to get a good look at him. I stood next to one of Papa's friends, Don Rodrigo de Gomez, who knew a little English. We watched as the pirates dragged the new fellow over to the giant. They threw him at the big man's feet and shouted in angry voices. The ladino was dressed in a filthy blue silk doublet which had once been very fine. Then I recognized the man: it was Pedro Garabito, wearing a coat I recognized from home. He cringed at the feet of the giant, pleading with him.

"Don Rodrigo," I whispered, "what are they saying?"

"Something about this fellow lying to them. They think he's a gentleman who is hiding his valuables from them."

"But anyone can see that he is not!" I said.

"It's his clothes, the blue coat."

I watched in disgust as he cringed there on the floor in front of the giant, telling him he would do anything as long as they didn't hurt him. The big pirate kicked him in the stomach which made a sickening thud. Then Pedro's captors tied him up and took him to the front of the church where they lashed him to the base of the altar so we could all see him. He sat there with his head hung forward not daring to look at any of us.

I was sure he would betray the Golden Altar to which he was tied, but he didn't. It couldn't have been because of any Christian feelings, I was certain. Could it be that he had never heard of the Golden Altar? How long would it be, I wondered, before someone was forced to tell the pirates about what lay under that coat of black paint? So far, I had not heard any of the townsfolk talk, even among one another about the change in our church. But I was certain they all were aware of it because most of them worshipped in this church and knew it like their own house. It was as if we all had made a silent vow to protect it.

Toward afternoon, we had another visit from Henry Morgan and Miguel. I tried to catch Miguel's eye to see if his conscience would make him give me word of Mama, but he did not look at me. Morgan walked up to the front of the church just as he had done the day before. He mounted the steps to the altar paying no heed to Pedro Garabito who was still tied there. Miguel, looking very grim, stood beside Morgan and spoke to us.

"Citizens," he said, "Captain Morgan wants you to know that he wishes you no harm. There were groans from the people.

"He only wants what, as the captor of this city, is rightfully his." Miguel paused a moment, cleared his throat, and continued, "Since you so unwisely sent the contents of the silver and gold storehouses out to sea before his arrival, the Captain feels it is your obligation to make it up to him." Miguel cleared his voice again. "Now there are many among you who are wealthy, and the Captain thinks it only right that you should turn over your wealth to him in order to gain your freedom and that of your families and friends. So until you people can produce enough treasure to have made his long, dangerous trip worthwhile, he will hold you ransom here in the Cathedral without food." Miguel paused again, took a deep breath and continued, "And to show you that he is serious, he has asked me to tell you that he will put one of you to death each day until you cooperate."

There were shouts and screams from my townsfolk. Henry Morgan seemed not to hear. He grabbed Pedro Garabito by the collar of Papa's coat and ordered Miguel to untie him. He yelled to a pair of men in the back who came, grabbed Pedro, and dragged him outside.

Miguel said, "The man who was just taken from here will be hung. He is accused of lying and hiding his wealth. Be assured that the same fate awaits any of you who do not come forth with your payments." After he had finished talking, Miguel turned his eyes to me and stared at me most fixedly. Silently, with his lips he formed the words, "I'm sorry."

Henry Morgan tapped him on the shoulder, and he spun around to face the pirate captain. Miguel listened to him and followed him around the church as Morgan examined each person, concentrating on the men, eyeing each one carefully. After he had covered the entire church, he turned and wandered among the people again, still followed by Miguel. At last he pointed at Don Rodrigo de Gomez and said something. A moment later, Miguel announced, "This man hangs tomorrow at sunset if the Captain does not get what he considers his due."

Don Rodrigo looked at Henry Morgan, his face drained of all color. "That is too little time," he said, "all of my worth sailed on those ships."

"Tomorrow at sunset," was Morgan's reply. Then he strode from the church. I hated the man more than I ever thought I could hate anyone.

Someone brushed my arm. It was Miguel. "Look on the floor," he whispered. Then he followed his captain out the door.

I scooped up a piece of paper, folded over several times to make it quite small. It held this message, written in a clear, elegant hand:

My Dear Marta,

You Mother is very ill. A friend and I have taken her to a safe place. She wants to see you and I have a plan to make it possible. Marta, I know it will be hard for you, but you must trust me one more time. Tonight, go to the storeroom where we hid together and hide yourself there. Then wait for a sign from me. Trust me. I am your friend.

I thought about his note for awhile, wondering if I should do what he asked. I wanted to believe him, but I didn't want to be a fool. On the other hand, I had nothing to lose. If he was telling the truth and he did help me escape, I would be able to find Mama. If not, I would not be any worse off. Besides, he had not looked at me like someone who was planning to betray me. Late in the afternoon, I carefully made my way to the storage closet at the side of the church and hid myself inside when no one was looking. Once inside, I hid in the shadows of a far corner, hoping I would be concealed from anyone who might look in. Once or twice I heard voices outside, but fortunately, the door stayed closed. I watched the light in the room grow dimmer and then disappear.

Just before sundown, I heard shouting and gunfire that sounded like it came from the plaza in front of the Cathedral. The shouts were English, and it sounded like the pirates were celebrating. One man would speak, and then there would be cheers from the group. After one last, loud cheer, the ceremony broke up and the voices and gunfire faded away, leaving only an occasional group of pirates passing by.

It seemed I had sat a good many hours on that closet floor before I finally had a sign from outside. "Psst, psst…," came a whisper from the little window.

I ran to a post just beneath it and softly answered, "Yes?"

"Marta, it's Miguel."

It was so dark in the closet that I could not see. It sounded like Miguel was at the window high above my head.

"Stay quiet," he ordered, "while I remove this window grate."

My chest tightened with fear as he worked to pry the iron grate from the window. The sound of his tool on the iron seemed awfully loud, and I was certain we would be discovered. Finally, the bars were off and Miguel stuck his head through the window. I was frightened and glad all at once.

"Ooph!" he exclaimed, "it's too tight, I can't get through."

"No! Stay there," I whispered. "Don't try to come in. I'll go out." I climbed onto a shelf directly under the window and found myself looking into Miguel s face. He was so close, it startled me. His head was sticking through the window, but his chest and shoulders were too big.

"Ah, Señorita," he whispered, "it's a lovely evening. I was wondering if I could have the pleasure of your company for a walk in the plaza." I couldn't help smiling.

"Well, I don't know," I answered, "you see, my *dueña* isn't here, and people would talk if they found me out alone with you."

"Let them talk. I know this isn't the proper way to do it, but would you mind coming out on this?" He passed a length of rope through the window and I grabbed hold of one end.

"Tie it to something solid in there," he said.

Holding the end of the rope, I climbed back down to the floor. Then I groped around in the dark searching for something that I could tie it to. Finally, I grabbed the door handle. I wasn't sure it would take the strain, but there was nothing else. It would have to do. I fastened the rope to the handle and climbed back up onto the shelf by the window.

"It's done," I said. "But I don't know how long it will hold." Miguel tugged on the rope and there was a soft crack from the wood.

"Come on out," he said. "You go down first. If it breaks it'll probably go with me. He withdrew his head from the window and hung outside so that only his hands were on the sill.

I climbed up and began to slide head first through the window. Everything went fine until I tried to pull the lower half of my body through. With my petticoats, I was too thick.

"I'm sorry," I whispered. "I'm going to have to try this again. I backed into the room, where I removed my petticoats. Then, I tried the window again. This time, I was successful. I clung to the windowsill while Miguel wrapped part of the rope around his waist several times.

Then he gave me the part that hung to the ground and said, "Here, take this and lower yourself slowly. It's not too far down. Don't be frightened."

I gradually let myself over the edge; the rope stung my hands as I slid down.

A quiet voice called up to me, and I froze. It was an English voice.

"Don't be afraid," Miguel whispered. "That is my friend, Eduardo. He's telling you it's not much further."

After climbing down and down, my feet finally touched the ground, and I found myself beside Eduardo who said something that I did not understand.

Then Miguel started down the rope. He was accompanied by the steady sound of ripping wood. Suddenly, there was a crash and Miguel fell the rest of the way, the rope still in his hand.

"Come, let's run," he said as he picked himself up and grabbed my arm. Away we went down the side street, Miguel, Eduardo, and I. We crossed the Calle Hospital and ran down another back street until we figured we were a safe distance away. Then we stopped and entered the courtyard of a darkened house. Eduardo handed me a cloth bundle and again said something in English.

"Marta," said Miguel. "These are men's clothes. Put them on. You will be safer if they take you for one of us."

I took the package and went behind some hibiscus bushes at the side of the yard. Eduardo had given me a pair of brown trousers of the sort worn by sailors, a white shirt, a bandana, and a pair of shoes. Everything smelled dirty. I tried to ignore the smell and not to think about the previous owner of the clothes. I removed my own clothes and placed them in a pile under the bushes. Then I put on the others and tied the bandana around my head the way some of the pirates did. I tried to hide most of my hair under the scarf. The shoes were too big. Even when I curled up my toes I couldn't keep them on my feet, so I left them and went barefoot back to where Miguel and Eduardo waited.

Miguel explained that Mama's fever had worsened after she was taken from the church to the Palace. Henry Morgan kept her locked in a bed chamber there. Last night he had an elegant dinner prepared for the two of them. He sent for her, and as she was being led into the dining room, she fainted. When Morgan realized how ill she was, he became angry and ordered her taken away.

Miguel and Eduardo were at the Palace when this happened, and they volunteered to do the job. They carried her to the lowest level of the Palace and installed her in a servant's quarters. She was very ill they said. Her fever was very high; she was breathing heavily, and they wanted to sneak me into the Palace so I could be with her.

We walked to the Avenida San Francisco, a broad street that passes in front of the Cathedral and the Central Plaza and finally arrived at the Palace. We walked along hurriedly, trying to keep away from the groups of pirates we found along the way. Before we approached the Cathedral, we crossed the street and walked through the Plaza, so we could conceal ourselves among the bushes and trees that grew there. I looked over at the Cathedral and saw guards at the doors. The windows were lit as if a midnight mass were going on inside. Halfway through the Plaza, our way was blocked by a group of pirates who sat around a fire they had built next to the fountain. Some played cards and others slept on the ground like animals. Not wanting to pass through that group, we turned and went back to the street. Passing under a tree, I felt something brush my shoulder. When I looked up to see what it was, I nearly screamed. Just above me, on the limb of a tree, hung the body of Pedro Garabito. He was covered with blood, as if he had been beaten, and he still wore Papa's blue coat.

"Come away, don't look," said Miguel softly as he pulled me along. "They left him hanging there as an example to your countrymen inside the church."

"How long has he been there?" I asked.

"Since sunset."

"And it will be Don Rodrigo tomorrow if the ransom isn't paid?"

"Yes."

I wondered what was wrong with Miguel that he would allow himself to join a group of men who would do such things, but I didn't have long to think about it before we arrived at the Palace.

We made our way around to the back and through a door which led down a damp, dark stairway to a narrow hall lined with doors. I could hear Mama coughing before we reached her room. Miguel and Eduardo directed me to a small cubicle only big enough for a narrow bed and a washstand. There, on the bed, lying curled on her side was Mama. Her eyes were closed. A rumpled blanket lay on the floor and a candle burned on the washstand beside the bed. I touched her forehead. She burned with fever. Her cheeks were flushed a bright red and her skin was wet and sticky.

"Mama," I called softly. "It's Marta."

She opened her eyes, but she did not see me. Instead she called Papa's name, "Antonio! Antonio!"

"No, Mama, it's Marta. Papa is in Peru."

"Antonio, help me!" She sat up suddenly and pointed at the wall. "Get him away! Help! Get him away!"

"What is it, Mama?"

She moved her arms wildly in front of her, screaming, "Get out! Get away from me!"

"Mama, there's no one here to harm you," I said to her. "Please lie down. You'll hurt yourself." I tried to pull her down on the bed, but she resisted me, lashing out at the air with her arms. "You can't take me! I won't go!" she yelled. Suddenly her body stiffened and she flopped down on the bed. There she lay, her whole body twitching and her eyes rolled back in her head so that only the whites showed.

"Mama! Mama!" I screamed. "What's the matter? Don't do that."

But she didn't respond. After what seemed an eternity, she stopped twitching and lay there limp and still, her eyes closed.

"Mama, can you hear me?" I whispered.

She didn't answer me. I wiped her damp forehead and put my ear to her mouth to check her breathing. It came faintly and slowly. Miguel brought me a chair and I sat beside her, praying that she would open her eyes and look at me and be all right again.

I sat in the candlelight, holding Mama's hand, willing her not to die, while Miguel and Eduardo stood vigil outside. The Palace was very still. Since almost everyone was asleep, the only sound came from water running in a fountain nearby. I must have dozed off because after an hour or so, I felt Mama's hand squeeze mine and I pulled myself to attention. Her eyes were open and she managed a wan smile when I looked at her. She said something I couldn't hear, so I leaned over her, putting my ear close to her mouth.

"Marta," she whispered, "you look like a boy in those clothes." Her chest rattled when she talked.

"They tell me I'm safer this way."

She squeezed my hand again. "I'm dying."

"No, Mama. Don't say that. You'll get better." I felt her forehead. "Your fever's better."

"Listen, child." She was overtaken by a fit of coughing

which shook her body as violently as a cat shakes a mouse between its teeth. When she could speak again, she said, "You are a strong girl and a good girl. You will survive these times, I know." She paused to rest, then she continued, "Lately we have had our disagreements. I was wrong in forcing Don Gaspar on you." My eyes filled with tears. Her eyes closed and I cried, "Mama!"

She looked at me and smiled. "I love you." Then her eyes closed again, and she fell asleep. I sat beside her sobbing quietly. A little while later she was dead.

Dawn had not yet come when Miguel, Eduardo, and I put her body in a cart and pulled it through the streets to my house. We buried her in a spot overlooking the sea until she could be given absolution and buried properly at the Cathedral. I wanted to stay and hide in the house, but Miguel said it wasn't safe. You couldn't tell when someone might come to ransack it once again. I wasn't sure I cared, but we found a place to hide in a modest candle shop off the Avenida San Francisco. I kept saying to myself, "Mama's dead. She's gone." But I couldn't really accept it. It seemed like a dream. I hoped I would wake up and everything would be all right again. It wasn't until later, after the pirates left that I truly grieved and mourned.

Rosa, after all this time, it is still difficult for me to write about Mama. I was not a good daughter. I often did things to annoy her and toward the end, as you know, we disagreed much of the time. Sometimes I dream that Mama is still alive and that we sit together on the patio and I tell her I'm sorry for the way I was. If only I had told her before she died. I am too melancholy to write more today. Until tomorrow.

Your loving cousin,
Marta

JANUARY 1671, PANAMA

This pirating business isn't for me. It's mean and nasty, and when I get home I won't have any part of it ever again. It wasn't so bad until we took Panama. Before that, it seemed like we were fighting for our lives. We were at war, you might say. It was either them or us. But when the decent citizens of Panama were rounded up and held in the Cathedral for ransom, I changed my mind. Father handles his animals better than those poor souls were treated. And the grief they suffered I wouldn't wish on anybody. The more I saw the Spaniards, the more I was convinced they weren't as evil as I used to think. They were good and bad, brave and cowardly, just like us.

The first time I remember catching myself wondering about the right and wrong of it all was when I watched the Captain command that beautiful Spanish lady to come to him at the Palace. She showed more quality than he did. She stood up to him from the start.

That day after we put out the fires we reported back to the Palace dining room, where the Captain supervised some servants who were laying a very fancy supper on a long wooden table with two places set at one end. The dining room was just down the gallery from the council chamber. Only the room where the treasure was being collected separated the two. I looked in as we passed and noticed the treasure room was fast filling up with loot.

Captain Morgan was dressed fit to dance with the queen. He must have raided the Governor's wardrobe again, because I know he didn't carry the gold-buttoned coat with the lace ruffles across the isthmus. His hair and moustaches were oiled and combed, and he smelled like he'd washed the trail off him. It must have taken a servant most of the afternoon to fix him just so. To look at him, you'd never guess the struggle he'd been through; you'd think he was a dandy, a fop who would shudder if he dirtied his hands. If that's what it takes to have the ladies fall at your feet, I'll have none of it.

When they brought the Spanish lady into the hall, the Captain went to her, bowed low and took her hand to kiss. But she was seized by a cough that rattled her person. Then she collapsed on the floor and lay there in a heap.

The Captain stepped back from her and shouted, "What's the matter, woman? Get up!"

She made no response.

"Get up I say!" He waved his arms at us. "Ned, help her up."

Ned lifted her head in his arms and said something to her in Spanish.

"What's wrong with her?" questioned the Captain in an irritated voice. "Is she afraid of me?"

"No, she's sick," answered Ned.

"Well, what is it?" The Captain drew away from her.

"I don't know," said Ned, "but her face feels very hot. Maybe it's the grippe."

"Well, get her out of here!" bellowed the Captain.

"I'll not have her around me. Get her out of here!" He stepped further away from her. "I've come too far and been through too much to waste my time mollycoddling any woman." He stormed from the room shouting, "I'll get someone else."

Ned glared after him, "That bastard!"

We carried the sick woman to a servant's room in the lower regions of the Palace where we nursed her through the night while she got sicker. She coughed more and harder; she breathed with a heavy rattle; we could see she was dying. She begged Ned to bring Marta to her and he promised he would.

That night, the two of us helped Marta escape from a window in the church. Then we brought her to see her mother. Early the next morning the poor woman left this earth. Just before sunup, the three of us buried her in the yard of her house.

That fancy house wasn't safe since looters were sure to come again, so we found a hiding place in the back of a candlemaker's shop. The front of the shop, which faced the market, was dark because of its shuttered windows, but the back opened onto a small garden with a fire pit. If we had enough food, we could hide there a long time. After looking in the jugs and boxes on the shelves, Marta came up with some oil and a box of salt, but not much else. There was nobody around the market, but we hoped some of the stalls might open later in the day so we could beg some fruit or fish. In the meantime, Marta suggested that somebody go back to her house for a sack of rice that she knew was stored in a shed.

I ran off to fetch the rice. On my way back, I noticed that fires had sprung up again in some of the buildings. The men must have discovered that the wine wasn't poisoned after all, because lots of them were staggering around, dead drunk. Later I heard that the Captain had started the rumor that the wine was poisoned to keep everybody sober. He should have known that most of those fellows wouldn't stay away from drink for long— poison or no poison.

The market never did open. Not a soul came to sell mangoes or papaya or fish or beans. The place stayed quiet and deserted all that day.

The next night after we caught some sleep, all three of us set off for Marta's house to fetch a bag of beans and any other food we could find. The city was lit by fires burning here and there, and this time it looked as if nobody cared to put them out. We had to be careful to stay away from bands of drunks who roamed the streets shooting off guns.

We got within sight of Marta's house and stopped dead in our tracks. Fire roared through the property. There was no saving it; flames covered every wall, and the terrible heat kept us from getting any closer. Marta took a deep breath, but she didn't say a word. Ned put his arm around her and said, "Come, let's get out of here."

At that moment, the roof caved in and at first the flames lessened; but then they gained extra strength and leaped higher into the sky. Marta buried her head in her hands; Ned turned her around and forgetting about being careful, we started back to our hiding place.

We hadn't gone far when all of a sudden two figures, one holding a musket and the other a knife, leaped from a doorway.

"Who are ye and where ye goin'?" It was Monkey's voice.

"Who are ye?" echoed Moon, who swayed from side to side. He was drunk again.

"It's me, Edward," I answered. "And Ned and the cabin boy off the *Sarah Jane*."

"The *Sarah Jane*?" asked Monkey, coming up close almost nose-to-nose with Marta. "I don't remember no cabin boy on the *Sarah Jane*." He put his knife against Marta's shirt and said, "What's yer name, boy?"

"Sam, his name's Sam," I answered.

"What's the matter, can't he talk?" Monkey pushed the tip of his knife against Marta's throat. "I said what's yer name?"

That girl is a wonder. Somehow, she understood the question, and in a soft shaky voice she said, "Sam."

"What? What'd ye say, boy?" teased Monkey pressing the tip of the knife against her throat.

"Leave him alone," shouted Ned. "He can't talk much. He's hurt."

Monkey turned sharp toward Ned, dropping his knife arm. "Well if it ain't Mr. Ned Green, the cleverest fellow in these parts. You know, Green, I can't say I was too downhearted when I heard the Spaniards had got ye. Too bad they didn't finish ye off."

He looked Marta up and down real hard and said, "He don't look hurt to me." Then he walked clear around Marta looking her over real careful "What kind o' hurt's he got that makes him so's he can't talk?" Moon interrupted in a thick voice, "Yeah, what's ailin' him so's he can't talk?"

I let Ned do the talking.

"You remember when we were fighting the Spanish horse soldiers?"

The two of them nodded.

"Well, he was kicked in the head and knocked unconscious. When he came to, he couldn't talk. He's just now beginning to get his voice back, but about all he can say is his name."

"Now," said Monkey. "Ain't that too bad."

"Too bad," echoed Moon swaying to and fro like a palm tree in the wind.

Monkey, put his hand on Marta's shoulder and said, "Say, boy, how come I never seen you around before?" Marta looked him straight in the face arid shook her head, but she didn't make a sound.

"He doesn't understand very well yet either," Ned said quickly.

Monkey pushed her away, saying, "Beats me where he's been." Then, pointing to Ned, he said, "Too bad it weren't you got kicked instead, Green."

Moon hiccoughed again. I looked past him down the street to see the smoke and flames on Marta's house. Monkey followed my look and said, "This here town's gonna burn to the ground tonight, right, Moonie?"

"Right."

"In an hour's time, there ain't gonna be nobody sober enough to put out anything bigger'n a twig. Right, Moonie?"

"Right."

"I thought the wine was poisoned," I said.

"So'd we 'til Moonie here got so thirsty he said he didn't care if he died, he had to have the wine. And he drank some and here he is walking proof that it ain't any more poison than it's ever been." He slapped Moon on the back making him stumble forward. "The word got around real fast and everybody left off searching for gold and went for wine instead. Now there ain't a man worth anything in the way of work except maybe the ones guarding the church." He grabbed Moon by the arm and said, "Come on, Moonie, let's go find us some fun." And the two of them turned and staggered off down the street toward what was left of Marta's house.

There wasn't any kind of order anymore in the city, what with drunkenness and carrying on everywhere. Fires were set just for the fun of it and before long, more than half the city was in flames. We went back to the candle shop half expecting to see it afire, but it hadn't been bothered. Ned said it wasn't safe for Marta to go out anymore. I knew he was right, but I could already smell smoke and I knew the fires were getting closer. We couldn't stay in the candle shop much longer. The old wooden place would go up the minute a spark hit it.

While we fussed about where to hide her, Marta was thinking about something else. She didn't care about herself, she said, but she couldn't rest until she did something to help her townspeople locked up in the Cathedral.

When Ned told her the only way we could do that was to find a million in gold for Henry Morgan, she said she knew of a little silver and some jewelry, but they were hidden in the well at her family's finca and it was too far to go. There would be no way to get there and back in time before they hung somebody.

"Morgan wouldn't settle for so little anyway," said Ned. "What he wants is a fortune."

"But it might delay the executions," she answered.

"No," said Ned. "It's too dangerous. If those drunken animals out there discover who you are, you won t have a chance. A young girl like you they would molest and torture until they were satisfied, and then they would kill you."

"But I can't abandon my friends in the Cathedral. We will all be killed unless we can pay off Morgan."

They kept arguing back and forth about it with Ned stopping now and then to translate for me. They shouted at each other for awhile and Ned pleaded with her, but in the end, she won and we set out for the Cathedral. The plan was to talk to the next person they were going to hang, a man named Don Rodrigo something or other, and get him to ask for more time so we could get the ransom at Marta's finca.

When we got to the Cathedral, Ned told Blackwort that Morgan had sent him to talk to the prisoner, Don Rodrigo. Blackwort let us in with a grunt and I calmed down a little when he didn't give Marta a second look. That girl was smart. She learned to walk like a boy real fast and after she smeared some dirt on her face, she looked as bad as the rest of us with the stinking clothes and all.

Don Rodrigo sat off by himself leaning against the seat in front of him. He had his head buried in his hands. When Ned called his name, he looked up at us with the saddest, weariest expression you ever saw. Well, when he discovered who Marta really was under the dirt and ragged clothes, he was real surprised. Ned warned him not to give her away, but if Blackwort had been standing by, he would have been real suspicious because Don Rodrigo came close to jumping up and hugging her. As it was, he sat there with his back to Blackwort and grinned at us, thanking us over and over again.

Ned grabbed him by the arm and pushed him over to Blackwort. He explained to the big man that Don Rodrigo had some valuables hidden out in the country and he had told us where to find them, but it would take a day or two to get there and back.

With a snarl and a nod of his head, Blackwort agreed to give the prisoner two days, but no more, before they hung him from the tree in the plaza. Don Rodrigo said something to him in Spanish. I think he was thanking him. But Blackwort didn't care and pushed him so hard the poor man fell to the floor. While he was still down, Blackwort kicked him in the stomach and grunted at him to get back to his seat. Don Rodrigo's face twisted with pain and he gasped to catch the air that had been knocked out of him, but he worked hard at not crying out. I left the church disgusted with the meanness Blackwort had in him. His evil looks didn't go far enough in showing the black soul inside the man.

Outside, it smelled like the whole city was on fire; the smoky air stung our eyes and made them water. Marta led us out of Panama along the back streets so we could stay out of sight as much as possible. Still we ran across drunks and looters. Lucky for us, they were too far gone to wonder who we were or where we were headed.

A mile or so out of town, we came to a fork in the road. One arm led up the coast and the other went back through the jungle to the mouth of the Chagres where our boats waited. At the Y, stood a barn, stable, and a little hut where an old man with a full white beard took care of six old horses and some pack mules. This man was Marta's father's groom and he told us that the Spanish soldiers had come and taken all the good horses and left the old nags behind.

The old man told us he had seen many citizens passing by on their escape from the city in the days past, but he didn't see anybody save a straggler or two in a couple of days. So far, he hadn't seen any pirates, but from the way he talked and the look in his eyes, I could tell he was pretty scared.

Marta asked him if he wanted to come with us, but he said, no, he would stay where he was and tend the animals that were left in his care. He wasn't about to leave his home for anything, he said.

We bade him goodbye, mounted the three strongest horses and headed up the coast road. Ned, I noticed, wasn't used to riding. He sat stiff in the saddle, but Marta looked like she belonged there. She rode as good as anybody I know.

Lucky for us, those old nags looked worse than they

really were, and we got some pretty good galloping out of them on the first part of the trip. It was a hot day and we stopped often to water the horses and take a drink ourselves. Sometimes we passed lanes leading into large cane plantations, but most of the buildings along the road were one-room huts where peasants and slaves lived. I can't say we didn't worry going along that country road. Marta's head turned like a nervous bird while she kept checking around us for bandits who live in the hills and swoop down on unprotected travelers.

The people we met had a thousand questions. They wanted to know if Morgan was headed their way. When they heard we were going to collect ransom for the citizens held in the church, some of them, dirt poor though they were, ran into their huts and came out with their belongings to add to the ransom. Marta put their glass prayer necklaces, cheap rings, and tin plates in her saddlebags, and we rode on.

By the time we finally got to Marta's finca early the next morning, those old horses were barely walking. Mine was so near collapsing right there in the road that I had to get off and lead him the last mile.

We didn't have much time to look around the plantation, but from what I could see, it looked like a rich well-run farm, not like ours where Father leaves most everything up to the lazy overseer. Seeing it, I thought that with the right kind of managing, our farm could produce three times as much sugar and cacao as it does. All of a sudden, thinking about our farm, I felt awful homesick.

The servants fixed us a good meal, and after a short nap, we loaded up fresh horses and started back toward Panama. It was late in the afternoon and not too hot, and the horses were fresh and young, so we made good time. Our bulging saddlebags made us feel more nervous than ever about bandits, and we watched everywhere for signs of them, Marta to the front, Ned to the sides and I to the back. My neck ached from looking back so much, so I turned in the saddle and rode backwards for awhile. Sometime before dark we had a scare when Marta sighted some men in the road up ahead, but they turned out to be peasants on their way home from the fields.

It was past midnight when we came to the stable just outside Panama where the old man kept the horses. There was no sign of the old fellow; he must have been asleep inside his hut. The same horses and pack mules stood there, dumb, hardly noticing us. Since we were afraid our horses would be stolen if we took them into the city, we left two at the stable, loaded everything onto the third and headed into Panama.

We couldn't have gone more than half a mile when we saw torchlight in the road ahead followed by voices and what sounded like a wooden cart creaking toward us. Quickly, Marta led our horse off the road and hid it in some trees. Ned and I just stood there not sure whether to meet whoever was coming or not. All of a sudden, without speaking, we both jumped into the ditch at the side of the road and lay there flat on our bellies, still as logs.

It wasn't long before the cart rolled by us. I'm sure they never would have known we were there if that horse of Marta's hadn't whinnied right then. At the sound of the horse, the cart stopped and a familiar voice yelled, "Who's there?"

Ned bolted out of that ditch in no time, and I followed him. There in the middle of the road, were Mr. Potts and Blackwort standing beside a cart as full as it could be of silver and gold and jewels. It must have held a good quarter of what was in the booty room at the Palace. Four Spanish prisoners were harnessed to the cart where two horses should have been. Blackwort held a whip, ready to strike; Mr. Potts pointed a dirk at us. Neither one of them relaxed even when they recognized us.

"What're you lads doing out here?" said Mr. Potts in a suspicious tone. He still pointed his dagger at us, his usual good humor gone.

"On our way back from the country," answered Ned. "We've been collecting ransom."

"Ye have, now, have ye?" said Mr. Potts. "And just who told ye you could leave the city?"

"Blackwort," Ned nodded toward the big fellow.

"That true?" Mr. Potts asked Blackwort.

The big man glared at both of us and nodded so slow that I wasn't sure whether he was going to answer yes or no.

"Well then, where's the swag?" asked Potts, "and where's the horse I heard. I swear I heard a horse." He looked past us out into the dark towards where Marta hid with the horse.

"The swag's on the horse out behind those trees," Ned said, pointing into the darkness.

"I'll get it," I said. Then I turned and stumbled over low bushes and rocks making my way in the dark toward Marta. When I got to her I made her understand that she should stay where she was while I took the horse back to the road. We were so quiet, not saying a word, but talking with our hands, that I'm sure Potts and Blackwort didn't have any idea there was a Spanish girl hid in those trees.

"Well, well," said Mr. Potts when I got back to the road. "And just why were you hiding all this?" His eyes narrowed and he said, "You weren't trying to keep this for yourselves, now were you?"

"No. We just didn't want anybody taking it before we got it back to the Palace," said Ned. "We didn't know who might be coming down the road and we didn't want to take any chances."

"I believe you, lad," said Potts putting his dirk in his belt. "It's just that some of the men, I'm not saying all of them, mind you, but some we've caught hoarding jewelry and gold that by rights should be put in the common pile to be divided up among us all." He stroked the nose of our horse and said, "The Captain don't think much of cheaters who do that."

Blackwort grunted and smacked the road with his whip so hard it made the dust fly into my nose and I sneezed. Then he grabbed the horse's reins from me and tied him to the back of the wagon.

"Blackwort and I are on our way down the road here a piece to where we can store all this loot by the trail leadin' home," Potts explained. "Captain says it'll be safer out here. He expects there'll be warships coming from Lima any time now, and we just might have to leave real fast."

"But that horse is carrying ransom for the hostages," said Ned. "I think we'd better take it to the Captain."

"And he'll have you turn right around and bring the beast back out here. No, you let us take him. Explain to the Captain what you've done. He'll understand." He looked slyly at Blackwort, who nodded in agreement.

Blackwort cracked the whip over the heads of the men harnessed to the wagon, and they strained forward until the cart, creaking and groaning, moved along. The horse shied to one side; then he followed behind.

Potts waved at us. "We'll be movin' along now. Be seeing ye lads." They left us standing there, watching them walk away with everything we had worked so hard to get.

When we knew they were a safe distance, we called to Marta and the three of us, tired as field slaves, walked toward Panama.

The city was ruined. The fires were pretty much out except for a few piles of rubble burning here and there, but from what we could tell in the dark, there wasn't more than a handful of wooden buildings left standing anywhere. Even the steady sea breeze couldn't take away the smoky smell.

When we finally got to the Palace, it was dead quiet. There wasn't a soul awake anywhere, not even a guard outside the booty room. We found three empty cots in a courtyard and collapsed on them to sleep 'til morning.

I woke up early with the sun and left my two friends asleep while I went to tell the Captain about the ransom we left in charge of Potts and Blackwort. I looked high and low for the Captain, but he wasn't in any of his usual places. When I climbed to the second floor to check the council chamber, I found the doors wide open and not a soul anywhere around. The door to the governor's bed chamber was open. I peeked inside to see if the Captain was sleeping, but he wasn't there. The room was a sorry sight with every door and drawer wide open and clothes and things hanging out of them, heaped in piles on the floor. The only thing that hadn't been messed up was the bed.

I walked over to the window and looked across the bay at some birds on the horizon. Then I don't know what made me do it, but I looked again and it struck me that those weren't birds at all, but sails. I counted at least five ships. Were those the warships from Lima that Potts talked about?

Quick as I could, I ran back to warn Ned and Marta who were still sleeping. "Ned! Ned!" I cried, shaking him. "Wake up!" But he slept on. "Ned!" I shouted louder, tugging harder at him. "Ships on the horizon!"

That must have gotten through to him because he sat up all of a sudden and blinked at me. "What? Ships?"

"Five at least."

I led him to a window where we could look across the

bay and there they were, a mite closer than when I first spotted them. By this time five ships had grown to twelve.

I heard a noise and turned to see Marta come toward us. Ned looked at her, and then pointed at the ships. "Lima?" he asked.

She leaned out of the window shielding her eyes from the sun's glare off the water and studied the specks in the distance. Then she turned to us, smiling, and nodded yes.

Ned looked at the mudflats that reached for half a mile from the Palace wall to the water line. "Looks like the tide's still going out," he said, "those ships'll be here with the next high tide."

Just then, Marta stuck her head out the window and yelled something in Spanish. Ned grabbed her and warned her to be quiet. I think she forgot for a minute that she was still surrounded by enemies.

"We'd better warn the Captain," I said. "Trouble is I can't find him."

"Let's try the Cathedral," Ned suggested. "It's my guess he's over there with Blackwort."

At first we thought Marta should stay behind and hide in the Palace, but she wouldn't hear it, so the three of us ran across the plaza to the Cathedral.

At first, it was hard to see after coming in out of the bright sunshine, but pretty soon my eyes adjusted to the light and I noticed that Blackwort wasn't there, nor the Captain. It looked like nobody was in charge. But the hostages were all still there, tired and sad. Then I heard Monkey's voice.

"That lad get his speech back yet?" He was slouched on the floor leaning against the wall next to the door. He held a sword across his knees and he pointed at Marta with his free arm.

"No," I answered. "It's getting worse. Now he can't say anything."

"Damnedest thing I ever heard of."

From the way he slurred his words, I could tell he was drunk. Two men lay crumpled near him on the floor, asleep from the drink.

"Where's Blackwort?" asked Ned.

"I can't say. He left me in charge before sunup. Went off somewhere with Potts."

"And the Captain?"

"Ain't seen him since yesterday."

"You'd better wake these fellows up," said Ned. "There are warships in the bay."

We left him there, the first signs of panic showing on his face, and went outside onto the steps of the Cathedral. Word of the coming ships was spreading fast and the plaza across the street was filling with men. There were shouts of "Where s the Captain?" and "I'm not waiting for him! I'm gettin' out of here."

Two excited men burst out of the Palace and ran across the plaza toward us.

"It's gone! All cleaned out!" one of them shouted, waving his arms about.

"What's gone?" asked Ned.

"The loot. The treasure. Everything we've squeezed out o' these Spaniards since we've been in this hole of a town."

Then another fellow dragged a white-bearded old man up the steps by the collar of his shirt. "I think this old 'un knows something, but I don't understand his talk." The fellow pushed the old man down on the steps in front of Ned and said, "Can you make any sense out o' his jabber, Green?"

It was the old man who cared for Marta's horses in the stable outside of town. He lay on the stairs, shaking with fear. Ned said something to him and reached down to help him up. When the fellow recognized Ned, he smiled and tried to embrace him, but Ned pushed him away and spoke to him real sharp. Then the old man talked to Ned in an excited voice with a lot of arm motions and pointing out away from the water toward the hills and the jungle.

A stunned look came over Ned. Then he kicked the steps and growled, "Those swine!"

"What is it?" I asked.

"Morgan, Potts, and Blackwort are gone with all the ransom and the horses and mules."

"The old man is daft!"

"He's not daft; he described the three of them beyond a doubt. It was them all right."

When the men heard about the double cross, panic really broke out. The ships were getting closer. It looked to me like they would be at the docks around mid-afternoon. That didn't give any of us much of a head start. My first instinct was to take off like the men flocking toward the hills and the jungle beyond, but then I came to my senses and remembered how we had almost starved out there. I think Ned was having the same thoughts because he looked at me just then and said, "Food."

He didn't have to say any more. I knew just what he meant. But we had to move fast to stock up for the trek and get across the isthmus before our ships left us behind. We were lucky to have Marta to help us.

—Edward

Marta's Letter to Rosa

FEBRUARY 1672, FINCA LAS BRISAS

Dear Rosa,

I am anxious to finish my story because I will soon be going on a trip. But I will tell you about that later.

After we buried Mama, Miguel and Eduardo wanted me to stay hidden until the pirates left. But I couldn't abide the thought of my countrymen being hung one by one while I hid from danger. Don Rodrigo was a dear family friend and I searched my mind for a way to save him. Then I remembered the things we had hidden in the well before we fled from the finca. There were some fairly valuable things in that well: silver plates, knives, forks and spoons, gold candlesticks, and some jewelry of Grandma's. It wasn't a fortune, but perhaps it was enough to buy one or two people's lives.

After I convinced the two boys to travel with me to Las Brisas, the three of us went to the Cathedral where Miguel and Don Rodrigo begged the giant for two more days before they executed anyone else. Fortunately, the beast's greed was stronger than his thirst for blood, and he granted us the extra time.

In the Cathedral, I was careful to check the altar. It was undisturbed, just as we had left it. All those prisoners knew, but not one of them told the pirates that under the ugly coat of black paint lay the most valuable thing in the whole countryside.

After departing the Cathedral, we rode to Las Brisas on some sad old horses that were all that was left in our stable. We spent only a few hours at the finca before we started back to Panama with the things from the well. We brought back everything except a pair of candlesticks that had been Mama's favorites. I couldn't bear the thought of the pirates having them.

In the middle of the next night, we left all the horses save one at the stable and journeyed the last mile into Panama on foot. Half the distance there, we were accosted by two pirates, that horrible giant and the first mate of Henry Morgan's ship. We didn't know it then, but they and Morgan were in the act of deserting their comrades and escaping with most everything of value. While I hid in some trees, they took our horse and its load from the boys, saying that they would keep it all safe. They did. They kept it all safe from everyone except themselves.

After we were rid of them, we stumbled on into the city, weary and worried that perhaps we were too late to save Don Rodrigo. As we passed through the plaza, I was relieved to see that there were no new bodies hanging from the mango tree.

Rosa, I find that I'm rushing on with this letter and in my haste I'm not telling you everything. When the boys and I traveled to Las Brisas, the city was aflame. Most of the invaders were under the influence of drink and they had lost all interest in quenching the fires. Indeed, I'm certain that many of the fires had been lit by that unruly gang.

Our house on the Avenida San Francisco was burnt

early on. I watched as the roof collapsed, but I didn't feel pain or grief or even loss. I remember thinking it odd, but I had a sense of standing out of my body and seeing myself watch as my home was being destroyed. It was as if it was happening to someone else. Have you ever felt that way, Rosa? It is very strange and a little frightening. Now Papa is having a new house built on the spot where the old one stood. He has named it Casa Carmen, in memory of Mama. The morning after Miguel, Eduardo, and I returned to the city was one of unexpected joy for me. We spotted Spanish ships in the bay, so close that they had to arrive in port by afternoon. Then the pirates themselves discovered that during the night, Morgan and his two henchmen had deserted them. By noon, most of the foreigners had fled, some vowing they would catch Morgan and kill him, others concerned only with saving themselves from the wrath of our rescuers. They left, still drunk, without anything but the clothes they wore.

Miguel and Eduardo were not so foolish as the others in their group. They asked my help in preparing themselves for the hard trek back across the isthmus. We raided the Palace storerooms and fixed them up with a good supply of rice and beans for their journey. I had been so glad to see the ships, I hadn't realized at first that Miguel and Eduardo would have to leave. But they did have to, of course. The Spanish soldiers would have killed them if they stayed. My joy was gone. I bade them farewell from the Palace steps. They made their way carefully through the plaza, staying out of sight of the citizens who had released themselves from the Cathedral and crowded the streets, crying out in disbelief at what had happened to their city.

Soon the Palace balconies and the promenade along the waterfront were crowded with people watching the approaching ships. Cheers and shouts and cries of "Hurry! Hurry! Catch the English satans!" rose above the throngs. I watched from the uppermost balcony of the Palace, praying that Papa and Roberto were on one of those beautiful ships, praying that two of the English satans wouldn't be caught.

Rosa, Papa is calling me. I will finish my story tomorrow.

Love,
Marta

Edward's Journal

JANUARY 1671, ABOARD
THE *HENRIETTA*

The sight of those Spanish ships sailing for Panama put
a scare into us and we knew we had to get out of there
quick. With Marta's help, we searched the Palace for rice
and beans and anything else that would be useful for the
trip. We stuffed bread, cheese, blankets, and torches into
some leather saddlebags that we found in the back of a
store room. I had the feeling Ned didn't want to leave.
Those sails kept coming closer, though, so we said goodbye
to Marta and made our way through back streets toward
the stable. We didn't think any animals would still be
there, but we figured it was worth a try. The stalls were
all empty, so we set off on foot along the trail to the Chagres, the saddlebags over our shoulders. I guess I should
have felt scared and peeved at the Captain about then,
but what I felt most was happy. I kept thinking about getting home where I would be free and life would be calm
and people were friendly with each other.

I didn't think about how I was going to get home. If
I had, I might not have been so happy. I could only hope

that some of our ships would wait for us at the mouth of the Chagres. If we got there and they were gone, we would be stranded with the Spanish hot on our trail. Ned thought maybe some Indians would take us to safety in their canoes, but I wasn't so sure.

The first night we lit a torch and, with the help of its light, had an easy time finding the trail. Not long after dark we came across four of Morgan's men lying there asleep in the trail, empty wine jugs scattered around. We called to them and one roused himself enough to look at us, but then he passed out again. We left them and moved down the trail. During the night, we passed more clumps of drunken men. We knew they were sure to get caught by the Spanish, but what could we do if they didn't stay sober enough to help themselves?

The next morning we came to the site of the wine poisoning and Ned's kidnapping. At that spot, the trail from Panama met the Chagres. If we had had a boat we could have climbed in and floated down the Chagres all the way to the North Sea. But there were no boats around, so we took a trail that looked like it went in the same direction as the river. This trail wasn't the one we had come in on. It took a sharp turn away from the river and I was sure we were going to get lost, but Ned said to have faith, that we were going the right way. I tried to have faith, but it wasn't easy when the trail ran farther and farther from the river.

We kept walking day and night knowing that the Spanish weren't far behind and that if they caught us, they would kill us, sure. On the third day towards nightfall, after stumbling down the trail for an hour or so, we both knew we had to get some sleep. That part of the trail ran along a hillside, and we climbed onto the downhill side, thinking we could hide there from the Spanish if they traveled at night. We each wrapped up in a blanket and sank underneath the bushes and vines where we would be invisible to anybody on the trail above.

That lucky Ned dozed off right away before he could feel the bugs crawling on him. I was just as tired, but it took some time before I could forget about the ants that crawled into my clothes, up my legs, and across my chest. They were everywhere, even in my armpits and groin, and I thought I would go mad. I must have passed a good part of the night jumping up and shaking things out of my clothes. Each time I lay down again, they would come back just as I was falling asleep. Finally, sleep got the better of me, and I dozed off in spite of the bugs.

Just before dawn, I was dreaming about home—tea and biscuits were in there, and so was Mother—when Ned shook my arm hard and I woke up.

"Someone's coming," he whispered.

I took a stick and made a hole through the bushes just big enough to see the trail above. Before I saw anybody, I heard the heavy tramp of horses' hooves. We held our breath while one by one, seventy horses passed above us; each had a Spanish soldier mounted on top.

We gave them a good head start before we came out of our hiding place to the level trail, where we made breakfast of cornmeal and water.

"You know, Ned," I said, "in a way, I was glad to see those soldiers."

"What?" He stopped chewing on his mush and looked at me like I was crazy.

"Since they're here, that means we must be on the right trail." We hadn't seen anyone for more than a day, and I had been sure we were lost.

He laughed and said, "You mean you've been following me along this trail for over a day thinking I was leading you wrong but not saying anything?"

"At first I figured you knew where to go, since you were so calm about it, but then I started to worry," I explained. "But I didn't have any better suggestions."

"When the Spaniards captured me, they told me about this trail," Ned said. "It leaves the river for a while, but up the way a bit, it meets the river again and runs beside it all the way to the North Sea. He took another bite of mush. Too bad Morgan didn't know about it on the way in. We could've saved ourselves a lot of work making a new trail."

After breakfast, we started up the trail, going slow enough to keep our ears open for sounds from the Spaniards ahead. Two or three hours had passed when we spied some birds circling in the sky.

"Buzzards," I said.

Ned shook his head.

We rounded a bend to find three more of the big black birds picking at a carcass at the side of the trail. They didn't fly until we got up close and shooed them off. Then they only went a short ways where they lit on the trail and perched there watching us, their beady eyes full of resentment.

They had been ripping at the body of a man who lay face down at the side of the path. By the looks of him, he had been dead for some time. He was all swollen up, and the birds and animals had had their go at him.

Ned looked at me. "Roll him over?"

"Might was well."

After we flipped the body over on its back, it didn't take much to figure out who it was. I saw the gold earring in his ear and I knew. "Potts!" cried Ned.

Ned knelt next to him and looked him over real careful. I walked away. It made me sick to my stomach to see Mr. Potts like that. Save Ned, he was the only fellow in the whole crew I could count on to treat me fair. He shouldn't have run off with Morgan and Blackwort, but he wasn't such a bad man.

"Throat's slit," said Ned.

I turned around and saw him get up and stand by the body. The buzzards still watched us.

"I wonder if they got Morgan and Blackwort too," I said trying not to look at Mr. Potts.

"Who?"

"The Spaniards."

"Ed, it wasn't the Spaniards who killed him."

"Who then?"

"His own kind. Morgan and Blackwort."

"How do you know?"

"He's been dead a long time, maybe a day, maybe more. The Spaniards we saw couldn't have done it, and if any others caught him, they would've tortured him first." He looked at the body and shook his head. "No, those two traitors killed him so they wouldn't have to give him a share of the swag."

It was impossible to dig a grave right there. We rolled the body into some thick bushes, and headed down the path again. I couldn't remember ever hating anybody so strong as I hated Henry Morgan and Blackwort. How could I ever have thought anything good about them? I told myself that when I was older I would make them pay for all the sorrow and death they had caused. Then I would write a letter to Marta and tell her that Morgan and his giant mate had paid for their malice. I liked thinking about that.

In the afternoon, the trail turned toward the river, and we were following it downhill when the quiet was broken by shots. We went on even more quietly and carefully, afraid to make any noise. Two hours later we caught sight of the Chagres River where the trail met it and followed it to the North Sea. Just when we saw the river, we heard the Spaniards chopping wood and calling to each other, and we dove for the bushes at the side of the trail.

We sat in the bushes and talked about our situation. It was sure that if we wanted to escape from the Spanish we had to get around them and reach the North Sea before they did. If any of our ships was still waiting at the river's mouth, it would sail at the first sign of Spanish soldiers.

From the sounds, we could tell the Spanish were setting up camp. We stood the best chance of getting around them if we waited until dark, so we sat there in the bushes, swatting at the bugs and hoping for nightfall.

After dark, we climbed onto the trail and headed toward the river. Soon we saw the light of their campfires through the trees. They were camped on the trail not far from where it met the river. When we crept closer to look, most of them were getting ready to go to sleep, except for the men who had sentry duty. One fellow sat by the fire picking his teeth with the spine of a black palm.

Ned tugged at my sleeve and we went up the trail far enough to talk without them hearing us. We had a problem. If we tried to go through their camp along the trail, one of the sentries would spot us. If we tried to pass them by cutting through the jungle in the dark, we were sure to get lost. There was only one way around them: in the river.

I wasn't sure I remembered how to swim, but what could I do? I couldn't give myself up to the Spanish, and I couldn't go back to Panama. I had no choice. It was the river or nothing.

We gave the men in the camp time to go to sleep before we crept down to the water and groped our way upriver far enough so we could swim out to the middle of the stream before we passed the camp. We sure didn't want to get caught on any snags right in front of those Spaniards.

At first I worried about snakes and crocodiles in the bushes there by the river, but that worry went to the back of my mind when I had to leave my boots and the saddlebag with all the food on the bank and wade out into the stream. Before we went into the water, we both ate as much as we could hold from the food supply, not knowing when we would have a chance to eat again. I pulled my diary out of the saddlebag, trying to think of a way to take it with me without getting it wet. It was a friend, and I wasn't going to abandon it on the bank of the Chagres to mold and rot.

Ned came up with the solution. "Your teeth," he said, "hold it in your teeth."

I followed Ned out to where the current was strong and the water rose to my middle. Although it was hard to balance, I told myself not to panic. I had to keep my sense if I wanted to see my home again. Even so, I could feel the panic starting to take hold.

Ned squeezed my shoulder and whispered, "See you downriver." Then he lowered himself into the water so only his head was showing, and he let the current take him. I watched his head bob downstream like a coconut that had dropped into the river from a palm along the shore.

When I couldn't see him anymore, I knew I should follow him, but I couldn't make myself do it. What if I'd forgotten how to swim? No one would help me there in the dark. Finally I got hold of myself, stuck my journal in my mouth, and plunged in. I felt like laughing when I discovered I could still swim. Ned had taught me well. I hadn't forgotten. Soon I was steering myself far out from shore and letting the current do the work. The water was warm and deep and, lucky for me, there weren't any exposed rocks to hit.

I caught a glimpse of the Spanish camp as I floated

by. The fires were still burning, but I couldn't see the sentries. I must have floated at least a mile. My jaws ached from clenching my journal, and I had trouble swallowing. I was beginning to think I couldn't hold onto the book any longer when I heard Ned calling me.

At the sound of his voice, I felt so happy I wanted to laugh. I swam toward the shore and as soon as I felt my feet touch the muddy river bottom, I grabbed the journal from my sore, cramped mouth and ran toward the shore. When we found each other, we stood there, soaked and cold, hugging and jumping up and down and laughing.

Lucky for us, the trail was close beside the river and we didn't have to go looking for it in the dark. It took us a while to calm down. Then we hiked along, soaking wet and shivering from the cold, but with no heavy saddlebags to carry. Even in the dark, we made good time, and by sunup we were a fair ways ahead of the Spaniards.

I was in the lead about mid-morning when I spied something shiny on the trail. It was a miniature of a girl with yellow hair in a gold, jeweled frame a little bigger than a doubloon.

"What is it?" Ned asked peering over my shoulder.

"Look," I put the miniature in his hand.

He turned it over and over. Then he looked hard at the picture. "She's pretty," he said, handing it back to me. "I wonder who she is."

Ned took the lead and we hiked on. I put the miniature in my pocket next to the diary and said, "This and my journal are the only things I have to show for all I've been through." We walked on awhile and then I said, "I wouldn't really want any of the swag knowing how it came from the suffering of those people in Panama."

Ned didn't hear me, I guess. He didn't answer. Then he slowed his pace 'til I came along side him and he said,

"You know, Ed, the most valuable thing in all of Panama was right under Morgan's nose the whole time and he didn't even know."

"What was it?" I asked.

He grinned, "The Golden Altar."

"You mean there really is a Golden Altar?"

"There sure is. It was right in the Cathedral all along. If Morgan had really looked, he would have seen it."

"You mean that ugly black thing with the baubles on it was the altar?"

"Yeah, I helped paint it myself."

I looked at him and shook my head. "You're supposed to hate the Spanish, remember?"

"And some I do. I guess."

I took the miniature out of my pocket and looked at it. "I guess we both learned there are good people and bad people everywhere, no matter whose soil you re on."

"I guess so," he said.

We trudged on, thinking that we had to be pretty close to the North Sea. The closer we got, the more I worried. What would happen to us if the ships had already sailed?

In the afternoon, we came to the mouth of the Chagres. What I saw there made my heart sick. Or maybe I should say, what I didn't see there made my heart sick. There was no sign of anything: no people, no pirogues, no ships, just some sea birds diving for fish. Our spirits fell, and we stood there looking at the empty bay that had once been filled with twenty ships.

We couldn't stand there for long because the Spanish were close behind. What to do? The river had grown too swift and wide to swim across. We could head down the beach, but sooner or later we would end up in Spanish hands at Portobelo. There wasn't much choice. We started down the beach, hoping to find a hiding place where we could stop and think things over. We hadn't gone far before I noticed something wooden behind the palms at the edge of the sand. We walked over to see what it was. It was a pirogue. It looked like it had come from one of our ships. Maybe it could take us back to one.

Without saying a word, we carried and pushed the boat across the sand to the water, floated her, and jumped in. Then we rowed out into the bay, fighting through the strong currents from the river. We aimed to get out of sight behind a point of land on the other side of the river's mouth. It was hard going, but with both of us using every bit of strength we had, we made slow headway across the choppy water.

When we got far enough out to see around the point, we caught sight of a single ship anchored a little way off-shore. She looked friendly, and we rowed straight for her, shouting with joy. When we got close enough to see sailors cheering us from her deck, both of us stood up and hollered and jumped up and down so much we almost tipped our boat over. We were saved!

The captain of the *Henrietta* was a good man who couldn't find it in his heart to leave his countrymen to the Spanish. He had stayed and waited in hope of rescuing his men while the rest of the ships sailed after Morgan and Blackwort. When we told him we were probably the last to escape, he gave orders to weigh anchor and sail toward Jamaica.

The *Henrietta's* crew told us that Morgan and Black-wort had slipped aboard the *Satisfaction* one night and sailed off without anybody knowing. The next day, men started straggling in and telling about Morgan's treachery. Most of the ships went in pursuit, but a few stayed behind to wait for us. Out of the thousand or more men who set out to conquer Panama, only a hundred came back. The day before Ned and I hiked out, all the ships except the *Henrietta* sailed off. I asked about some of the men who had been on the *Satisfaction*. No one could remember seeing sad old Higgins, but two sailors reported sighting Monkey and Moon in a group that staggered out of the jungle the morning after the *Satisfaction* disappeared. They sailed aboard the first ship hot on Morgan's tail.

Ned says he will come home with me and work on the farm for a while. He talks about going back to Panama. He talks about England, too, but I don't think he'll ever go. I hope he stays with us a long time. Who knows? Maybe with his help, we can make the farm pay. I've taken care of my half of the debt to Henry Morgan, and judging from the way he ran out on me and the rest of his men, I don't think he'll be coming around to collect the other half. If he ever does, it's for sure I'll set him straight.

I'm not the same lad I was when I left home. Now I know what it is to be starving, to be scared witless, to witness cruelty and death. I've seen supposed friends act no better than beasts and supposed enemies show kindness. People aren't always what they seem.

True, the only things I have to show for it all are my diary and the miniature I found on the trail. Still, my head is full of thoughts—thoughts and pictures and smells and sounds. In a way, they are treasures, too.

—Edward

Marta's Letter to Rosa

FEBRUARY 1672, FINCA LAS BRISAS

Dear Rosa,

I must finish this letter to you in one sitting at my writing table, for I will soon be leaving on a journey and it may be a long time before I have another chance to send you word. My mind lies with the trip ahead, and it takes quite an effort for me to concentrate on the events of a year ago. The house is quiet now, it being siesta time, so I will take up my favorite pen and tell you the end of my story.

Papa and Roberto came on one of the first ships to anchor in the harbor, and early that afternoon the three of us were reunited. Their fleet left Peru as soon as they had word that Henry Morgan was marching on Panama. While I waited for them to land, I thought about how I would tell them of Mama's death. I wanted to save them pain. But when I saw their beautiful faces in the crowd disembarking from the boats, all my planning rushed from my head. After they recognized me in my filthy disguise, we hurried into each others' arms and none of us could stop our tears.

Papa and I hugged each other. "Mama's gone," I sobbed.

Then I blurted out the story. They interrupted often, asking me to explain something or to repeat things they had difficulty believing. When I had told them everything, the three of us leaned against the seawall in front of the Palace. Papa put his arm around me, and we stood silent and drained while horses and soldiers congregated around us getting ready to go in pursuit of the invaders.

A ship was sent to Taboga to tell the citizens who were hiding there that it was safe to come home. Later the next day, Grandma and Jaime returned to us, and I told my story once again.

The Governor had been killed the day Morgan seized the city, but his son survived, and he invited us and others whose homes had been destroyed to live in the Palace until we could travel to our fincas. We lived there for nearly two weeks before we could get horses and a carriage to carry us to Las Brisas.

Before we left the city, many of the soldiers had returned from hunting the pirates. Henry Morgan and the giant escaped, but many, if not most of the pirates perished in the jungle. Our soldiers caught and killed a large number of them and there were still others who died of fever. I tried to find out if there had been any youths among the dead. I asked every officer, I met. Nobody seemed to know.

This year has been one of sorrow and melancholia for us. Recently, I have felt more cheerful, and Jaime and I are beginning to tease each other once again. Papa is still not himself. He has shown little interest in farming or shipbuilding, things he once cared for very much. Roberto has taken on many of Papa's responsibilities in the city, and it is he who oversees the building of our new house.

Grandma and I share the responsibilities of running the house, while Jaime has surprised us with his talent for managing the finca. I often go into the fields with him and watch him deal with the slaves. He does it naturally and well. When I see him like that, I sometimes wonder if Miguel and Eduardo are doing the same thing in Jamaica. I think of Miguel's strange accent. I see his face at the window and in the church. I think of the three of us hiding in doorways and walking through the night from Las Brisas and watching Spanish sails come into the bay. I wonder if they escaped this land, or if their bones lie somewhere along the jungle trail. I am not sorry that most of Morgan's men did not reach the North Sea alive, but I hope my two friends are doing what Jaime is doing right now. Will I ever know their fate?

Well, Rosa my story is finished. As I said, it may be some time before I write you again. In two days, I leave for Lima with Roberto to trade silk for silver. He hints of a young man there who he thinks might appeal to me. It seems I will inspect and be inspected. Grandma has had the maids sewing day and night making me piles of new dresses, and I'm really very excited. I've never traveled before. I'm also a bit worried about this young man. When I try to picture him, I see only Miguel or Eduardo. What if he is another Don Gaspar? I have made it clear to my family that I will not be forced into marriage. But perhaps I will find this young man appealing. It is something to think about.

Your cousin,
Marta

About the Author

LINDA BROTEN STRALEY was a wife, mother, teacher, cook, knitter, gardener, reader, world traveler and unpretentious lover of family and friends. She died in August 2019 after 77 years of a full life. A native of Bellingham Washington, she graduated from Smith College in 1964. Immediately upon her college graduation, Linda traveled to Guatemala where she taught school for several years. Panama was her home in 1970 where she lived with her husband Hugh, and two sons Ben and Nick. After three years in Panama, in 1973 Linda and her family returned to the Pacific Northwest where they put down roots in Seattle. For over 20 years Linda was on the faculty of Seattle Academy of Arts and Sciences where she taught Spanish and provided college counseling.

With her knowledge of Central America and fluency in Spanish, Linda devoted several years of reading, research and writing that resulted in this Panama adventure story for young adults. Written in 1982, the book was a project that eventually took a back seat to her devotion to teaching. It was found shortly after her death on a shelf in a storage room. *The Atar of Gold* is published as a memorial to Linda's careful research, to her love of teaching, of Latin America, of children and of world literature.

– Hugh Straley

CPSIA information can be obtained
at www.ICGtesting.com
Printed in the USA
FSHW012004080420
68985FS

9 780999 364635